Aug 22
W

'...under your skin'

Teresa Driscoll, *I Am Watching You*

'You won't know who to trust in this twisty,
absorbing and intricately plotted family thriller'

T. M. Logan, *The Holiday*

'The pages keep turning in this suspenseful tale of
secrets, lies and suspicion. Unmissable'

Imran Mahmood, *You Don't Know Me*

'An utterly compelling story of female competition
with plenty of twists'

Heidi Perks, *The Whispers*

'A plot that knocks you sideways. I loved it'

Phoebe Morgan, *The Wild Girls*

'Completely absorbing from start to finish'

Celia Walden, *Payday*

'A twisty, pacy thriller asking questions about who we really
are, what's important to us and whether we really know the
people close to us'

Gilly MacMillan, *The Long Weekend*

'A fiendishly twisty page-turner . . . an unputdownable read'

Emma Curtis, *Invite Me In*

'An emotional, immersive domestic drama filled with secrets,
suspense and twists!'

Sam Carrington, *The Couple on Maple Drive*

'Kept me in heart-stopping suspense throughout'

D0183247

ABOUT THE AUTHOR

Jane Corry is a former magazine journalist who spent three years working as the writer-in-residence of a high security prison for men. This often hair-raising experience helped inspire her *Sunday Times*-bestselling psychological thrillers, *My Husband's Wife, Blood Sisters, The Dead Ex, I Looked Away* and *I Made a Mistake* which have been translated into over sixteen languages and sold over a million copies worldwide. Jane was a tutor in creative writing at Oxford University, an RLF Fellow at Exeter University and is a regular contributor to the *Daily Telegraph* and *My Weekly* magazine.

We All Have Our Secrets

JANE CORRY

PENGUIN BOOKS

PENGUIN BOOKS

UK | USA | Canada | Ireland | Australia
India | New Zealand | South Africa

Penguin Books is part of the Penguin Random House group of companies
whose addresses can be found at global.penguinrandomhouse.com.

Typeset by Jouve (UK), Milton Keynes
Printed and bound in Great Britain by Clays Ltd, Elcograf S.p.A.

The authorized representative in the EEA is Penguin Random House Ireland,
Morrison Chambers, 32 Nassau Street, Dublin D02 YH68

A CIP catalogue record for this book is available from the British Library

ISBN: 978-0-241-98902-9

www.greenpenguin.co.uk

MIX
Paper from
responsible sources
FSC
www.fsc.org   FSC® C018179

Penguin Random House is committed to a
sustainable future for our business, our readers
and our planet. This book is made from Forest
Stewardship Council® certified paper.

To my amazing family (nothing like this one!)

Prologue

'We are here to establish the following points: The identity of the deceased. The time, date, location . . .'

The coroner pauses for a nanosecond.

'. . . and the cause of death.'

There is a hushed silence.

But inside, my head is spinning.

Death is a word unlike any other.

It can strike at any time.

It might be long overdue.

It can be a merciful release.

It might be a crime.

But if so, who did it?

A stranger?

Statistics show that the murderer is often known to the victim.

Frequently it is a family member.

A wife?

A husband?

A son?

Or maybe a daughter . . .

WANTED!

*COMPANION/CARER FOR RETIRED LAWYER, YOUNG AT HEART.
NOW WITH LIMITED PHYSICAL MOBILITY BUT STILL IN POSSESSION
OF FACULTIES WITH GSOH AND KEEN ACADEMIC MIND. DOES
NOT WANT TO BE MOTHERED! NURSING BACKGROUND USEFUL
BUT NOT NECESSARY. APPLICANTS SHOULD BE HAPPY TO TALK
AND BE QUIET AT APPROPRIATE TIMES, HAVE A PASSION FOR
ROCK AND ROLL, ENJOY A GLASS OF WINE OR TWO AND BE
CAPABLE OF COOKING A JUICY STEAK. (NO VEGETARIANS OR
ANY OTHER -ARIANS, THANK YOU!) NO GLUTEN-FREE EATERS
EITHER. MUST ALSO BE A DOG LOVER. APPLY TO HAROLD
GENTLE, WILLOWMEAD HOUSE, WILLOWMEAD, CORNWALL.*

PART ONE
Emily

I

Black tights. That's what I need to buy on the way home. Fifteen denier, medium size. Perfect for that knee-length slinky dress from Hobbs I treated myself to last week. Or will that look too sexy for a first date?

What if it does? For goodness' sake, I'm nearly thirty-five. I should have more confidence at my age.

Then again, I don't want to make a mistake. Too many of the numerous wedding ceremonies I've been to in the last ten years have ended in a decree absolute and a pair of broken hearts.

Far better to wait until I find the right person. And this time, I've got a good feeling. He's single. Smart. Interesting. And he understands the pressures of my job. Take today. I wasn't meant to be on duty. I could be having a relaxing afternoon getting ready for my date. But we were short-staffed so I volunteered.

'Nurse! I told them I don't want any kind of intervention. Absolutely nothing. Do you understand? It's *not* in my birth plan.'

Mrs Smith's voice jolts me back to the delivery room. I must have been talking to her while letting my imagination wander. How could I have done that? I usually have my mind one hundred per cent on the job in hand. Nothing is more important than bringing a child safely into the world. Apart, of course, from saving a life. Although sometimes the two are the same thing. I know a bit about that too. But now isn't the time to go into details.

'I understand,' I say calmly, trying to pick my words with care. 'But there's a possibility that baby might need help in turning.'

'*Turning?*' snorts her husband, who strikes me as the kind of man more accustomed to giving orders than receiving guidance. 'You make our baby sound as though it's a bloody car.'

'Is turning dangerous, nurse?' asks Mrs Smith. Her voice is tinged with panic and I feel for her.

'Baby often does it naturally,' I say, again carefully choosing my words while supporting the head and waiting for the next contraction.

I only just finish my sentence before the monitor breaks into loud bleeps to show the fetal heart rate is decreasing. (I usually ask my mothers if I can call them by their first name, but Mr Smith had declined on his wife's behalf.)

'What's that noise?' they both ask together.

'Don't worry,' I say reassuringly.

This isn't good. The consultant should be here by now but he's got heaven knows how many other patients to attend to. I have to act quickly.

'I want you to take a deep breath,' I say slowly.

'How the fuck is that going to help?' she screams.

When I started training as a midwife, I was taken aback by the number of seemingly calm women whose behaviour would alter so dramatically during labour.

'*Do* something for my wife, can't you?' booms Mr Smith.

It's normal to be angry when you're scared. I get that. More than they might realize.

4

'Breathe in and out,' I say, evenly, even though inside my heart is racing. Good. Here comes a contraction! She cries out in pain. I try my favoured method of distraction. 'Do you have a nursery at home?'

They're the kind of couple who would have a room specially prepared. I can see it now. In the corner there will be a little lacy crib. A chest of drawers brimming with everything you could ever need for a newborn. Nursing pads at the ready. And toys. So many toys! Rustic wooden blocks, a velvet-pawed bear, a mobile that plays a lullaby when you pull the string. A husband who comes in and puts his arms around my waist . . .

STOP! I can't afford to lapse into more daydreams. What has got into me?

'Yes,' says Mrs Smith. 'We do.'

The pain of the contraction has subsided for a minute. I can see it in her eyes. My gaze locks with hers. She needs to trust me. Then her body will relax.

Nearly there now.

'What's a bloody nursery got to do with it?' snaps the husband. He has a wide silver ring on his left hand. I wonder how long they have been married and whether they'd been trying for a baby for some time. Somehow – don't ask me why – I have a sneaking suspicion that they're one of those golden couples who were lucky first time.

I really thought I would be a mother by now. But I've never been a great judge of character when it comes to men. Yet tonight will be different. I just know it. When George and I met last week during a caesarean, it was lust at first sight as we gazed at each other across the operating table. I hasten to add that this quickly led into a mutual respect as we each did our bit during a rather complicated delivery.

'Well done,' George said to me afterwards.

'You too,' I replied flushing.

'Have you got time for a coffee in the canteen?' he asked.

We couldn't stop talking. 'I saw this great film the other night,' he said, before telling me all about it over a couple of flat whites. Every now and then, he'd run his hands through his hair as if he was nervous. Rather endearing!

The only fault I can find in George so far is his slightly irritating habit of grading everything on a scale of one to ten. 'I'd give this coffee a five,' he said. 'What do you reckon?'

'I'm not sure I can be so precise,' I answered truthfully.

'Really?' He seemed quite surprised. Oh dear! Had I said the wrong thing? But then he still asked me out on a date, which was a relief. I could put up with the grading stuff. After all, I have some irritating habits too. Don't we all?

Yes! Baby's turning on his own with another contraction. There's a whoosh and out he comes. I am overwhelmed with elation. My relief is palpable; I've never lost one. I'm not sure I could go on if that ever happened to me. Even if it wasn't my fault – even if there was nothing I could have done – the guilt would be too much to bear.

'Here's your beautiful baby boy,' I say, swiftly running an eye over him, drying him, putting a hat on his dear little head and gently placing him on his mother's chest. Baby to mother, skin to skin. A lump forms in my throat. Silently, I say the words I always do when a baby is born. *Bless this child.*

It's not that I'm religious. It's because birth is an event

6

so extraordinary and yet so common, that people do not always recognize it for the miracle it is.

There is nothing like witnessing this first meeting. That locking of eyes between mother and child. The mother's face that says, 'You are my mine. My flesh and blood. My child who will live long after I have gone. Trust me. I will kill anyone who hurts you.'

But I, the midwife, am usually the first person to touch this miracle. My hands are the first to feel a brand-new human being enter the world. Birth never loses that sense of wonder for me. With every delivery I feel privileged to be there; to have played my part.

Suddenly Mrs Smith isn't who she was two minutes ago. She's a mother, with tears of joy streaming down her tired face. 'My son!'

She clasps him protectively, her wet cheek against his. I feel a flash of jealousy. I know I shouldn't, but I can't help it. I want to be her. I should have been. And I might have been if it hadn't been for –

'Thank you, nurse,' says the husband.

As usual, I refrain from replying that, actually, I am a midwife, not a nurse.

His previous anger and doubt have evaporated. It's understandable. People are often frightened about labour as they have no experience of it. The support of the midwife can make all the difference.

'I just need to weigh him,' I say gently, 'and do a few tests.'

He's alarmed. 'But everything's all right.'

It comes out as a statement even though I suspect he means it as a question.

I pop him on the scales and check him from top to toe. 'Perfect,' I say, giving baby back.

The placenta is coming out too. Good. I take it next door to the sluice room. There are usually two of us on duty but today we're short-staffed so it's just me. I have to leave the parents alone while I do this. It doesn't take long.

And then I hear a deep rich voice from the other room. 'How are we doing?'

It's George. Or to give him his full title, George Chester, the new consultant obstetrician.

'All good,' I say, hurrying back in, my heart pounding. 'Mrs Smith has a very healthy baby boy.'

'Excellent!' he beams. 'I'll be back shortly to check up on you both. But rest assured, you've been in experienced hands with your midwife. On a scale of nought to ten, our Emily is a ten!' He picks up my notes. 'Just like your baby's rating on the Apgar score, which I see she's just filled in.'

I can feel myself flushing. The Apgar score is used to measure a newborn's health.

Then he gives me a quick look as he leaves. Oh dear! I'm conscious of feeling flushed and sweaty. I hope this won't put him off. I'll have to make sure that I look my very best tonight to make up for it.

'My shift is over now,' I tell the happy parents. 'I'm going to hand over your care to Flora, another midwife, now. It's been lovely to meet you.'

'Thank you so much,' they say as one.

They were scared before. That's why they'd been snappy – especially the father. But now they have their little baby safe in their arms, all is well.

'I've a feeling I might have sworn at you when it was all happening,' says Mrs Smith. 'I'm really sorry.'

I squeeze her hand. 'Believe me, I've heard far worse. Birth is one of the most traumatic experiences you can go through.'

They'd taught us that during our midwifery programme. But I'm aware that my words suggest I've been through it myself. It makes me feel like a fraud. Sometimes when I deliver a child, I pretend it *is* mine. Crazy, I know. But I can't help it.

Shortly afterwards, I am cycling back to my flat, humming happily. What a wonderful day! I've helped bring a brand-new person into the world. And an attractive, single, interesting man is taking me out for dinner! But first I'll treat myself to a long hot shower (there's no bath in my small rented flat) and I might even attempt to style my corkscrew auburn curls.

Those curls are possibly my best asset. If truth be told, they are my *only* asset. Otherwise the rest of me is pretty ordinary. Medium height. OK nose. High cheekbones inherited from my mother which make me look 'happy' even if I don't always feel it. Slightly rounded shoulders from bending over patients, although I try to pull myself up straight when I catch my stoop in the mirror. But people often remark on my hair.

'Such a lovely colour,' Mum would say when she brushed it for me as a child. 'Like a golden sunset. Never cut it, Emily. It suits you long.'

As I wend my way through the traffic, ringing my bell when someone dives across in front of me, I spot a chestnut-seller on a street corner. It's the last day of September. How I love this time of the year! It's still light when I leave work (providing I've been on a day shift) and the leaves on the trees glow like flickering candles with those glorious oranges and yellows.

And then I remember. I've forgotten to call Dad.

I try to ring him every day but today has been manic. I didn't even have time for lunch. Just a rushed cereal bar which I wolfed down while racing from one ward to the next. If I don't ring now, he'll be onto his second gin and lost in one of his old films. My father has a vast collection of DVDs, all neatly numbered. Favourites like *The Quiet Man* with John Wayne.

My mother used to enjoy them too. Their evenings together had been the only time of the day she'd allowed herself to sit down. Not that she would ever complain. Mum had thrived on rushing around: playing tennis, making jam from damsons in the orchard, helping out with reading at the village school, singing in the choir, running the book group, going on little trips with Dad after he'd retired. But then she'd suddenly got tired. Very tired. One of the first signs of leukaemia, apparently. But she wasn't even sixty. Much younger than Dad. The doctors *had* to do something . . .

Even now, I can't believe she's not here any more. Four years gone already. How is that possible?

Dad's lonely. I know that. Time and time again, I've suggested he moves up to London so I can keep an eye on him, but he always dismisses the idea. 'Why would I want to leave all this for a shoebox?' he demands, waving his hand at the Chesterfield sofa and the oak corner cupboard filled with the blue-and-white china my mother had religiously dusted every Thursday. (She 'tackled' a different room on each day of the week. The list is still pinned on the inside of the pantry door in her clear, loopy writing. It gives me comfort.)

He had a point. Willowmead, the sleepy Cornish seaside village where I grew up, is picture perfect. It belongs to a postcard. Honey-coloured church. Pale pink, blue and cream cottages with thatched roofs. And over it all, Willowmead House dominates, with wisteria dripping down in purple clumps from the eaves onto the worn, red Georgian brick.

As a child, I'd loved it. We'd swim in the sea, ride along the beach after school, gather for impromptu barbecues. But then we all grew up and went in our different directions. When I come back, I can only take so much of small-village life and then I'm itching to get back to the buzz of the capital's theatres and shops, and to the hospital, where there is always someone to talk to.

Someone who knows me as the new Emily. Not the old.

Yet in the last year I've noticed that Dad has become frailer. He's ninety-four, although he looks younger.

My father is a good-looking man. Mum was always teasing him about that. 'They'll think you're my toy boy!'

'With a thirty-year-plus age gap?' he'd scoff.

But he enjoyed the flattery.

People sometimes remark on how he bears a passing resemblance to the actor Donald Sutherland. Maybe that's because of his bold nose, deep voice and arching eyebrows, with eyes that switch from loving to piercing according to his mood. In recent years he's grown a silver beard, which gives him a certain gravitas. When we're out together, I've seen more than one woman of a certain age give him an admiring look.

But the truth is that he really needs some help. Of course, he wouldn't dream of a live-in carer. I know that if I suggested that, he'd bite my head clean off. Dad's a very private person. An alarm around his neck would give me some peace of mind but he won't hear of it. 'It would make me feel old,' he says. I bite my tongue to hold back the words 'But you *are* old, Dad'. He used to have a cleaner but she left last year.

'She said I was "too difficult",' he'd declared when I asked him about it. 'Took offence when I ticked her off for moving the whisky bottle. Honestly, nowadays people are so sensitive.'

'It's not always what you say, Dad,' I reminded him. 'It's how you say it. You didn't accuse her of hiding it, did you?'

'Well, she did, didn't she? Even though she denied it.'

Oh dear! 'You're not in a courtroom now,' I said gently.

He'd harrumphed at that but it had clearly struck a nerve. 'Your father always has to be right,' Mum would say in a 'that's fine' voice. But sometimes it wasn't.

To be honest, this is why I don't always feel inclined to visit Willowmead as often as Dad would like, but I do ring every day. How could I have forgotten?

I pull off the Harrow Road. Propping my bike against a wall, I try to call him. No answer.

I try again. And then again.

'Hello?' barks a deep, clipped voice.

'You're there,' I say, my heart flooding with relief.

'Of course I'm here. Where else would I be?'

'I was just worried, that's all.'

'Why?'

Because he might trip on the step when going out of the French windows into the garden or slip on the tiles in the conservatory or forget that the kettle has to be taken off the Aga. So many reasons to worry, any of which would infuriate him.

'No real reason,' I say.

'Good. Then I'll get back to my wildlife programme, shall I?'

Other daughters might be offended by this. But I know Dad. At fifteen, he was one of the youngest to fight in the Second World War. He fibbed about his age because he wanted to fight for 'king and country'.

I've often pressed him for memories but he won't talk about it. Yet I sense they have made him steely.

Dad's the type who doesn't believe in taking paracetamol for headaches. He belongs to the 'you just have to get on with it' brigade.

But at the same time, he is quite capable of showing unexpected flashes of love and emotion. When my first love, Nick, broke up with me just after my eighteenth birthday, he even gave me a hug and gently told me there were plenty more fish in the sea. And when I insisted that I then wanted to become a midwife instead of going into law, as he'd done, he was surprisingly supportive. 'You must do what you want, my girl, although I have to say that with a brain like yours, you could earn a great deal more in a law firm.'

But it wasn't money I wanted. It was magic. Ever since I'd been small, I'd been fascinated by babies. 'Why can't I have a brother or sister?' I would constantly ask my mother.

'Because sometimes it just doesn't happen,' she'd say. 'Besides, your dad and I are getting a bit past it now.'

I was aware that Dad was older than my friends' fathers, but because he was young at heart, it didn't seem to matter. Dad was as fit as a fiddle: always swimming in the sea, where he taught me to perfect my crawl.

'Such a daddy's girl,' my mother would say, laughing, when we came home dripping wet, full of that amazing adrenalin that only the cold water can give you. 'You wouldn't catch me in the sea in November!'

Shrugging off these memories, I get back on my bike after telling Dad I'll ring tomorrow. I'm still on a high after work. There isn't much that can give me that whole body-tingling feeling these days but, however many lives I help to bring into this world, each one still feels magical.

Then my mobile begins to vibrate aggressively from my basket. Please don't let it be George to say he's been delayed, or, worse, cancelling our date. Once more, I pull into a side street.

'Emily?'

It's my senior midwife. Her voice has an edgy, chilling tone. 'I believe you were in charge of Mrs Smith.'

'That's right.'

'I think you'd better come back.'

There's something foreboding about the way she says this.

'What's happened?'

'Just come back, Emily.'

'Tell me. Please.'

I listen with mounting disbelief. This is impossible. No. NO!

'I'm on my way,' I whimper.

I begin cycling furiously back towards the hospital. It's getting darker. Too late, I realize I should have switched on my lights. I need to pull in again.

Then it happens. So fast that I don't see the shape until it's right in front of me. There's a scream. Mine. I wobble. For a split second, I realize I could go either way. The right or the left.

As my head hits the road, I have a flash of 'this can't be happening'.

Then nothing.

2

Three Days Later

The woman in front of me on the train is in her second trimester, at a guess. Bump nicely rounded, which sometimes suggests a boy.

Ankles slightly puffy. She needs to watch that. Constantly getting up and down to go to the loo. Rather too often, in my view. Maybe she has a urinary infection. I hope she's told someone about that.

Stop, I tell myself. You're not in charge of her. Or of anyone else, for that matter. Not now.

There's a jolt as the train swerves to the left. The Cornwall to London railway trip was one of the biggest adventures of my childhood. 'Hold my arm, Emily,' my father would tell me when we made our annual visit to the West End for a pantomime. 'Now close your eyes and we can pretend we're on a fairground ride!'

I'd snuggle up against his big, warm, secure coat. 'Let's go!' I'd say.

My mother, who would be sitting opposite with her knitting or a *My Weekly* magazine, would give us one of her indulgent smiles. 'You two have got such imaginations,' she would say.

'Of course we have,' my father would reply jovially. 'It's

the only way to enjoy life. Now duck, Emily. Quickly! We're going under a bridge.'

I'm going under that very same bridge now. Of course, there's no need to duck, just as there wasn't then. But it doesn't stop me doing it simply out of habit.

The pregnant woman opposite gives me an odd look. I feel silly. Embarrassed. I want to tell her that my head is still hurting from my fall, but that this is nothing compared with the frantic beating of my heart.

I want to tell her – anyone – about what happened three days ago. I'd explain that, if I look a little jumpy, it's because this is the first time since then that I've left my one-bedroom rented flat on the outskirts of Deptford because all I could do was lie on my bed and think 'How did this happen?'

My mind keeps going back again and again to the Smiths. *We want a natural birth.*'

To George, the consultant obstetrician. 'On a scale of nought to ten, our Emily is a ten! Just like your baby's rating on the Apgar score, which I see she's just filled in.'

To the bike. The dark. The phone call from the maternity unit. Those fifteen-denier tights that I never bought. Why am I even thinking about them? To the fox that shot out in front of me and that awful realization that I was toppling, falling, hitting the ground. Hard.

Then the voices.

'She's coming round.'

'She was only out for a few seconds.'

Looking up to see the flock of strangers who had gathered round me.

'Does anything hurt?'

'No.' Just my head. But I didn't want to admit that. It was hard to tell if the pain was emotional or physical. Thank goodness I'd been wearing a helmet.

'Do you have anyone we can ring?' asked a voice. 'A husband? A partner? A child?'

These kindly strangers had taken me at my word. Yes, I was certain I felt fine. I had a work meeting to get to. I had to see my superior. To face people. Everyone would be talking by now. '*Did you hear about Emily? She's been suspended. There's going to be an internal inquiry. Maybe a referral to the Nursing and Midwifery Council . . .*'

I could ring and say I'd been knocked off my bike. It was the truth, wasn't it? Besides, what good could my presence do at the hospital? None at all. Not now.

I managed to make my way home and then had a dim memory of falling asleep.

When I woke, with a splitting headache, I realized I must have slept all day. It was dark again. I still hadn't called the hospital – or had I? I left a bumbling message on my senior midwife's answerphone and went back to sleep again. The following day there was an envelope on the doormat. An official one with the hospital stamp.

Statement needed . . . you have a right to be accompanied by a witness or union representative . . .

I've been reading and rereading that letter all the way down from Paddington, just in case the wording might have rearranged itself. Perhaps it really says it was just a mistake. Everything is fine. Come back. We need you.

Who am I kidding?

And then another thought. Scarier than them all.

If I can't do my work, who am I?

I'll never forget my first birth. Until then, I'd thought that delivering a baby was a procedure. Checking the cervix to see how far it was dilated. Watching the fetal heart rate on the monitor to make sure all was well. Reassuring the patient. Helping her to breathe and push at the right times.

All this is important, but it's more than that. The real magic is that glimpse of the cusp between nascence and being. And the reward for witnessing the void? Unadulterated joy. A feeling that wells up inside you when you put that slithery miracle into the mother's arms and you see her face. That utter purity of love. That passion. And that fierceness. Yes. It took *me* by surprise too. It needed another midwife to explain it to me during my training.

'It's maternal instinct,' she'd told me. 'You suddenly become aware that this child depends on you. Nothing else is as important. You will die to save it. Life will never be the same again.'

I want that.

I crave that total kind of love.

And there's only one person left in the world now who can make me feel better.

Daddy.

The woman with the round bump is looking at me in an odd way again. Maybe it's because I am tearing up the letter with its official wording into long strips. Then I rip those strips into half. After that, I take each one and furiously scrunch it into a small ball before gathering them up and placing them in the litter bin between carriages.

There. It's gone.

They can't get me now.

19

3

The train's about to stop. I pull down my holdall from the rack. I haven't brought much. I couldn't think clearly when I was packing. Besides, some of my things are still in my old childhood room. The one overlooking the sea.

I can glimpse it now. Coming round the corner. The late-afternoon sun glinting on the water. A passenger behind me gasps. 'Isn't that beautiful?'

Yes, I want to say. *I grew up with it*. I took it for granted then. All I wanted to do was head for London's bright lights. But they're not so bright now.

I have extinguished them.

I glance behind me. I can't see the pregnant woman but I wish her luck in my head. I hope her midwife takes good care of her when it's her turn. The local taxis are hovering but I stride past. I need the walk. It will take almost an hour but that's fine. It will give me time to get my story straight.

Someone says hello but I keep my head down, pretending not to hear. I don't know who it is. And I don't want to. I need to be alone.

My mobile rings. It's the maternity unit.

Decline.

I take the coastal path. It's October now. Only three days from when it happened but already a fresh new month has begun. My favourite season of the year. At least, it was.

There's no fence at this part of the cliff. Just a sheer drop. The council relies on common sense and responsible dog walkers. Not a woman who's been told to stay away from work while evidence is being gathered against her.

Nearly home now. I can see the ladder that leads down from the café to the beach. In Victorian times, this was the only way to get down there. Then they built a steep path. Now there is a choice. Sometimes you see tourists who take the more adventurous option but then get dizzy.

I'm aware that I feel dizzy now myself. I take a pause. Maybe I should have had my head checked. There's no bruise, although internal bleeding doesn't always have any outward signs. But I can't bear the thought of entering a hospital. Not after what happened.

My head clears and I can see it now. That charming, warm old red-bricked house with the dove-grey slate roof. The buddleia is still out with its sweet scent like honey that makes me stop and breathe it in every time. And there are the wide, inviting sash windows. Willowmead House.

How long is it since I was here last? Three months? Maybe even four? I should have come sooner but my conscience means I never say no to an extra shift if we're short of staff. If only I had, then it might have been another midwife looking after the Smiths. She might have done things differently.

'I'm fine,' my father had always assured me during those daily phone calls.

Memories flood my mind as my worry mounts with each step. Dad taking two daily newspapers from opposing ends of the political spectrum, so he could keep a 'balanced view'. Dad playing his beloved Chuck Berry and

Buddy Holly 45s on that old record player of his, which is 'perfectly serviceable'. Mum's dressing table, still exactly as it was before she died, with its silver hand mirror and half-empty bottle of Blue Grass.

Past the old stable with the weathercock on top. As a child, I'd had a horse. There were always 'loan ponies' being offered by farmers or people whose children had moved away and needed someone to exercise them. We'd race each other along the beach, Nick and I . . .

My mobile rings again. The maternity unit. *Decline.* I have an urge to hurl it into the sea but I can't. It might be Dad.

I gently touch the crowning glory of Willowmead House – my mother's roses, still in bloom, clambering up the trellises; a vivid reddish orange, like burning sunsets. The colour of my hair. The only concession my father has made to getting 'help' was to increase Joe the gardener's hours. Despite being in his eighties himself, Joe would always check in on Dad for me. This would inevitably end in him receiving an earful. 'Stop fussing,' Dad would say crossly when he rang to complain about my interference. 'You mustn't bother Joe about me.'

It was never easy to predict whether Dad would be warm or snappy.

Peeping through the windows of my father's study, I see those familiar bookshelves lined with Yeats, Chaucer, W. H. Auden and other much-loved bedfellows. He'd wanted to read English but his parents had expected him to follow the family tradition of law. Dad had complied, but I always wondered if he regretted that decision. My mother and I would wait with bated breath for him to return from court. If he'd won a case, he'd crack open a bottle of wine. If he hadn't, he'd retreat to his study and we'd both lie low for a bit.

Finally, the front door. Solid oak, painted black with a brass knocker. A Victorian iron boot scraper bought by Dad from a local auction years ago. The sound of a dog barking. Zorro – an enormous flat-haired, camel-coloured cross-breed of unknown origins whose party trick in his youth was to leap onto your lap and then proceed to lie on his back, kicking his legs in the air while almost squashing you – is not quite as lively as he used to be now he's almost twelve. But at times he still behaves like a puppy.

I knock. My heart thumps as I hear footsteps on the other side, crossing the stone-flagged hall with its old and slightly frayed apricot rug, purchased in Egypt on my parents' honeymoon. One of many elaborate stories. Some true. Some (I suspect) not.

I hear the latch on the other side of the door being released.

'Dad,' I prepare myself to say. 'Something happened at work.'

Then it opens.

I stand there, my unspoken words drying in my mouth. Before me is a living, breathing painting from one of my father's Renaissance art books. She has long dark hair that curls down to her low-necked midnight-blue top. Her soulful eyes match the colour perfectly. This woman possesses one of those faces that is lit up from within. Her teeth are impossibly even and white. She is supermodel tall. For a second, I am reminded of a six-foot-plus Penélope Cruz in a film I once saw with Nick.

'Hello,' she says. 'May I help you?'

May she help *me*?

'I'm Emily,' I say.

'Ah!' She claps her hand to her forehead and laughs. It is a tinkly laugh that feels forced. Artificial. 'Of course. *Emilee!* The daughter of Harold. Forgive me.'

Harold?

My mobile rings again. Maternity unit. *Decline.*

'Who are you?' I demand.

'Je suis Françoise,' she says as if I should already know. She flicks a strand of hair back from her heart-shaped face. 'Don't you want to answer that phone?'

'No,' I say. 'I would like some answers myself.'

She beams at me. 'Then please come in.'

4

Please come in?

A stranger is welcoming me into *my* house?

And she is wearing one of my mother's aprons, no less! A lemon-yellow apron that I hadn't touched since she'd died. An apron that, when I'd cuddled her, had been imbued with that comforting Blue-Grass-fresh-baked-sponge-and-home-made-strawberry-jam smell. I hadn't been able to face putting on any of my mother's aprons after her death so I'd left them neatly folded in the huge kitchen dresser. Yet this Françoise has gone right ahead and helped herself. The apron would smell of her now. Not Mummy.

She would not have been as brusque as I had been just now to this woman. 'Excuse me,' I say, 'but I'm a little confused. Are you here to help with the house?'

I'm politer now. It's more like me. Then again, who am I now? The midwife who . . .

I stop that train of thought in its tracks. I can't think about what happened. Stay in the moment.

Her eyes are dancing. There's a brief, deliberate, pause. 'In a way,' she says.

What does she mean? It's almost as if she's playing games with me. I've seen that in my job. Maternity units are no different from other workplaces.

I'm not going to ask any more questions. Instead, I try

to walk ahead of her but she is immediately at my side, as if she is my minder. Frustrated, I toss my coat on the large wooden chair by the grandfather clock in the hall. I head for my father's study.

'He is not there,' says a voice behind me. 'Your papa is digging in the garden.'

But he doesn't dig! It's also nearly dusk. My father always reads in his study at this time. I glance at the clock to confirm the time, remembering hours spent with Dad explaining how the hands relate to its moon-and-star-speckled face. And though he likes to gaze over the lawn, with its magnificent cedar at its centre, he never ventures out into the garden. Rarely did, to be honest. That was my mother's domain.

I'm moving quickly now. Striding through the sitting room with its faded pink-and-blue Liberty-print sofas, the well-stocked drinks cabinet, the marble chessboard set for a game. I make my way to the French windows, which are flung open.

There he is. Kneeling over a pot on the patio.

'Emily!' he says, looking up. 'I'm putting in some daffodil bulbs.'

He speaks as though I have just returned after popping out for a few moments.

I kneel down next to him. 'That's nice, Dad,' I say softly. 'But the wind is whipping up. Don't you think you should come in now?'

His hands are gently tucking a bulb into the compost, rather like they used to tuck me into bed when I was small. 'Françoise says fresh air is good for me.'

'Why exactly is Françoise here?' I ask carefully. Years

26

of experience have taught me that you have to tread softly where Dad is concerned.

'To look after me, of course,' he says. His eyes look almost pleading, like a child's.

'But *I* am your daughter,' I say. 'I can do that.'

'How can you? You live in London. Besides, I need help with Zorro. I can't get Joe to do everything. He's getting on, like me.'

He rises to his feet now and stumbles a little. I attempt to steady him but he pushes me away. 'I can manage, thank you.'

'I try to be here, Dad,' I say. 'But I'm working.'

Even as I say it, I realize that's not true any more.

'I know that. It's why I decided on a carer.'

'Well, you didn't tell me. Anyway, you always said you'd hate having a carer.'

'No I didn't.'

I know better than to argue right now.

Dad almost trips over as we step through the French windows but I take his arm. This time he doesn't shake me off, but my heart is thudding at the close call. I ease him into his armchair, noticing that it's in a different position from usual. It's one of a matching pair and has been moved closer to its twin. The one that Mum used to sit in.

'I didn't want to bother you with the details,' he says in a slightly softer voice. 'You're always so busy.'

'But we talk every day. You could have said something then . . .'

He cuts in. 'Anyway, Françoise applied and she's perfect.'

He sounds almost dreamy. Please don't tell me he's getting soft on her! At a guess, I'd put her in her twenties.

'How old is Françoise?' I ask.

'I'm not sure,' he says vaguely. 'But she's had experience in looking after people.'

Is that so? 'Did the agency you used check her references?'

He's getting up and heading for the whisky decanter. 'Françoise didn't exactly come through an agency.'

In my head, alarm bells are clanging. 'What do you mean?'

'I just put an advert out in *The Lady* magazine. Or was it *The Oldie*? I can't remember.'

'Dad! This is absurd. You can't do things like this. You've brought a complete stranger into our home without any references.'

He tosses down his whisky in one gulp and pours another. As he lifts his glass, I notice a crop of liver spots on his hand that surely hadn't been there on my last visit. 'I didn't say Françoise didn't have references. I said she didn't come through an agency. In fact, she brought a letter with her from people she used to look after in Lyon.'

Dad used to be a lawyer. A good one. A sharp one. How can he be so stupid?

'What if the letter was a fake?'

He laughs, tapping the side of his nose. 'What do you take me for, Emily? A besotted old fool who's going to fall for the first pair of decent legs he's seen for a long time?'

I wince. My father never used to be so crude.

'I rang them, didn't I? My French is a bit rusty but I got the gist. I spoke to the manager of a home where she was a carer and she was most complimentary.'

'How did you know that if your French is rusty?'

Dad waves his arms around airily. 'I know a "fantastique" when I hear one. Anyway, I'm perfectly happy with Françoise. She reminds me to take those blasted tablets, she sorts out my clothes, she makes these amazing cheese soufflés and she can play chess.'

'So I noticed,' I say tightly.

I have to admit that Dad looks better than he did on my previous visit. Despite my giving him some lovely cashmere jumpers for his last birthday and Christmas, he'd previously insisted on sticking to his old ones, especially the navy-blue cable-knit with holes in the elbow. Now he's wearing smart dark green cords and a cravat. He even seems to have put on a bit of weight; before, he was painfully thin. There's a mouth watering smell drifting out from the kitchen right now.

'Onion soup,' says my father, as if reading my mind. 'Then lamb chops.'

'But I don't eat meat.'

'Since when?'

'For ages, Dad. But I am a pescatarian.'

'A what?'

'It means I eat fish.'

He makes a harrumph noise. 'I don't hold with all that business. When I was your age, we ate what we were given and were grateful for it. I'll have to ask her to cook something else. You are staying for dinner, aren't you?'

'Actually, Dad,' I say, 'I'm here for a few weeks.'

'Are you?'

It's not the enthusiastic reply I'd hoped for.

'I've got some unexpected leave,' I say. Now doesn't seem the right time to tell him the whole truth.

'So why don't you use it to go somewhere more exciting?'

I kneel down on the carpet next to his chair and put my arm around him. 'I thought I'd spend some time with you instead. You know. To catch up on those weeks I haven't been able to get here.'

'Months, more like,' he mutters.

I pretend I haven't heard. He's right, of course, but I have my reasons.

'I thought we might take some trips together,' I say.

He shrugs. 'I'll need to check with Françoise. We're having a little break in St Mawes next week.'

What?

'How are you getting there?'

'I'm driving.'

'But you promised you wouldn't.'

'No I didn't. I said I'd ask the doctor and she reckons I'm fine to carry on. Now stop worrying! It's all sorted. You could come with us if you like. Couldn't she, Françoise?'

For someone so tall, this woman can slip into a room without making any noise. She must have very sharp ears – or has she been listening at the door all along?

'Of course.'

As if I need this woman's permission to accompany my father on a trip! I give her a pointed stare, but she just flashes back a sparkly grin.

'I am so looking forward to seeing the sights,' she trills. Her voice is high-pitched and girlish. It sets my teeth on edge.

'The countryside around here, la campagne, she is very beautiful.'

'It,' I correct her. 'We say "it" is very beautiful.' I know her English is better than my French but I can't help myself.

She frowns. 'Thank you, Emilee. I will write that down.' I bristle at her mispronunciation of my name – dragging out the last syllable almost like a sneer.

'And it's *Em*ily,' I say. 'Not Emil*ee*.'

She bows her head. 'I try to practise my English. It needs improving, I think, although Harold, he says she – it – is not so bad.'

I can feel the shame rise in my chest. What is it about her that is getting my back up so much?

'Perhaps you would like to go to your room before we eat?' she asks.

And there she goes again – treating me like a visitor in my own home.

'Ah,' says Dad. 'There's just one thing, Emily. The guest room has had a touch of damp. So I suggested Françoise move into your old room.'

Just perfect!

It's not like me to be sarcastic and I don't like it.

'Please. Do not worry.' Françoise is doing a very good job of looking repentant. 'I will move out. Ce n'est pas un problème.'

'Are you sure?' asks my father. 'Perhaps you could . . .'

Any minute now and he's going to suggest we share.

But Françoise cuts in. 'I could help find someone to cure the damp!' she trills. 'Such a lovely house, but she needs some care, n'est-ce pas?'

'Great idea – thank you, Françoise,' beams my father.

My blood is simmering as I remember the countless

times I've offered my help and Dad has overruled me, telling me it's unnecessary.

She drifts gracefully towards my father's chair. I watch, incredulously, as his arm shoots out and she takes it, gently easing him up. Then they walk together to the kitchen with a cosy familiarity, as if they've done this for years.

I follow behind.

I don't like this. Not one little bit.

France, 1944

I was eleven when I heard about the battle at Dunkirk on the radio. 'All those lives lost,' my mother had wept.

Even then, as a schoolboy, I'd been desperate to get out there and do my bit.

And now, here I am — only just making it before war ends, according to rumours. I'd held my breath when they'd questioned my age as I signed up.

'No papers?' they asked.

'Everything was destroyed when our house was bombed,' I replied. 'And you're eighteen?'

'That's right.'

Just as well that I'm tall for my age.

I clamber off the landing craft — one of the few lads not to have retched my way over the Channel — and stare around.

'Finis,' I mutter, as I stride up the beach, the soft yellow of the sand at odds with the stark barbed wire coiled thickly across its surface like some gargantuan snake. Apart from us, it's surprisingly quiet.

'Can you speak French?' my sergeant asks, overhearing me.

'We learned it at school, sir.'

I don't mention I was top of my class.

'Then you've got one up on most of us. And I'm Sarge to you. What's your name again?'

'Gentle. Harold Gentle.'

'Get in one of the trucks ahead then, in case we need a translator.

And make sure you don't bloody live up to your name. We need tough men, not pansies. Our job is to wipe the bastards out. Got it?'

I nod. 'Where are we going, Sarge?'

'It's not your job to ask questions. We've got a war to fight and –'

He never gets to the end of his sentence. There's a terrible noise that deafens me momentarily, setting my ears ringing. Men are falling to the right of me, puppets crumpling to the floor, their strings severed. Limbs catapult into the air.

'Mines,' someone yells. 'The Jerries have mined the bloody beach!'

5

Dinner is awkward. Despite the delicious melt-in-your-mouth sole, which Françoise has miraculously cooked at the last moment after filleting it herself. (Naturally, the conversation is stilted.) I keep trying to find out more about this woman presiding over the table but my father continually interrupts to enthuse about a soap they're clearly watching together. It's a show my father would never have watched in a month of Sundays when my mother was alive.

They loved to watch arts programmes together, especially about painting. Mum had been a keen watercolourist. Dad would frame every one, all of which are still hanging on the landing; something Mum had claimed she was embarrassed about (although I know she was secretly chuffed).

'Do you watch television, Emilee?' asks Françoise.

'Not much,' I say shortly. I don't add that I prefer to walk or read or just sleep. I'm always exhausted after shifts.

My father doesn't ask me anything about work. Even though this makes it easier to hide the horrible truth, I can't help feeling hurt at his lack of interest.

I observe Françoise eat, analysing her every move. She holds her fork daintily, continental-style, and turns down my offer of potatoes. No wonder she's so slim. Then she takes a tiny sliver of Stilton, which she serves before the dessert.

'We usually have cheese at the end of a meal in England,' I point out.

'But why?' she says, as if I am mad.

I am about to explain how Dad likes things a certain way, but notice that he is giving me a cold stare as if to say 'Don't be rude'. So I hold my tongue.

Relieved that the meal is over, I retreat with them to the sitting room. We listen to some jazz. 'The singer is called Sarah E. C. Byrne,' says my father. 'She married her bass player. Françoise told me that. Wonderful, isn't she?'

Indeed she is.

'Françoise, play us a tune would you?' Dad asks.

My mouth drops as I watch her stride towards the piano – *my* piano – and proceed to play a jaunty tune. I recognize it instantly. It's 'Reelin' and Rockin''. My parents used to jive to this, grasping hands and spinning each other round the living room, while I watched and laughed. It was never long before one of them (usually Mum) would beckon me to join in and we'd end up in a giggling heap by the end of the song.

Now I can't stop my right foot tapping along in tune, even though it feels like a betrayal.

'Bravo!' exclaims my father, clapping when she finishes.

Françoise dips her head in acknowledgement. Then he staggers up and actually kisses her on the cheek.

I know it's only a chaste kiss, the kind that you might give someone after a dinner party. But can't he see what a fool he is making of himself? Maybe he really is falling for her, but she's young, talented and beautiful. Surely she can't feel the same way? Yet she seems far too involved for this to be just another caring job.

'Please,' she says suddenly, startling me from my thoughts. 'Emilee must play too.'

Very clever.

'I'm afraid I'm rather tired,' I say.

'I would be enchanted to hear you,' she says. 'Your father says you started when you were small.'

Reluctantly, I take her place. I used to know several songs by heart, but it's been so long and my fumbling hands can't seem to find the right notes. My brain is whirling with worries: the phone calls, the missed meeting, the letter, Françoise, my father.

'Another time,' I say after a few false starts. 'I think I need an early night.'

When I'm home, Zorro always sleeps on my bed. He curls up next to me and often I wake up to find his paws around me.

But not tonight.

Instead, he stays firmly by Françoise's side, following her up to the damp spare room. Traitor!

An hour or so later I go downstairs to make a hot water bottle, my bed feeling chillier without Zorro's warmth. As I pass the sitting room, I glance inside. Dad is sitting in his chair and she is standing behind, her hands resting on his shoulders. She must have come down again.

'What are you doing?' I blurt out.

She looks at me with cool eyes, as if I have no right to ask. 'I give your father a massage. His shoulders, they ache him.'

Even if that's true, a massage is far too intimate for my liking.

I lie awake for ages. Françoise's occupancy in my bedroom has left it with a sweet-smelling perfume that churns my stomach. Moreover, my brain can't settle.

Supposing the investigation goes against me? What will I do if I can't be a midwife any longer? And even if I am allowed to continue, whispers and rumours will surely follow me everywhere I go.

I'll never be trusted again. Quite rightly.

If only Françoise wasn't here, I'd have poured all this out to my father. He'd have listened calmly, as he always did, and then given me his wise advice. He'd have made suggestions. He would have called one of his lawyer friends. He would have said that none of us are perfect.

Maybe, I tell myself, I'll get up early and catch him on his own. He's always been an early riser, like me. We can go for a gentle stroll. Yes, that's it. It will be like the old days. Him. Me. Zorro. Zorro would never turn down a walk.

There's a creak from the landing. Voices whispering. I get up and listen through the door.

'Bonne nuit, Harold!' I hear.

It's nearly one in the morning! What are they doing up so late?

I try not to think of the implications – it's too much for my brain to take in after the week I've had. I go back to bed and sit upright, watching the moon casting its silver light over the sea. Eventually, I must have dozed off because the next thing I know, the pale dawn light is filtering between the gap in the curtains and my door groans softly as it opens.

6

Zorro leaps onto my bed, nudging me. 'Come on,' he seems to say. 'Let's get out.'

So he's remembered me again! Quickly, I slip into some well-worn jeans and my blue mohair jumper – a cosy old favourite.

Dad will be up now. We'll go together and I'll tell him everything. But as I tiptoe down the stairs, I can smell coffee. A tall figure in a flimsy pale pink dressing gown is lifting the kettle off the Aga. She turns round. Françoise's long hair is not loose like it was yesterday. It is in a long, neat plait, which lies artfully down her right shoulder.

My headache, which started after the accident, immediately comes back, pounding in my temples.

'Emilee! You are up. Did you sleep well?'

'Not really,' I say tetchily. 'The thing is, several questions kept going through my mind.'

Is it my imagination or does she look a little nervous?

'What kind of questions, Emilee?'

I resist the temptation to correct her pronunciation again. There are more important things to discuss.

'About you, actually.'

Her face changes. Only slightly, but enough. Being a midwife has made me an expert in reading people. A glimmer of a smirk, a quick flick of the eyes – I had seen it all. I know what this means. Françoise has something to hide.

Then it occurs to me that I might be losing my touch because I'd clearly missed something in George's face when I'd last seen him. That's a two out of ten for me. Maybe less.

'Is there something you would like to ask me, Emilee?'

'Yes, actually. For a start, I wondered how old you are . . . if you don't mind me asking.' I added the last part hastily in case I sounded too blunt.

She beams. 'Not at all. I have twenty-four years.'

'I *am* twenty-four years *old*,' I say, unable this time to stop myself.

She beams. 'Thank you, Emily!'

Is she being sarcastic? Surely she can't be grateful for my caustic corrections?

'And what do your parents think of you coming over here?'

Her smile vanishes. Her eyes flutter downwards. 'My parents, they are both gone.'

'Oh, I'm so sorry.' Another flash of shame at my probing – did I judge her too quickly? Yet at the back of my head, a tiny, nagging voice wonders if that isn't just a little bit too convenient. I silence that voice. At work, I was so often praised for my empathy and here I am grilling a young girl who has lost her parents young. Still, I can't shake my uneasiness.

'My father says you have a letter as a reference.'

Her eyes are back up now, holding mine steadily. 'That is correct. You would like to see it?'

'Yes please,' I say.

There's a definite tension between us now. She knows I don't trust her.

'D'accord,' she says. 'Wait there.'

While she's away, I open the cupboard for the sugar, but a row of cans looks back at me. I also see that my mother's list of daily jobs (*Clean kitchen floor; wipe down fridge . . .*) has gone.

'Voilà,' says a voice behind me. 'It is the home where I used to work in France. I went straight there from school. Maman was ill, we needed the money.'

I scan the comments, which are glowing: *Excelle dans son travail . . . Très professionnelle.*

There is a number at the top with a seven crossed through, continental style. I use the message pad by the phone to make a note of it, sensing Françoise watching me. I feel uncomfortable. Yet I have every right, don't I?

I'll call later when I am alone.

'The cupboards have been rearranged,' I say.

'Yes. I clean them all. Then I put back in a better place. It is more sensible, I think.'

'I prefer the way they were before,' I say, the imperious tone in my voice betraying my true feelings. 'And where is the list that used to be inside one of the doors? Dad doesn't remember to do things himself – he needs prompts.' I don't add that I need the reminder of Mum too.

'There was a piece of paper but it fell off. I put it in a drawer. Here.'

She gives it to me. I look at my mother's handwriting. *Be kind to her*, the words seem to say. But I can't.

'How do you remember what to do and when?' I ask. In my training, it was drilled into me. Medicines had to be locked away in a certain place. Checks to be made on mothers and babies in the correct order . . .

'I write down my rota on my iPhone.' Her expression has soured, all pretence lost. Her voice is heavy with resentment. 'You are not happy with my work?'

'I did not say that. I simply want things the way they were.'

'Très bien,' she says stiffly.

Very well. I can still remember my schoolgirl French.

'Where's the sugar, by the way?' I add.

Françoise's tone is sullen. 'I give it away to the food bank.'

'Why?'

'It is not good for your father. He is pre-diabetic.'

I bite my lip. I didn't know that. Not that I'd admit it to her.

'I am très careful with his food. Already, his blood sugars are down.'

Her firm tone takes the wind out of my sails. I find myself unable to speak. I've been trying for so long to get Dad to lose some weight but he wouldn't listen to me. Yet this woman has succeeded where I have failed.

I watch as she gets down on her knees and starts laboriously moving the mugs out of their new place and back to the old.

'You don't need to do it right now,' I say.

'I think it is best,' she snaps without turning round.

Zorro is pawing at me. 'Soon,' I say. 'Wait for Dad.'

'He will be asleep for a while,' Françoise says, with a hint of satisfaction in her voice.

'How do you know?' I reply sharply.

'Because he never has breakfast until nine.'

'That isn't true. He's always been an early riser.'

'Now I work for him, he can lie in later.' She looks at

Zorro. 'He doesn't have to walk the dog so early because I am here.'

'Well, now I'm here too,' I say.

Grabbing the lead, I stride out of the back door, my body pulsing with pent-up irritation. As Zorro tears off over the fields, I call the number I wrote down.

A voice answers almost immediately.

'I am ringing from the UK to check a reference,' I say.

'Of course.' The woman speaks perfect English. 'I have been expecting this. It is for Françoise Alarie?'

I am taken back. 'Yes. I believe she worked for you?'

'Vraiment! Mademoiselle Alarie was very satisfactory. We were sad when she left, but pleased she has found a good job in England.'

'Can you tell me exactly what her role was for you?'

'Françoise began as a cleaner but she showed such care and empathy with our residents that she became a carer.'

'Did she have the necessary qualifications?'

The voice is mildly reproving. 'When people are dying, they do not always need someone with a certificate to hold their hands. Kindness and a practical nature are, in my experience, more important.'

'Dying?' I repeat, stunned.

'Yes. Our home specializes in end-of-life care. Did Françoise not tell you that? She was wonderful at easing our residents through the final part of their journey.'

My mouth is dry. Easing them through? End of life?

A terrible thought comes into my head.

No. That's crazy. Isn't it?

7

Am I jumping to conclusions? The question goes over and over in my mind as I lie in bed unable to sleep again that night.

Then again, you read about it all the time. Con men fleecing old people out of thousands to tarmac perfectly good drives or fix roofs that don't need mending. Fraudsters ringing at random and demanding bank details. Couples who change their wills at the last minute and leave their money to the gardener or the neighbours because one of them was 'so very kind' when their grown-up children weren't around to help.

This Françoise Alarie might just as well have flounced into Willowmead with a balaclava on her head instead of a tight pair of jeans and a revealing top.

'I hope your dad marries again,' Mum said towards the end. 'He's not the kind of man who does well on his own.'

I'd always thought he was too old to find someone else, but now look at him. I'd watched him ogling her earlier this evening as he and Françoise did their chair yoga together before dinner. Chair yoga!

'That's right, Harold. Now lift your arms! Perfect.'

Other than walking Zorro, he's always hated any kind of physical exertion. What makes it worse is that he was never the kind of man to look at another woman. He adored my mother. Never had eyes for anyone else. It just doesn't stack up. Now his tongue is almost hanging out of his mouth.

I can hardly tell him that he's making a fool of himself; I know he'd get all defensive and tell me I'd got the wrong idea. I need to think about this. Very carefully.

Being an only child, I've always been close to my parents. When Mum died, Dad and I clung together in our grief. I know I haven't been able to get down here as often as I should. But it's always hard with shift work to plan anything, let alone a trip all this way.

Eventually I fall into a troubled sleep. I wake very early, when it's still dark, with the whisper of an apricot morning streaking the sky. I go downstairs and Zorro is already there, standing by the coat rack in the hall, sniffing at the chic, expensive-looking suede jacket that Françoise wears.

There is no sign of the owner herself.

'Shall we go for a walk on our own again?' I whisper conspiratorially.

He's still nosing at the coat. The right-hand pocket to be exact. Swiftly, I unzip it and put my hand in. And what do I find? Cubes of Cheddar cheese.

Of course! So that's why he is so affectionate towards her. We don't even give Zorro dog biscuits.

'So she's been bribing you, has she?' I snort, as I slip the lead over his head and open the back door. 'Bet she's got a stash of other treats up in her room. No wonder you're so keen to go up with her every night.'

Zorro gives me a baleful look. 'You're just like all men,' I say, heading for the beach. 'Unable to resist.'

George's face flashes in my mind's eye. He hasn't returned the desperate 'I'm in trouble' call I made to him last night. I wish I hadn't now. It's not as though we'd even had that date. But it would be nice to have his support.

Zorro and I are walking down the wooded footpath, bordered by juicy blackberries, ripe for the picking. We reach the flat part without me even realizing. My feet are on autopilot while my mind runs wild.

Zorro is bounding ahead. It's steep here, with no hedging. When I was a child, I'd fallen badly, rolling down to the cliff's edge. My father had thrown himself forward and grabbed my arm just in time. It was one of the few occasions he'd ever been angry with me. 'Never do that again, Emily,' he'd thundered. 'You could have been killed.'

Now, as I look down at the beach below with its sharp rocks, jagged and jutting like some huge fossilized sea creature's mouth, I shiver.

'He's only cross because we love you so much,' my mother had soothed.

I am in my mid-thirties. No husband. No children. Possibly no career now. If Françoise takes away my father, I will have nothing.

My head begins to ache again. I know I ought to get it checked out but the last place I could bear right now is a doctor's surgery.

I carry on walking, picking up speed until I'm running full tilt. Then, at last – the sea. It stretches out before me like a glassy plain. I often swam in the winter as a teenager. Why not now? I didn't bring my costume but I could strip down to my underwear and put on my jeans afterwards.

Then Zorro starts barking. Not a bark of warning, but one of anticipation. He's racing ahead on the beach towards an approaching figure.

I'd recognize him anywhere.

8

I hold my breath as he gets nearer.

The first boy who held my hand, at fourteen, when we walked back from school together. The boy who would share an ice-cream cone with me as we sat on the wall overlooking the sea, swinging our legs in time with each other. The boy who, just before my seventeenth birthday, had kissed me during our evening strolls, bare feet in the cool sand. The first who had pressed himself against me. Who had announced, after our A levels, that perhaps we ought to 'have some time apart'. The boy who had broken my heart. Shattered it in thousands of pieces.

The man who had returned to our home village some years later, as the new partner in Dad's old firm, and with a wife who was seven months pregnant.

'Did you give Nick the job?' I'd asked Dad accusingly.

'Of course not,' Dad said. 'You know I'm not involved in the business any more. I understand it's hard, but you have to try and put the past behind you.'

Easier said than done. If I am fully honest with myself, Nick is the true reason I can't face coming home as often as I should.

'Hi,' I say, heart pounding and palms sweaty, forcing my voice to sound normal. 'Down, Zorro. Down.'

'It's all right.' Nick bends down to give Zorro a pat. 'Good to see you both. I heard you were back for a bit.'

'Just using up some holiday leave so I can spend some time with Dad,' I say. Subtly, I try to take him in. He still has that boyish look about his face, although his blond hair is shorter and there are lines around his eyes. My mother used to say that he reminded her of Robert Redford.

'I expect he's pleased to see you. I hear he has a live-in carer now.'

'Yes,' I say brightly, giving nothing away.

'French,' he adds.

'That's right.' My head's throbbing again.

'How about you?' I ask. 'Is the family well?'

Each one of those words sticks in my throat. I have to squeeze them out one at a time in a false jolly voice. This is possibly the longest conversation I've had with Nick for years. And yet it still hurts.

'Actually, Sophie and I aren't . . . well . . . we're having a break.'

I feel my heart rate step up a notch. It's even harder to keep my voice neutral than it was before. 'I see.'

He shoves his hands deep in his pockets and glances down at the sand. How often did Nick and I come down here as night settled in? The waves had lapped at our feet as he had pulled me towards him.

'It was her idea,' he says. 'Things haven't been great for some time. She felt that it was better to put things on pause sooner than later, while Billy was still little.'

Billy. An image of a small boy with a shock of blond hair just like Nick's flashes into my head. I passed them on a visit home last year: Sophie, Nick, their son dangling in between, grasping each of their hands and looking up at them with total trust. My heart had filled with longing, regret and the sharp pang of jealousy.

'I'm so sorry,' I say. 'Are they still living in the village?'

His voice is raw with pain. 'They've moved nearer Sophie's parents so they can help while she goes back to work.' He swallows hard. 'Still, Billy is coming down this weekend to stay with me over half term. I can't wait.'

I look at him directly for the first time. Until now, I've been trying not to. He knows me so well and I'm scared of what he might see in my eyes. Not only this ridiculous infatuation, which I can't seem to move past, but every terrible event of this week. My suspicion towards Françoise. My pain over the Smiths. My fury towards George. It can't just be *my* fault. But who will believe me? A midwife against a consultant . . .

'So,' he says, 'how long are you staying, exactly?'

'I'm not sure,' I say, careful not to mention the real reason I'm here.

'Your father must be pleased to have you back.'

'I'm not sure about that either.'

The words slip out before I can take them back.

'Why?' He looks at me with that intense gaze I recall so well.

'Oh, nothing really.'

'Are you sure?'

'Well . . . Dad seems rather attached to this Françoise.'

'Ah.' Something gives in his eyes. 'I did wonder. Well, I expect he's glad of the company.'

'I know. It's my fault for staying away too long.'

He shakes his head. 'I'm not saying that, Emily.'

I used to love the way he said my name. Now it's more clipped. Detached.

'We all have our own stuff going on,' he continues. 'But she's made quite an impression in the village.'

I feel a surge of jealousy. 'Has she?'

'Well, with some people, anyway. She helps out with the food bank and has joined the sewing committee to repair the samplers at church.'

I want to tell Nick that I'd rung the number on her only 'reference'. That she'd specialized in end-of-life care. That she'd been good at helping people 'through the final part of their journey'.

I could have told the old Nick. The one who is still eighteen in my head.

But I know he'll think I'm overreacting. That I'm being overemotional – like I always have been.

Maybe he'd be right.

'I'm going to head back now,' he says. 'Lovely to see you.'

He reaches out a hand. It all feels horribly formal.

'Lovely to see you too,' I say, flustered, colour rising to my cheeks as he walks away.

My heart feels flat. Sad too, at what might have been. Then I tell myself there's no point in dwelling on the past.

No time for a swim now. I need to get back to the house to see what Françoise is up to.

I glimpse her long wavy raven hair – unplaited today – through the window of the study as I reach the house. What is she doing there? I go in through the back door, settle Zorro in his basket and then tiptoe to the study as quietly as I can. She looks around, sensing my presence.

There's a quick ping from Dad's desktop. She must have just closed whatever she was working on.

'Your father . . . he has asked me to alter the details for our trip to St Mawes,' she says. 'I have added a third bedroom so you can join us.'

She makes me feel like an interloper.

'How do you know his password?' I say.

'He gives it to me.' Her voice is cool and authoritative.

Then she gets up from my father's desk. 'I do not see Zorro this morning.'

'No. I was up early and took him for a walk with me. By the way, I would prefer it if you didn't give him cheese to eat.'

Too late, I realize she'll know I found it in her coat pocket.

'I found a piece on the hall floor,' I add hastily.

She knows I am lying. But she's too smart to confront me.

'Very well,' she shrugs, nonchalant.

Then I see it. Sitting by my father's computer. 'Is that Dad's credit card?' I ask.

'Oh yes. Thank you for reminding me.'

Casually, she picks it up and slips it in her pocket.

'He's given you permission to use that?' I ask.

'Of course. I do not steal it.'

'I didn't say you had.'

She is looking at me steadily. 'D'accord. I go to prepare his breakfast now.'

There's no getting away from it. She knows I don't like her. And I know she doesn't like me.

9

There's a change of plan. We're going to the Lizard before St Mawes. Not only that. But we're staying at the hotel we used to go to with Mum every year.

'I want our guest to see as much of the south-west as possible,' Dad announces over dinner that night.

Our guest? The hired help, more like.

Françoise's eyes are shining. She looks directly at me as she speaks. Challengingly. 'I cannot wait! The Lizard, this is at the end of the country, non?'

'It's the southernmost point of the UK mainland,' I reply coolly. 'It's a favourite of ours.'

I stress the 'ours'.

The journey takes just over two hours. My father drives. Just like he always did. He likes to be in control. I'm relieved to find that, despite his age, he still has a keen eye for the road, although unfortunately he hasn't lost his irritating habit of providing a running commentary. 'Look at that idiot in the Volvo? Can't he see a right of way when there is one?'

'You need to turn right at the next junction,' I say, studying the map.

'On the ball as usual,' says my dad approvingly. 'My right-hand batman, you are, just like the old days! Remember when your mother got us lost in the middle of Dartmoor because she got the roads muddled up?'

I giggled. 'We might not have got out if it wasn't for that farmer who told us to follow his tractor.'

'Sometimes I think she pretended to be inept at map reading so you could shine instead,' says Dad.

I'd never thought of it like that. But it would be typical of her kindness. Mum was always boosting my self-esteem. Telling me I could do anything if I wanted. What would she think of me now, after what had happened in London?

Françoise sits in the back with Zorro. She is rather pale and quieter than usual.

'Are you all right?' I ask, my professional concern creeping in.

'I am often sick when I sit in the back of a car,' she says faintly. The thought comes into my mind that maybe she's jealous of the 'do you remember' conversation between Dad and me.

'Then you and Emily must swap seats,' says my father, glancing in the rear-view mirror with a look on his face that can only be described as genuine care. 'You should have said before, Françoise.'

'I do not want to take your daughter's place,' she says softly.

'Nonsense,' he retorts. 'Emily doesn't mind. Do you, Emily?'

Just as I've started to feel natural with Dad, he undermines me again. But it would look churlish to say that yes, I do mind. Very much. In fact, it makes my headache start up again.

'Of course,' I say with as much grace as I can muster.

'That's settled, then. There's a lay-by ahead. I'll pull in there.'

I get out and Françoise does the same, looking even paler than before.

'Thank you, Emilee,' she says.

'Avec plaisir.'

It comes out with a sarcastic undercurrent that I had not intended to slip out.

My father gives me a 'that's not very nice' look and once more I feel like a scolded child. I'd forgotten how parents can do that, no matter how old you are.

After a couple of miles, Françoise is back to her usual perky self. 'Your colour has returned,' says my father, glancing across at her.

'I feel better,' she chirps. 'Thank you so much, Emilee.'

'It's nothing,' I say, gritting my teeth.

My phone pings. A text from Nick. So he still has my number.

Good to see you again. Would you like to meet up for a coffee sometime?

My heart jumps.

But my head is cautioning. What if it all goes wrong again?

I text back:

How about a walk?

That's better. More neutral. Capable of being interpreted as a friendly stroll. I have enough going on without adding heartbreak into the mix.

Besides, how can I even think about romance after the Smiths?

'C'est magnifique!'

I sit up. We can see the sea glistening before us. The beautiful hotel, with its red brick and a wide drive leading up, is just as I remember it. Below are layers of cliffs, each as rugged as the next. As we get out, the wind whips my hair.

'Hold my arm, Harold. The wind, it blows hard. You might fall.'

Françoise is there before me, steadying him as they make their way up to the door.

'Lock the car, can you, Emily?' calls out my father, tossing the keys.

I follow them with their two cases and my holdall, wondering whether Dad even wants me to be on this trip. All that warmth during our map-reading reminiscences has disappeared. Now I feel like the hanger-on.

I unpack a few things but it's clear that Zorro needs a comfort break. I take him along the narrow footpath at the top of the cliff, careful to steer him away from the edge. The gorse is in full bloom, its bright yellow flowers like stars, camouflage for the bushes' prickly stems. A bit like people. An attractive outward appearance can distract others from the inner, darker part.

We're out longer than I meant to be. There's no time to change out of my scruffy jeans. As I head to the dining room, I can see my father with Françoise – in a figure-hugging red jersey dress – at the far window overlooking the cliffs. Her head is tilted to one side as she listens attentively to whatever he is saying.

No doubt he's describing the formation of the rocks or giving her some facts about the local area. My father is good at that – always keen to impress with his encyclopaedic knowledge of seemingly everything. I wonder for a minute if Françoise finds him as fascinating as I do, or whether she is just putting on a good show.

'I'm sorry, madam,' says the waiter as I start to walk towards them. 'Dogs are not allowed in here.'

'But they always used to be,' I say.

'The rules have changed, madam. There is a special area next door for eating if you want to keep your dog with you. Or you can leave him in the room.'

Zorro hates being left on his own in places he doesn't know. 'I just need to tell my father,' I say. I try gesticulating but he is still jabbering on to Françoise. She glances across at me briefly yet she carries on listening intently, her head cupped in her hand. Wilfully ignoring my waving arm.

'I can tell him where you are,' says the waiter.

I detect a look of sympathy on his face that makes me feel even more pathetic.

I make my way to the dog-owners' area and order a crab sandwich. It's delicious, but every mouthful sticks in my throat. With no one to talk to, my head starts buzzing with everything I've done wrong since last week.

I keep going over the hospital scene again and again in my head. What did I miss? The birth had been slightly delayed, but it wasn't out of the ordinary. Of course, I should have phoned the union for help straight away after my senior midwife had rung me but it feels too late now. I just wanted to talk to Dad first. To ask his advice on what to do next. But I'd been thrown by Françoise's presence and now I'm here and so is she, and the longer I leave it, the harder it is to say. And this situation with Françoise feels more pressing every day. How long will it be until she's had enough of his waffle and finally commences her end game to get what she wants? I'm presuming it's money unless – please, no – she's after marriage.

It's all too much. My head is aching again. And then I hear it. Her laugh, like the jangle of wind chimes in a warm summer breeze.

I go out into the corridor. 'Ah there you are, Emily,' says my father. 'We waited but you didn't come down so I'm afraid we ate without you.'

I try to explain about being directed to the dog-owners' room but he isn't listening.

'Shall we take a little stroll now?' Françoise suggests.

'Great idea,' says my father. Apparently all Françoise's ideas are great.

'I must change first,' she coos.

Good. It will allow me time with my father, alone.

'Dad,' I begin, carefully after she leaves. 'I can see that Françoise is very helpful but –'

'She is, isn't she?' he says cutting in.

'I just wondered if you are allowing her to be just a little too familiar.'

He frowns. 'What do you mean?'

'Well . . . I gather you let her use your credit card.'

'That's right.'

'Is that wise?'

His eyes are boring into me like skewers. 'Why not? I trust her.'

'She used to work with the elderly,' I say.

'I know that.'

His tone of voice is sharpening even more.

'She specializes in end-of-life care,' I venture uneasily.

'What are you saying, Emily? That I'm going to pop my clogs?'

I give a nervous laugh. 'No. Of course not. But . . .'

'Je suis prête!'

I stop. That was quick. In a few minutes, Françoise has transformed herself from a 'lady who lunches' into 'country casual chic' with skinny jeans, ankle boots and little zip-up leather jacket complete with a jaunty white beret with one of those small tails on top. I have a sudden juvenile urge to pull it off. I clasp my hands behind my back.

'You look lovely, my dear,' says my father.

She preens. 'Merci, Harold.'

I want to throw up.

The wind has dropped now. The grounds in front of the hotel are dotted with lush palm trees and bordered with autumn-flowering blush roses. We stroll through them, pausing briefly at the bench overlooking the imposing cliffs.

'I have never seen anywhere so beautiful,' breathes Françoise.

Oh, come on! I want to say. I mean it's lovely, but she's going over the top to please Dad.

'What about the French countryside?' I ask. 'I'm sure that's beautiful too.'

'I only know Lyon,' she shrugs. 'When I was a child, we did not have the money for family holidays. And when I started working, my wages were needed for Maman and our rent.'

'Then we must make sure you enjoy this little break, mustn't we, Emily?' says my father.

'Yes,' I say as sunnily as I can. 'We must.'

This is the way forward, I suddenly realize. I will flatter Françoise from now on. I will praise her more. I'll be friendly, wait for her to open up. Then maybe, sooner or later, she will make a mistake.

Everyone makes mistakes, as I know all too well.

Zorro is pawing at my ankles. He wants to go further but I sense that Dad isn't up to it.

'You go on,' he says. 'We'll just sit here for a bit.'

I agree reluctantly – feeling like a child who has been dismissed so the adults can have some alone time. When I return to the bench a while later, it's empty.

So they've just abandoned me again!

Then I hear a high-pitched scream that sends cold shocks shooting through me.

'Harold! HAROLD!'

France, 1944

The convoy of lorries rattles along the narrow roads, high hedges obscuring the land on either side.

We swerve suddenly to avoid the rotting corpse of a cow.

'Why doesn't someone move it?' I ask the man next to me.

'Maybe it's a decoy,' he says tightly. 'Free meat. For all we know, son, a Jerry might be waiting in the hedge to gun down anyone who stops.'

Nausea rises up from my stomach and into my throat. I've only been in France for two hours but I've already seen enough death and gore to last me a lifetime.

'What do we do if we meet a German soldier?' I say, trying not to tremble.

'Point your gun at him. Your average Jerry will surrender pretty quick. Some of them don't want to be here any more than we do.'

'Thanks,' I say. Despite the horrors on the beach when we landed and the fear of everything ahead, I feel proud to be here for my country.

'Pleasure, lad.' He puts out a hand. It feels rough, as though he's a working man. 'The name's Albert Evans. What's yours?'

'Harold Gentle.'

I'm aware my hand is shaking with nerves. He can probably feel it.

'Tell you what, Harold. This will help.'

Reaching inside his camouflage jacket, he produces a bottle of whisky. 'Take a slug of this.'

I swallow it gratefully. The sweet burn makes my sickness feel better already and numbs my brain in a rather pleasing fashion.

'Thanks,' I say, rather loudly in my enthusiasm.

'Shh. We don't want the others having any.'

Then he takes a slug himself and slips it back. 'You're a young kid,' he says. 'You need a bit of Dutch courage. Have this an' all.'

He puts a cigarette in my hand. I've never had one before. It makes me cough but it also helps me feel older than I am. Ready to take on anything.

We go on for a couple of hours and then the sound of an engine roars overhead.

'Pull in,' yells the sarge. The driver almost rams us into the hedge in an attempt to get out of sight. 'Down under your seats everyone.'

Shaking, I do as I'm told but not before sneaking a look upwards. The plane's got black crosses on the wings.

This is it, I tell myself. Strangely, I feel calm. I'd rather end my life _doing_ something other than sitting at school while countless faceless others are giving up their lives. The authorities seemed to understand that. Maybe that's why they accepted my lie about my age without asking for proof.

'I'd have done the same as you, son,' my father had said proudly when I told him. 'If they hadn't turned me down for my dodgy chest, I'd be out there myself.' He slapped me on the back. 'Good luck, lad. Don't tell your mum. I'll sort it when you're gone.'

The plane is circling above us, bringing me back to the present.

I never even said goodbye to her, my mum. And now it might be too late.

'DOWN,' yells the sarge again.

The explosion is so earth-shatteringly loud that it feels like I'm being sucked into a huge wave, the air pressure roaring in my lugholes.

Then it stops. There's an acrid burning smell. I begin to choke with the smoke. So does everyone else. I open my eyes. We are still here. All of us. The vehicle is intact.

61

'That was a piece of luck,' says the sergeant.

We stare at the ball of fire in front that used to be a German fighter.

We move off. There is just room to squeeze through. As we pass the burning aircraft I see a hand inside the cockpit. Waving. Silently begging for help.

Stop! I want to say. What has got into me? I came here to kill Germans, didn't I? But this is a human hand. Suddenly this war feels very real. And instead of feeling heroic, it seems hollow, cruel, evil.

But what can I do? The Jerries will kill us if we don't kill them first.

And so we drive on. That hand still in my head.

10

'Harold!' Françoise screams again.

Zorro is barking frantically. I have to hold him back to stop him running forward.

My stomach freefalls. I spot the two of them, standing on the edge of a sheer cliff. Below, the sea is churning with angry grey waves.

She is clutching his arm. I see my father sway. For a minute, I think she is pushing him. I shoot forward, my breath gasping in my lungs, my feet pounding. Françoise is pulling him back up. 'Hold on to me, Harold! Hold on!' she is yelling.

I reach them. Grab hold of his other arm. Together we get him to the bench. Dad's face is ashen.

'What happened?' I shout.

'It was my fault.' My father's voice is hoarse. Scared. 'I wanted to show Françoise the view.'

'How can you be so daft?' I yell at her. 'He's an old man.'

'I do not want to,' says Françoise tearfully. 'But he sets off before me. I go there to stop him.'

Can I trust her word? My gut instinct says no.

'Stop arguing,' snaps my father. 'I've already told you. It was my fault. If it wasn't for Françoise, I might have died.'

He clutches her arm tearfully. 'I owe you my life.'

'You owe me nothing, Harold,' she says. 'You are safe.

That is all we want.' She turns her wide eyes on me. 'Isn't it, Emilee?'

All *we* want?

I see what she's doing. Making my father more and more reliant on her. Putting him deeply in her debt. But if I say something, I will look petty. Jealous even. I remember my earlier resolution to play along.

'Yes,' I say. 'Of course it is.'

Dad spends the rest of the day resting. He doesn't come down for dinner. 'I'm a little shakier than I realized,' he says when I knock on his door. 'You girls eat without me.'

I invite Françoise to join Zorro and me in the doggy dining room but she declines. 'I think I have an early night,' she says. 'It was such a frightening experience, n'est-ce pas?'

She pauses, as if expecting me to congratulate her again for saving my father. Despite my resolve to get on her good side, I can't bring myself to say anything.

I go to my room to fetch my book, then realize I've left it in the car. As I go outside, the moon is shining down, projecting a milky path on the midnight blue waves below. For a moment, I feel peace descending. The sea always does that to me.

My father's car is the old-fashioned type where you have to turn the key in the door lock but, strangely, it's already open. Dad's words come back to me from when we'd arrived. 'Lock the car, can you, Emily?'

I had. I'm sure I had. Hadn't I? But the more I think about it, the more I begin to wonder. I shake my head with a jolt, I must have just turned it the wrong way. Nothing's been taken. But it's still unsettling.

*

When Françoise comes down for breakfast the following morning, I am waiting for her with Zorro at the foot of the stairs after our walk.

'Have you seen Dad?' I ask.

'Only before bed,' she replies.

I try to hold on to my resolve to be bright and kind while restraining Zorro, who is intent on licking this woman's hands. Traitor! 'I thought you were both having early nights,' I say.

'I check on him before I retired,' she answers. 'We had a mug of cocoa together.'

'In his room?'

'That is right.'

I try not to show the hurt on my face at being left out of yet another ritual. But then I notice something. My heart starts to race.

'Those earrings!' I blurt out.

She touches them, one at a time. Her fingers are long and slim, unlike my short, squat ones. 'They are beautiful, oui?'

I stare at the round, blue sapphires set in gold. 'They look just like a pair my mother always wore,' I say. The thudding from my chest is so loud that she must hear it. They cannot be. She will correct me now.

'They are.' She flashes those perfect white teeth. 'Your father, he presented them to me last night. He wanted to thank me for saving his life.'

I cannot speak with shock. My mother had left her jewellery collection to me. I was worried about taking it to London – in case it got lost or stolen – but Dad had told me to leave it with him, where it would be 'safe' until I was ready.

These particular earrings, which had matched her deep blue eyes, had been her favourite. As a child, I'd gaze at her delicate beauty as she put them on before a dance or fancy dinner. '*I know how much you like these, darling,*' my mother had said with her soft smile. '*One day you will have them, I promise.*'

'Good morning,' says my father.

He beams at us both. You would not know that yesterday he had had such a close brush with death. Just one step more, the loosening of Françoise's grip, and he'd be gone.

'Good morning, Harold,' beams Françoise.

'How are you, Dad?' I ask. Despite my effort to sound calm, I can hear the strain in my voice.

Inside, I am boiling. Bursting to ask him what the hell he was thinking, giving this girl my earrings. But I have to hold it in. Wait until she has gone, I tell myself as they go into the dining room together. Zorro and I will hover outside, no matter how long they take.

Eventually they come out. 'I must freshen up,' she says, 'before our shopping trip.'

'Shopping trip?' I repeat.

'Yes,' booms my father. 'I thought we would take Françoise round some of the gift shops.'

'Just one thing,' I say. 'Did either of you go out to the car last night?'

They both look at me. 'No,' says Dad. 'Why?'

'I found it unlocked.'

'Perhaps you forgot to secure her,' suggests Françoise brightly.

'You must be more careful, Emily,' says my father.

Is it me? Or is this woman trying to make me doubt myself?

She glides off. The waiters all watch her go, with admiration on their faces.

'Françoise is wearing Mum's earrings,' I say tightly.

'That's right.' Dad is looking at me steadily. 'I wanted to thank her for saving my life.'

'Saving it or nearly pushing you off herself?'

'What do you mean?'

'I saw her, Dad. She had your arm.'

'Don't be ridiculous, Emily! She was pulling me back.'

Our voices are raised. People are glancing over curiously.

I try to control my voice. He needs to take me seriously. 'You can't give away what Mum left to me. It's not yours to give.'

'She actually left them to me to bestow at my discretion.'

'That's not how I remember it.'

Dad's eyes go hard. 'Well, it's true.'

I love my father, but, like I've said before, he can never be wrong. To him, it's a sign of weakness. Mum used to say it was because of his job. A lawyer has to be sure of his facts.

'Why did you bring the earrings in the first place, anyway?' I demand.

'I was going to give them to you as a surprise.'

'And why didn't you?'

'I changed my mind.'

There isn't a hint of embarrassment, of wrongdoing. Another hangover from his courtroom days along with his proclivity to elaborate, to embellish or bend the truth to his favour. When I was growing up, Mum would always tell me to leave it and not argue back. But right now, I can't.

'So instead of giving them to me, you donated them to a total stranger?'

67

'She's not a stranger. Really, Emily. I don't know what's got into you. You haven't been the same since you came back. Not that I saw you for months before that.'

'I told you. I was working.'

'Everyone works, Emily. But they can still spare time to see their elderly father. Can't they?'

So he *is* cross with me for being away for so long, even though he'd said he understood.

'I'm sorry.'

'And now, just because I have found someone to keep me company, you're jealous and acting like a spoilt child.'

Dad stands up. He has his hand on a side table as if steadying himself. 'I would have thought better of you than that, Françoise.'

'I'm Emily. Not Françoise.'

'That's what I said.'

'It's NOT,' I retort.

And with that, he makes his way upstairs. I'm aware that people walking past are staring at me. Mortified, I make a quick exit myself.

I walk Zorro again. He doesn't need it, but I have to clear my head.

Had I been too hasty? No.

Could she have tried to push him? Yes. Maybe.

Should I tell Dad what had happened on the maternity unit? I want to but I don't feel that I can trust him. I'm not even sure he'd be on my side. His scorn would be unbearable. It would make it all even worse.

When I get back, my father is in the lobby. His bags are

68

packed. He is tight-lipped. 'We're going home now,' he says flatly.

I'm taken aback. 'What about St Mawes?'

'No. Françoise says she prefers to go back.'

'Why?'

His voice is clipped and cold. 'She wanted to know why I was upset, so I told her what you said about the earrings. She is distressed that you thought so badly of her and says she does not feel comfortable now being on holiday with you.'

'This is ridiculous. I'm the one who should be upset.'

I stop as Françoise comes down the stairs, as if on cue. There's a brief flash of triumph on her face as she stares at me.

And then I realize. This was all set up.

This woman is clever.

And she's dangerous.

She flaunted those earrings this morning knowing what my reaction would be.

I'm pretty certain too that she did try to push Dad off that cliff and then 'save' him to get his lifelong gratitude.

We drive home in silence. My father opens the front door. He makes a gesture for Françoise to go in first.

There's a small pile of post on the floor. She bends down to pick it up. One has a French stamp, I notice. Another looks official. Françoise inspects it and looks up.

'This one is for you.' She hands the letter to me.

It has an NHS logo on it. And, stamped in blood red across the front: CONFIDENTIAL.

11

I put the letter from the hospital in my chest of drawers. Still sealed.

If I don't open it, then I can say I haven't read it.

That's not a lie. It wouldn't mean I didn't get it. Receiving something is one thing. Absorbing the contents is another. I haven't lived with my father for all these years without picking up some of his lawyer's tricks.

Perhaps I shouldn't have given Willowmead as my contact address on my hospital file. But at the time it seemed best because it was more permanent than a rental address that I might leave at any time. I go downstairs. Dad is nowhere to be seen. The door to the sitting room is open. Françoise is at the piano. *My* piano. Her fingers move fluently across the keyboard. Her face is set, her expression different. There's a look of determination. Concentration. Fire brimming in her eyes. It scares me.

Then she stops. Her eyes close. It's as though she is sleeping upright.

I stand for a minute, just watching. Then she shakes herself, stretches and sees me. Her face immediately sharpens. 'Emilee,' she says. As if I could be anyone else. 'I am sorry. I meditate. Do you practise it?'

'No,' I say, rather taken aback. 'I don't have time.'

'You must. It is so calming. And you can do it anywhere!'

Then she tips her head in that way she does with my father. 'Do you have some time? I want to talk to you.'

Her voice rings with an impressive display of hurt. If she thinks I'm going to apologize over the earrings, she has another think coming.

'How is your head?' she asks.

'My head?'

'Yes. You said it gave you pain.'

'Did I? When?'

'In the car. You were half asleep I think but you kept saying, "my head, it throbs".'

'My head is fine, thanks,' I lie quickly. 'Have you seen my father?'

'He has gone to bed early.'

'But we haven't had dinner.'

She shrugs. 'He is tired.'

He hadn't even said goodnight to me. In the past, even if we'd had a disagreement, he'd always make sure we ended the day on good terms.

'I think I make an omelette,' she says. 'Would you like one too?'

'No thanks,' I say shortly. The prospect of making small talk over supper puts me off the idea of eating altogether.

'Quel dommage,' she says. 'Your father, he likes my omelettes very much. I make them with herbs.'

I need air to get away from this woman, so I take Zorro down to the beach. I love the sea at night. It's beautiful during the day, but when it's dark, it takes on a different identity. The moon streaks a silver trail through the waves, which are strangely still after the roughness of the Lizard coast.

'Evening,' I say quietly to a pair of fishermen with their lights and rods. You always get someone here whatever the hour. I often wonder what they think of when waiting for the fish to bite. Are their minds whirling with worries like mine? Or are they able to have that blank, peaceful silence in their heads that I have tried for so long to achieve?

'Emily!'

I jump.

It's Nick. Coming up from behind me. The tide is going out, leaving bare fresh sand and removing the tell-tale crunch from the shingle.

'I'm sorry. I didn't mean to startle you.'

'It's all right.'

I'm not surprised to see him. We've both always been drawn to the sea. It wasn't far from here that we . . .

No. I won't allow myself to think of that time. We've both moved on.

'How are things?' he asks.

We seem to have fallen into step. We're walking together now, side by side along the shore.

'Fine,' I say but the word comes out like a sob.

'I know you better than that,' he says quietly.

You used to, I almost say.

Under the light of the moon, I can see his eyes are soft, sympathetic. This both scares and comforts me. 'Do you want to talk about it?' he adds.

Once more, I can't make up my mind. Since the Smiths, I hesitate over every decision. Scared of getting it wrong.

'Is it your father and Françoise?'

I stiffen. 'Why do you say that?'

'Because of our last conversation.'

I try to remember exactly what I'd said. Something about not trusting her. But that was before our trip to the Lizard. I can hardly say that I think Françoise tried to push my father over a cliff. I have no proof.

'Let's just say that things aren't very easy at the moment,' I say. My mind shoots back to that hospital envelope in the drawer. 'For all kinds of reasons.'

'I'm sorry. It's the same for me, actually.' He sighs. 'I never thought I'd end up getting divorced.'

'That must be really hard,' I say, hiding my surprise. So they're not just on a break. It's over.

'Thanks.' He's looking down. Avoiding eye contact. 'It feels as though it's happening to someone else.'

I get that. 'Is there any chance that you and your wife might be able to work it out?'

I inwardly cringe at my words *your wife*. Nick's words, when we were teenagers, are still etched on my heart. '*I will never find anyone else like you. Never.*'

'It doesn't look like it at the moment.' He's looking up now. Gazing directly into my soul. Just as he used to. Or is that my imagination?

'It's Billy I'm worried about,' Nick continues. 'He's eight. Too young to understand everything but old enough to know that something's going on. It's confusing for him.'

'It must be,' I say gently. 'I mean, I know I don't have children of my own but we get plenty on the ward, coming to see their new brother or sister.'

'I bet you're really good with them.' His voice sounds deliberately lighter.

I'm embarrassed now. It feels as though he's trying to compensate for the fact that I'm childless. There have been times when I've thought of going to a sperm bank, to be honest. One of my Scandinavian doctor friends did that. She now has a beautiful little girl and is 'perfectly happy'.

But would it be fair on a child to be brought up by one parent, especially when I'm at work so much? Yet maybe it's better than two warring ones.

'Actually,' he says, 'you know I said Billy was coming to stay? He's here now. We're going to take a picnic down to the far side of the beach tomorrow. Would you like to join us? It's going to be sunny according to my weather app.'

'I'd love to,' I blurt out, taken by surprise. What have I just done? You can't go back. Everyone knows that. Especially not after what I did. Perhaps Nick just feels sorry for me. Poor Emily. Still on her own. And now some young French woman is cosying up to her dad. Everyone finding someone, except for her.

'Great.' He seems genuinely pleased. 'We'll pick you up, shall we? Is ten-ish all right?'

Zorro comes bounding up.

'Can I bring him too?'

'Of course. Billy loves dogs.' He squats down on the sand and tickles Zorro's tummy. 'I always wanted one but it didn't seem fair with us both working.'

There it was again. *Us*. Always an 'us'.

As he speaks, the moon goes behind a cloud. The beach is suddenly very dark. 'Shall I walk you home?' he asks.

'No thanks,' I say, forcing myself to speak lightly. 'I'll be fine. See you tomorrow.'

Then he moves towards me. My heart races. His cheek

brushes mine. His smell is still the same. Lemony. Salty. Right.

'Goodnight, Emily.'

There's something about the way he says my name that sends thrills right through my body, like a shock of electricity.

'Goodnight,' I gulp.

I walk back with Zorro now on the lead, my head whirling. That kiss wasn't a romantic kiss, I tell myself. It was just a friendly goodbye. Tomorrow isn't a date. It's merely a friendly invitation. He's married.

Separated and talking about divorce, says a hopeful voice inside me. There's a big difference.

I wipe Zorro down and then take him up to my bedroom. He whimpers for a moment outside Françoise's room but I have a piece of cheese ready, which I've taken from the fridge on the way up. He wolfs it down, barely swallowing. Two can play at this game! Zorro doesn't need any more persuading. On my bed he goes.

Just before I go to bed, something makes me go to that drawer. I'm not going to open it. I'm not, but . . .

I stiffen. The envelope from the hospital isn't in the same place. I'm certain I put it under my blue mohair jumper. But it's now under the red one next to it. I pick it up. The seal looks slightly out of kilter as though it has been moistened and then put back.

There is also a faint whiff of cigarette smoke in my room. I knew it! I saw a faint yellow nicotine stain on Françoise's fingers the other day. My father abhors smoking. So do I. Yet if I tell him, he'll probably stick up for her. But she has been in my room. Of that I am certain.

'Bitch,' I say out loud.

Zorro sits upright, his ears pricking.

My mind goes back to Françoise's curious look as she handed me the letter with *CONFIDENTIAL* stamped on it.

So she knows.

Or rather she knows something I don't even know.

Reluctantly, I peel open the envelope which comes apart easily – more proof that it's been tampered with. I scan the contents, my heart sinking. I feel sick.

Your presence is required . . .

12

After reading the letter, I almost cancel my day out with Nick and his little boy. How can I pretend that everything's OK with this hanging over me? I can't get out of this any longer. I have to give a formal statement about what happened. What else did I expect? That it would all go away? Of course not. So when I go down to breakfast and find Françoise and my father already eating, I am feeling distinctly edgy. And that's before I hear Françoise's voice.

'You want more whisky marmalade, Harold? I think there is too much sugar in it, n'est-ce pas? Why don't you try this nice healthy chickpea spread I make, especially for you!'

She's fawning over him in such a way that I want to retch. She's wearing a skin-tight jogging outfit: pink Lycra leggings, sweat band. The lot.

'Thank you.' My father glances at me. 'Morning, Emily.'

'Morning. Did you sleep well?'

'Like a log.'

Françoise frowns. 'But a log is wood, non?'

'It's an English expression,' says my father, in a much kinder tone.

'I'm going out now,' I say abruptly. I can't pretend any more.

'It is a good idea,' beams Françoise. 'I go running this morning when everyone is still asleep.'

'So I see,' I say, glancing at the outfit. I can't seem to speak nicely to Françoise, however hard I try.

'Do you not want to eat something first, Emilee?' chirps Françoise. There she goes again. Ever the hostess. 'Why do you not taste my fruit compote? It is another of my recipes. Very healthy.'

'No thanks,' I reply, snapping a banana off the bunch in the middle of the table.

Neither of them asks me where I am going. Good. Then Zorro barks at the sound of tyres on the gravel drive.

'Isn't that Nick's car?' asks my father, glancing out of the window.

'Yes,' I say casually.

'You're going out with him?'

What am I? A teenager?

'I'm having a picnic with him and Billy.'

'He looks a very handsome man,' says Françoise, staring out of the window. 'He is the solicitor, is he not?'

She is blushing. Has she met Nick already?

'Yes. I'll see you later. Unless you'd like me to stay with you, Dad, and keep you company?'

'No. You go. Françoise is going to read to me before our coffee break.'

'We are perusing *Winnie the Pooh*,' says Françoise.

But that's *our* book! I feel a pang of jealousy as I remember cuddling up with Dad as a child, poring over the illustrations of Tigger and Eeyore and Rabbit.

'I thought you preferred Dickens or Raymond Chandler, Dad?' I ask.

'I find this more comforting,' he replies swiftly. 'And it is helping Françoise with her vocabulary.'

'Sounds like you've got the morning sorted, then,' I retort. 'See you later.'

'Be careful,' says my father. 'I remember that Nick would take those country roads too fast for my liking. I hope he's safer now.'

'I'm sure he is, Daddy,' I say.

And for a minute, I see the caring father I knew before Françoise arrived. If only she wasn't here, everything – well, not quite everything, but enough of it – would be all right.

13

It's always the same when I meet friends' children. I get on really well with them, but it's their parents who make me feel awkward, saying things like, 'I'm sure it won't be long until you have one of your own.'

But it's not like that with Nick and his son. From the minute I get into the car with them, it seems natural. It's almost enough to put the letter out of my mind. But when I remember its demanding wording, my heart accelerates. Time is running out.

'Is that your lunch?' asks Billy, leaning over my seat from the back and eyeing my banana. His cheeky smile is so like his father's that it takes me back. Nowadays, Nick's smile has lost that youthful jubilance. It's more careful, guarded.

'Actually, it's breakfast and lunch.'

'Strap in, Billy,' says Nick, as he starts the engine.

'Did you know that bananas can float in water?' says Billy.

'Wow! Actually, I didn't.'

'It's not much,' says Nick.

'Yes it is, Dad. Floating bananas are a big deal.'

'To eat, I mean.'

'I was in a bit of a rush. But it's OK, thanks. This will do me fine.'

'She can share ours, can't she, Dad?'

I'm touched by his concern.

'It's Emily, not she,' says Nick.

'Sorry.' Billy rolls his eyes. 'Dad's a tickler for detail. Mum says it's because he's a slister.'

How cute! Some words are quite hard to get your tongue round when you're small. I glance across at Nick but his eyes are steady on the road.

'It's solicitor, not slister,' he says.

'See what I mean?' Billy rolls his eyes again, but they sparkle with good humour. Such a sweet little boy. 'Dad's made us this yummy picnic. So there's plenty to go round. I'm glad you've brought your dog. I love dogs but Mummy is allergic to them.'

So not quite what Nick said then. People tell fibs for different reasons. It occurs to me that maybe Nick's wife might not be allergic to dogs at all. Then again, it's none of my business.

'Are you sure you don't mind him in the back with you?'

'It's cool. Oooh. He's licking me!'

'Zorro,' I say warningly, but Billy is laughing and so is Nick. The look in the little boy's eyes as he strokes 'my own boy' brings a lump to my throat.

It's like this for the rest of the day. We play games on the beach. We talk. 'Did you know that the oceans provide over ninety per cent of living space on the planet?' asks Billy.

I didn't!

We make a small fire in a disposable barbecue that Nick has brought and then toast marshmallows. It's even warm enough to swim. When we were young, we'd swim all the year round. You soon warm up when you get moving. I've brought my costume with me, just in case. Billy has a wet suit.

'He's like a little fish,' I say, as we clamber out.

'He is, isn't he? We taught him when he was really young.'

'That must have been nice,' I say wistfully.

We're walking side by side now. I'm burning up. Is Nick looking at me? I suddenly feel naked, my costume too flimsy.

Billy has run ahead and is drying himself on a stripy towel. I could see his mother packing up his weekend bag. It must break her heart not having him with her all the time. I'm not sure I could cope with that.

'Our son is the best part of our marriage,' says Nick quietly. 'But we got together too quickly . . .'

He stops. I know what he's going to say. It doesn't take much to work out that Billy is eight and that his parents got married seven and a half years ago.

'How about you, Emily?' His eyes have locked onto mine, just as they used to. I couldn't look away if I wanted to. 'How is work going?'

I want to tell him. Nick would understand. The old Nick, that is. I don't know the new one. He belongs to someone else.

'Great,' I say brightly. 'Couldn't be better.'

'Have you decided how long you're staying?'

'I'm not sure. I've got some leave to use up and it's quite quiet at work so I'm leaving it open.'

Quiet at work. Who am I kidding? He seems to swallow the lie anyway.

He nods. 'Well, it's wonderful to have some time with you.'

'Come on, you two!' bosses Billy, dancing up and down in the sand. 'Get dressed.'

'I'll just nip into the woods there and sort myself out,'

I say, shivering. I'm beginning to get cold now, and not just because the sun has gone behind a cloud. Glimpses of swimming with Nick, way back in time, are flooding into my head. The feel of his skin against mine . . .

My phone goes as we get into the car. The maternity unit again.

Decline.

'Feel free to take your call,' he says.

'It's OK,' I say. 'It can wait. I'd rather enjoy this time with the two of you.'

'We've loved it too,' says Nick.

Ping. A text message. The wording is exactly the same as the letter.

URGENT REMINDER OF TOMORROW'S MEETING TO GIVE FORMAL STATEMENT

A shiver goes through me. I might be able to pretend I haven't received a letter. But I've opened this text. Their software can probably confirm it. There's no denying it now – I'll have to face the music.

'I don't want Zorro to go,' says Billy when we pull up outside Willowmead House. The two of them are entwined in the back. 'Can we have another picnic tomorrow too?'

'If Emily would like that,' says Nick.

'I would. But I have to go back to London for a few days.'

It's not until I say those words that I finally make up my mind. Maybe I already knew it. The text and the letter leave me with no choice. My presence tomorrow was not requested. It was demanded.

'Will you definitely be back or could you stay up there?'

asks Nick. His voice is neutral. It might be a pleasant question. Or it might show interest. It's hard to know. I no longer trust my judgement.

'I'll be back,' I say firmly. *Maybe*, I add silently, *for good*.

Then – so fast that it's over almost before I know it – he leans across and gives me a light kiss on my mouth.

It's been years since he's done this. But it feels so right. Like coming home.

We both glance at the back seat. Billy is hugging Zorro. Had he seen us? Even if he had, it could just have been a friendly kiss. The sort friends give each other. Maybe it was just that.

I feel a thud of disappointment. That's when I realize I wanted it to be more.

When I get to the door, I find my keys are not in my handbag although I am sure I put them there. I must have left them in the house.

I bang the big old-fashioned knocker. No one answers. But the spare key is still under the stone round the side of the house.

I let myself in. There's my key, sitting in the bowl on the hall table. How very odd.

There is also a note in my father's writing.

Gone for a drive. Don't bother making supper for us.

Maybe this is the time to make my exit. The two of them can't ask any awkward questions.

I leave another note.

Have to return to London for a few days. Will be back as soon as I can.

Hastily, I gather a few things together. I don't intend to stay long.

On my way out, I can't resist taking a peek into Françoise's room. She's been into mine, so it's my turn.

Her dressing table is neatly laid out with all kinds of cosmetics. Lipsticks. Powder. Perfume. Brands I couldn't afford on my pay packet, even if I wanted to. She doesn't seem short of money. Where does it come from?

And what's this in the top drawer. A packet of herbs?

Her voice comes back to me.

'*Your father, he likes my omelettes very much. I make them with herbs.*'

Herbs belong in the kitchen, surely. Why is she keeping them in her bedroom? I put them in my bag to inspect more closely later.

I'll come back as soon as I can. Meanwhile, there is only one person I trust to keep an eye on Dad in my absence.

Joe is up a ladder, pruning the roses at the front. He's been our gardener since I was a child. He seemed as old then as he does now. At any other time, it would have been reassuringly good to see him.

'How are you, lass?'

I love the way he still calls me that.

'All right, thanks, although I'm worried about Dad. I've got to go away for a bit and I wondered if you could keep an eye on him.'

He clambers down. 'To be honest, I've been worried about your father too. He hasn't been himself since that young French lady arrived.'

My skin starts to tingle. Not in a good way. 'What do you mean?'

'Well . . . it's clear she's cosying up to him, if you don't mind me saying.'

So I'm *not* going mad.

'Always sitting next to him, rather close. Can't do enough for him. And he's got a bit sharp with me. Ruffled a few feathers in the village, he has. Her too.'

I think back to what Nick had told me. 'I thought Françoise was very popular.'

'Not with everyone.' He rubs the side of his nose. 'I might be speaking out of turn here. But there's something I feel I have to tell you.'

My skin is prickling now. 'What?'

'The missus does a bit of cleaning for your solicitor friend. The one who dropped you off just now.'

'Nick?'

'That's right.'

'She says that last week, just before you arrived, your father and that French woman went to see him. They had a very early appointment, before the office usually opened.'

'Why?' I whisper. Even though there's no one else around, it seems too big a thing to say loudly. Then I remember Françoise's flushed face when Nick had arrived to pick me up.

'I don't know exactly. But after they left, my missus went in to clean. There was a file on the desk. And on top was this big document with some official-looking lettering on the front.'

He looks at me steadily.

'It was your dad's will.'

PART TWO
Françoise

14

I was the tallest in my class. All 185.4 centimetres of me. Or, as the English would say, nearly six foot one. This used to embarrass me. But no more. I take care to wear my height proudly. And I have learned to see my nose as 'strong' rather than large.

Be proud of who you are, especially your name. Remember that Alarie can mean 'all powerful'. It was a piece of advice Maman gave me on the day I came running back from school in tears because the other girls had called me a giraffe.

'Those who are taller, see more of life,' she told me. This was one of her lessons that I never forgot. She had many more.

'Put yourself in someone else's shoes,' she would say. 'It helps to understand their motives. Remember, Françoise. Everyone has a reason for doing something in life. If you can find the key, then you will always be one step ahead.'

I cannot help wondering what Maman would have thought of ninety-four-year-old Harold Gentle and, in particular, his daughter Emilee. If she was a friend, I would teach her how to make the most of those high cheekbones with my highlighter and blusher. I would encourage her to wear more flattering clothes instead of those old jumpers and creased jeans. And I would offer to plait her hair, which is *extraordinaire*. Like a burning flame.

But this woman is no friend. Emilee is a bad daughter who does not do her duty. Doesn't she realize how fortunate she is? She does not deserve a papa like Harold.

If life was fair, I would have had a father like him.

I also wonder what Maman would say about this huge house, which was filthy until I arrived. The only food in the kitchen was cereal and mouldy cheese. And it is oh so cold! The boiler is always expiring. Also – incroyable! – there is no shower. Only a big cold bath with brown stains underneath the taps and round the edges. What was Emilee thinking of, leaving a helpless old man like this?

'Françoise?' calls out a voice from the room next door. 'Where are you?'

I feel a sigh coming up through my body but I push it back down. You need sympathy, not irritation in my job. It must be so hard and demeaning to have an old body that cannot walk without difficulty any more, let alone run. How frustrating to have a mind that can't find a particular word until it inexplicably pops, some minutes later, into the brain. In my experience, some deal with it better than others. But I have to say that Monsieur Harold Gentle is not an easy man.

He is a caméléon – a 'chameleon'! (Not so different from the English!) At times he can be oh so charming. If this man was younger, he would be handsome – almost like a film star! That deep, powerful voice that holds you in a spell, makes you feel special.

But at other times, there is a ruthless streak. I have seen that in the way he treats his daughter. Just look at how he insisted on giving me those lovely sapphire earrings. I was not to know they had been left to Emilee by her maman.

If it wasn't for her own bad behaviour to her papa, I might feel almost sorry for this woman.

Stand up for yourself, I want to tell her.

I stood up to my own father when I was a small child. 'Do not shout at Maman like that,' I had said.

I can still see them now. My poor mother cowering on the bed we all shared, her hands covering her eyes. My father close up to me. His face mottled and red, like an angry beast. 'Do not tell me what to do,' he had growled.

I remember this so clearly because it was the last time I saw him.

I do not allow myself such memories very often. The past is to be left behind. That's what Maman said. The present is the one to think about in order to make the future bright.

Naturellement when making my plans, I had not taken Emilee into account. Harold had already told me she had her own life in London. And then, before I know it, she is here! Watching my every move. Suspicious. Hostile. Her eyes narrowing like a snake's.

I am glad she has gone back again. It is so much more relaxed now at Willowmead House. But she should have said au revoir properly instead of leaving a note. Her poor papa was so upset. How could she leave him, so vulnerable, with a near-stranger? For all she knows, I could 'take him for everything he's got', as the English say. He is so trusting that this would not be difficult.

'Françoise?' calls out the voice again. 'Are you there?'

'Oui, Harold. I am making your coffee.'

'What is taking you so long?'

Old people can be so rude. My mother was the same. It

is as if they reach a certain age and decide they can say and do what they want, just like a toddler. Still, who is to say what we will be like when we are that age? A carer needs much patience.

The trick, I have learned, is to swallow your frustration when an elderly person does things that don't matter, such as wearing a shower cap on your head all day (like one of the old ladies in the home where I worked) or breaking wind (I believe the English word is 'fart').

At the same time, you must be strict with the things that *do* matter, including taking their medication. Of course, you do not stand over them with a whip. You present it as something positive. 'I know this doesn't taste nice and that it is the last thing you want to do,' I will say to Harold when I give him the painkillers which the doctor has prescribed for his rheumatism. 'But it will make you feel better. Then afterwards, you can have a chocolate, yes?'

A good carer – and I pride myself on being that – will know what to do if someone gets anxious or aggressive. You distract them. When Harold frets because Emilee is not back yet, I tell him that maybe the trains are delayed and that she will be home soon. Sometimes, I tell him to close his eyes and think of his thoughts like passing clouds. 'Just let them float by,' I say softly. 'Imagine that a stream of warm sunshine is pouring down on your head and through your body. This is nice, yes?'

It is a form of meditation that Maman taught me. Some people think this is a waste of time, but I find it helps me to relax as much as the people I am caring for.

Carefully now, I spoon coffee into the percolator. Then I open the cupboard door and get out a packet of yellow powder. Just one teaspoon. So good for the joints. I used to do this for the old people I cared for in France. 'My angel,' Maurice used to call me.

I get a lump in my throat just to think of him, although there are others I would rather forget. One cannot help having favourites. There are some cases that squeeze your heart more than others. Harold, of course, is particularly special for entirely different reasons.

Then I arrange a lace cloth on the tray I found at the back of the linen cupboard. It is rather old fashioned with blue-and-white daisy stitching. I wonder if Mrs Gentle made it.

She sounds like a nice lady, from the chat I have heard in the village. Someone told me she did something called 'meals on wheels' for people who could not get out to eat. She also helped out with reading at the local school. There are photographs of her in what Harold calls the 'drawing room'. She is no beauty but her face has a certain softness about it. Almost naive. What would she think of all this now? Would she approve of me? I hope so.

On top of the tray I place his mug with 'Dad' written on it. Harold tells me that Emilee gave it to him on La Fête Des Pères – what the English call 'Father's Day'. He insists on using it for morning coffee.

Myself, I prefer hot water with lemon. It can be good for the digestion.

I put two biscuits on a plate. They are still warm from the oven. They are Maman's recipe, although they do not taste quite the same with these English ingredients. How I miss French butter, so rich and creamy, melting before you even touch it with your tongue!

'Thank you, my dear,' Harold says when I go into the sitting room. He seizes on the biscuits and wolfs them down as if he hasn't had breakfast only an hour or so earlier.

'Is this a new brand of coffee?' he then asks, taking a sip.

'Yes,' I say. 'It is nice?'

'There's a rather interesting punch to it.'

Good. He is drinking it.

'Do you think Emily is all right?' he asks suddenly.

There's a crumb on the side of his mouth which he hasn't noticed. I would like to brush it off for him but Harold is a proud man. The elderly have already lost so much. They must not be allowed to lose their pride too.

'Emilee seems the sort of woman who will always cope,' I say carefully.

'Really? There are times when she worries me.'

'She was upset about the earrings,' I remind him. 'You should have asked her first.'

He shrugs. 'I know. But I was so grateful to you for saving me on that cliff.'

'All people would do the same,' I reply quickly. But inside, I am still trembling. It was very close. One false move over that steep edge and one of us could so easily have fallen. I could tell from Emilee's eyes that she blamed me. But he had insisted on going too close. '*I am an adult*,' he had barked. '*I can do what I like.*'

Harold's moods could change so quickly. I did not like to argue in case he went over the edge.

'I would like to give you lots of presents,' he says now.

'And cause more problems with your daughter?' I shake my head. 'It is very kind of you, Harold. But I think it is not a good idea. Now, shall I read to you?'

I pick up a magazine from the coffee table. Harold's sight is not what it was and he likes me to read the 'Down Memory Lane' piece. It is written by readers who share their stories from the past. I rather enjoy them.

This month's is from a woman who was evacuated to Devon during the war, to a blacksmith's family. She liked it so much that she didn't want to return home to London afterwards.

'You should write about your past,' I say to him. 'What did you do during the war, Harold?'

A strange look comes over his face. At first I think it is fear. Then disgust. And now anger. His voice rises. It is loud and furious like the waves from the sea, which must be strong today because I can hear them, even from the house.

'Can't you think of anything else to talk about?' he booms.

I move my chair away. I do not like it when people shout. It brings back memories of my own father.

'I am sorry.'

Tears trickle down my cheeks. I cannot help it.

Then, almost instantly, Harold's face softens. 'No, my dear. It is *I* who should be sorry. Please. Play to me.'

He waves his hands towards the piano. Bon. I need a distraction. Blowing my nose, I get up and make my way to the stool, which needs mending. The embroidery is coming loose. I will fix that later. I like to have a purpose.

Then my fingers take on a life of their own. I am back in Lyon. At the piano in the nursing home. Maurice is sitting by my side. Showing me the names of the notes. 'Listen, Françoise,' he is saying to me. '*Truly* listen with

95

your whole being and your soul. You can tell when it is right. Your body will dance.'

He taught me well. Maurice used to be in a rock-and-roll band when he was young. 'You're my rock chick,' he would joke, holding out his old, gnarled hand with the blue veins standing up. 'Will you jive with me?'

'I would be honoured,' I'd reply. And then we'd launch into 'Roll Over Beethoven', and before long everyone in the home would join in – or try to. We must have made a sight with all those walking frames and sticks! Often, I would stay beyond my shift. But the smiles on all of their faces was worth it. 'You are a dose of good medicine,' the matron would say.

It was the piano that helped me charm my way into Harold's house. What a coincidence that I knocked on his door in the same week that he placed the advertisement. He presumed I was there because I had seen it. Luckily, no one else had yet applied. He did not ask me how I learned about the position in France. Perhaps that is because his mind is muddled.

When he asked me in for an interview, I saw the piano and asked if I could play. His eyes moistened and I knew I had hooked him.

'I don't suppose,' he said, that you know a tune called "Reelin' and Rockin'"?'

'Of course!' I said. I was surprised. I'd have thought Harold would prefer something slower.

It got me the job. I am sure of it. When letters arrived from other applicants, Harold told me to put them in the bin. 'I am happy with you, my dear,' he said. 'I do not need anyone else.'

I too am quite settled as Harold Gentle's carer.

Yet now, as my fingers fly across the keyboard, I find myself back in France. At the village hall dance. I am resting my head against a young man's shoulder. Then I lift up my face and his lips brush mine.

'*Please,*' says Jean-Luc in my head, '*come to Paris with me.*'

'*I cannot,*' I say. '*I have to care for Maman.*'

All of a sudden, there is a huge crash, interrupting my reverie. The cup of coffee has fallen from Harold's hands. 'I am so sorry,' he says. 'I don't know why that happened.'

He is crying. 'It's all right,' I say, gently wiping the tears running down his confused, wrinkled face. 'No harm done.'

'You won't tell me off?' he asks.

'Why should I?'

'My wife might.'

'But Harold, she is not here.'

'Jean does not like a mess,' he weeps. 'She is very fussy.'

Harold gets himself muddled at times but this is the first time he has thought his wife was still alive. I must watch this. Ordinarily, in my old job, I would mention it to the relatives. But Emilee is gone.

'It's only coffee . . . and it was not hot,' I reassure him. 'I have a special mixture I can make to get out the stain. Now let's get you upstairs and I will find you some dry trousers. Afterwards I will give you one of my back massages.'

'Thank you, Françoise.' He grips my arm as we walk towards the stairs. For an old man, his grasp is strong. 'What would I do without you?'

15

Later, when Harold has his nap, I walk to the post office. Willowmead is so pretty. There is something very special about a small village by the sea. The waves are high and there are lots of tiny black figures in the distance riding their surfboards, ripping through the waves. For a minute, I am behind Jean-Luc, gripping his leather jacket and laughing as we dip and dive through the traffic on his motorbike.

But no. I am a different Françoise now.

I pause outside the butcher's window and then go in. 'Excusez-moi,' I say, pointing at the tray. 'What is Scotch egg?'

The man looks at me as if I am mad. 'It's sausage and breadcrumbs wrapped around an egg,' he says.

'But why is it called Scotch?'

'No idea, love. Want to try one?'

Before I can answer, he puts one in a paper bag and hands it over.

'How much, please?'

'No charge.' He chuckles. 'You're living up at Mr Gentle's place, aren't you? You'll be back for more. He's very partial to them himself.'

I sit on the sea wall and take a bite. Delicious. So too is the view. Imagine! Across the water is France. For a minute, I feel a pang of homesickness. Then I swallow the last mouthful, put the bag into a bin and walk on.

I came here for a reason. And I must get on with it.

As I turn the corner, something else catches my eye. It's Nick, Emilee's friend, in the car park opposite. The solicitor that Harold took me to visit just before Emilee arrived. He is talking to a pretty woman with long blonde hair. A little boy is standing next to them with a small suitcase. Then Nick takes the woman in his arms, kissing her. The little boy is clinging to her legs. They look to me for all the world like a family that cares for each other deeply.

Then Nick looks up suddenly and sees me watching. Immediately he steps away from the woman. Does Emilee know about this? I saw them down on the beach when I was walking on the cliffs before she went to London. Any fool could tell from their body language that there was something between them, even though the child was there too. Whatever my personal feelings are towards Harold's daughter, I do not like a man who plays around.

Walking up through the pretty high street with flowers spilling over hanging baskets above me, I take another look at the pink envelope in my hand. It has taken me some time to write the right words and even now I am not sure.

'A stamp for France?' asks the woman in the post office, as if she is not asked for one very often.

'Oui,' I say.

'And how are you getting on, looking after Mr Gentle?' she asks.

'Very good,' I say.

She unpeels the stamp and presses it onto my letter. 'I heard that Emily was back for a while but is in London now.'

'That's right,' I say.

If she expects me to gossip, she has picked the wrong person.

'So it's just the two of you together, then.'

'Mr Gentle needs someone to be with him at his age,' I say sharply. I do not like the implication behind her words.

She says something quickly that I do not understand.

'How much for the stamp, please?' I ask tightly.

I pay her and then watch her place my pink envelope in a bag on her side of the counter.

I walk to the door and then turn back.

'I am sorry,' I say. 'I have changed my mind. May I have it back?'

'You can't have a refund – it's already processed.'

Her forehead is a river of lines. She needs to use the right cream and do the facial exercises Maman taught me, every night. Beauty, as every French woman knows, is hard work when you do it properly. But it is worth it.

'Excuse me,' I say politely. 'What is a refund?'

'It means getting your money back,' says a voice behind me.

I turn around to find the lawyer again. Nick is very handsome, with hair the colour of sand and bright blue eyes, like the sea on a beautiful day. He is taller than me, too. I can see why Emilee has the hots for him. But my instinct tells me that there is something untrustworthy about this man.

'I do not want my money back,' I say. 'I just want my letter.'

The woman pushes the envelope back across the counter, along with a look that suggests I am mad.

Maybe she is right.

'Thank you for explaining,' I say shortly to Nick.

'No problem.' He seems a little nervous. 'Is Emily in today?'

'No,' I say. 'Emilee has gone to London.'

'Already?' He is clearly disappointed. 'When will she be home?'

'I think this is none of your business,' I snap, remembering how Emilee blushes when Nick's name is mentioned. Even though I do not like Harold's daughter, I do not care for men who disregard other people's feelings. 'You have a wife and son, n'est-ce pas?'

He looks taken aback.

'But . . .'

I do not give him time to reply. Instead, I push past him. 'Adieu,' I call back over my shoulder.

Good riddance, as the English say.

That man means trouble. I can smell it.

Meanwhile, I am relieved I have taken the envelope back from the post office woman.

After all, you cannot write a letter to the dead.

16

Actually, you can write a letter to the dead. And you can send it.

The danger is that the wrong person will receive it.

Someone else might have opened my envelope in Lyon, even though I had marked it *Confidentiel*. The landlord, perhaps. He was always so nosy. Or the new tenant.

I hope he or she remembers to water the purple and red bougainvillea flowers on the balcony. Maman and I used to be very conscientious about that.

How I loved our little apartment! It was easy to take care of, unlike this big rambling Willowmead House, where dust seems to take pride in settling in corners I wiped down only the day before.

But I cannot go back to my old home now. Not after what happened.

It haunts me still, especially when I wake bolt upright in the early hours. During the day, I try to drive it out of my head with washing and cleaning and caring. Yet it is not enough. That is why I write the letter. I pour out all my feelings; my emotions; my heart.

Ma chère Maman, je suis tellement confuse

In fact, I have never been more confused.

Maman used to say that it can be good to release your feelings by writing to someone you find it hard – or impossible – to talk to.

It had helped when I was writing it. But I find I cannot post it. Besides, it had served its purpose. It had helped me to make up my mind about what to do next.

'*Even if you tear it up, the words will help to clear your mind.*' This had been another of Maman's tips.

And now I rip the letter, piece by piece and throw it in a bin on my way back to Willowmead House. I run the name over on my tongue. My mother and I never had a home with a name. Just an apartment with a number. Does Emilee realize how lucky she is to have such a beautiful place with a father who loves her?

I let myself into the house with the key that Harold has given me. I hope he is more careful with others who are less trustworthy. Joe the gardener, for instance.

The other day, I catch – or is it 'caught'? – the man napping in the greenhouse. He woke with a start and his face filled with displeasure that I had found him out. I hope it will be a lesson to him. You should not sleep when you are being paid to do a job.

The house is silent. Just the ticking of the grandfather clock in the hall. It has a face with a silver moon and pale yellow sun. When I first saw it, it brought back a fleeting memory of a tall clock in my grandparents' farmhouse in the countryside in Normandy. They are long dead. Who knows where the clock is now? Things disappear in time. Not just treasured objects; memories too. And I have no one to pass mine on to. I might be young but I have seen death many times and heard people talk at the end. It makes you think of these things.

I run my finger along the mahogany table in the hall where I place the post every morning.

The table, she has responded well to my polishing – so shiny that, I'm satisfied to see, I can make out the outline of my face. '*There are two things you can do to make yourself feel better in life,*' Maman would say. '*Clean your home from top to bottom so you feel in control. And do good to others. Both bring warmth to the soul.*'

I think this is why I love caring for others. To me, it is more than a job. It is a vocation. I've heard some complain that it is no more than 'bottom wiping'. And yes – I have cleaned up many people in my time. But there is an art to it. You have to reassure them that you are happy to do this for them in more than words. A warm smile can go a long way to preserving someone's dignity.

'Do not be embarrassed,' I would say to Maurice in the nursing home if he had another 'petit accident' before reaching the bathroom. 'It is my honour to help you.'

'Thank you, Françoise,' he would reply. 'You are such a kind girl.'

Those words were worth more to me than my small weekly wage.

Caring means listening too. It is being there in the small hours of the night when the world seems like a lonely place.

'I have never told anyone else this before,' my patients would often say before confessing to a past indiscretion, something that might seem very minor but was weighing on their conscience. 'When I was a child,' whispered one lady, 'my brother was sent to his room for a day because my mother thought he had taken the last slice of bread. But it was me. We were so hungry. He didn't want me to get into trouble but now I feel terrible, especially now he is gone.'

Poor woman. 'Would he want you to feel guilty if the positions were reversed?' I asked.

'No,' she said firmly.

'There you are, then,' I said reassuringly. 'So you must not fret either.'

'Thank you, Françoise,' she said. 'I had never thought of it that way.'

Then I gave her a gentle kiss on the cheek. I cannot help it. Sometimes it is impossible not to get involved.

'Never underestimate the weight of guilt,' my supervisor used to tell me. 'Or the relief which comes from a reassuring squeeze of the hand.'

I think of this now as I watch Harold sleeping in his chair. His mouth is open wide. Perhaps he was reading when he dozed off because his glasses have fallen down his nose and his newspaper has flopped onto the carpet.

Gently, I place his glasses on the table next to him and fold the paper neatly. He does not stir. His coffee cup is empty. Très bien! Then he has drunk the yellow powder.

17

Harold is still asleep, with Zorro lying by his feet. Such a big dog! I have never seen one like him before. He could belong to a circus! He is stretching out now and lying on his back in the most extraordinary position with his legs in the air. I am reminded of a kangaroo in the way he bounds across the room, even though he is old. How I love him! He brings an energy to this house.

'Shhh,' I whisper. 'You will wake your master.'

I too need some peace. With any luck, I have an hour or so before Harold wakes. So I put Zorro's lead on him and we walk down to the sea.

I cannot leave it alone. It is so beautiful. The waves almost make me forget why I am here. I am lost in their dance; mesmerized by their light. Once, my mother took me to Saint-Malo. It must have been after my father left. It was just the two of us. Maman and me.

I do not know how we had the money to travel. Perhaps her client paid our expenses. My mother painted pictures of people; something I took for granted when I was a child and only later realized the special talent she had.

We stayed in a small pension with a bathroom that we shared with others. Then we walked to a big house nearby where I had to sit in a huge room with curtains that fell from the sky to the soft white carpet. There I watched my

mother draw a small girl, of about my age, in a pretty violet organza dress with a wide sash. I had never seen such
a lovely dress before. The girl kept fiddling but I sat very
still. My mother had warned me. 'They have only allowed
you to come with me because I have no one to care for
you. So you must be good.'

It was boring, sitting there for so long, but I made the
time pass by making up stories in my head. Wonderful
complicated stories about another life when I lived in a
palace and wore violet dresses with sashes.

In the evening, my mother and I would have a bowl
each of thick onion soup and hunks of warm crusty
bread, served by the landlady of the pension. There was a
piano in the dining room.

I noticed my mother kept casting her eye to it.

'Puis-je en jouer?' she asked la patronne.

'Bien sûr.'

My mother could play the piano? I had no idea.

I listened, mesmerized, as her fingers flew across the
keys. Other guests at the pension drew nearer. 'She is a
musical magician,' breathed one.

At the end, everyone applauded her. One man tried to
press money into her hand. 'You are so kind,' she said.
'But please, keep it for yourself.'

'Why didn't you accept?' I asked as we went up to bed.
'You are always saying we have to be careful.'

She gave me that lovely smile of hers. 'Because,' she
said, stroking my hair, 'sometimes it is enough reward in
life to give pleasure.'

'Where did you learn to play?'

'Your grandmother taught me.'

How I wish she was still here. But they are all gone. It is just Maman and me.

'Can I learn to play the piano too?' I asked.

Her face dropped. 'We have no room in our apartment, chérie. And even if we did, we cannot afford one.'

We might if you accepted tips, I thought to myself. 'We could start saving,' I said hopefully.

'That would take a very long time.'

'But it is possible, yes?' I persisted.

'Everything in life is possible,' she said, 'except one thing.'

'What is that?'

She shook her head. 'One day, I will tell you.'

The child's parents must have been pleased with the portrait, because on the day it was finished, we went down to the harbour to eat mussels. Never before had I been served by a waiter. He even bowed to me. It was as if my princess daydreams had come true! Afterwards we went for a walk along the harbour ramparts. Such a long way down! I held on to Maman so she did not fall.

'Can we stay here for ever?' I asked as we walked back along the cobbled streets towards our room.

She patted my hand. 'I am afraid not.'

'Is that the thing which is not possible?'

She smiled again, but it was a different one from before. It was one of those comforting smiles that she made if I fell over and bruised my knee. 'No. It is another.'

'Then there are two things which are impossible?'

'Not exactly. I will explain when you are older.'

'Hello again!'

108

Is this man following me? Saint-Malo, with its cobbled streets and worn battlements, evaporates. I am here, in the present day, by the sea, with that blond lawyer striding towards me. Zorro is running towards him excitedly.

'Hello, boy.' Then Nick looks at me. 'Françoise!'

I do not care for his familiarity. 'I prefer Mademoiselle Alarie,' I say, standing tall.

'Of course. I'm sorry.'

The wind is blowing. It is carrying our voices as well as the waves.

'I'm glad I saw you,' he says. His voice has a slightly nervous quality. 'There's something I wanted to clear up. When you saw me in the car park with . . . with my wife. I –'

'It is none of my business.' I turn to walk on but Zorro has other ideas. He is pawing at the man.

'I think you may have got the wrong idea,' he continues. 'My wife was taking my son back and I was simply saying goodbye to her.'

Does he think I am a complete idiot?

'I do not want to hear.'

'But I'm worried, you see, in case you might mention it to Emily.'

'Please, I have already said. It is none of my business. Your matters are private, just like my own.'

I wanted to remind him of that. I wouldn't want him to tell Emilee about the meeting Harold and I went to at his law firm.

His voice sounds desperate. 'I don't want to upset her, you see.'

Enough is enough. 'Why do you not ring her and tell her this?'

'I would, but her mobile is switched off.'

I did not know that. I'd have thought a caring daughter with such an elderly father would have it on at all times. Suppose Harold is ill and I need to contact her?

'I'm afraid I cannot help you with that. Come, Zorro.'

The dog doesn't want to go. Luckily, I have some cheese and ham to bribe him. (In my opinion, he does not get enough treats! Emilee is very strict.) I walk back up the cliff towards the house. But I don't feel comfortable. Despite my reassurance to Nick, is it not my duty to tell Emilee about him kissing his wife? Or am I tempted to do so because it will give me a certain amount of pleasure to hurt her?

I do not like this thought inside me but maybe she deserves it, at least a little. Emilee is selfish – she should have given up her job and moved here to care for her papa just as I gave up my Jean-Luc and my job to care for my mother.

As we approach the house now from the back, I see that the big doors to the garden are open. A man is standing on the patio, holding up his arms to the sky as if embracing the fresh October day. When I get nearer, his arms slump to his side and he sinks down on a chair. I realize it's Harold, but for a moment I saw him as he might have been as a young man.

'Emily,' he says. 'Where have you been? I have missed you.'

'It is not Emilee,' I reply gently. 'It is Françoise. Do not worry. I am back now. Zorro and I went for a walk.'

His eyes are wide with terror. 'But the Germans. Did they get you?'

Germans? Harold would have only been a schoolboy when the war ended. Certainly too young to fight. But it must have left its mark. I shudder. I can still remember some of the stories my mother told me, passed down to her by her mother. Her neighbour had hidden a young English pilot in a chicken coop. Both were shot dead. Another had been bombed by our own side by mistake. A whole family dead. Even the baby.

'No. I was quite safe.' I pat his arm soothingly.

Sometimes it is simpler not to disagree with fantasies. Why deny this pleasure? Much better to agree and move on. Only the very young and the old can pretend and get away with it.

'Shall we eat now?' I ask, leading him gently back into the sitting room.

'Yes please.' His voice is docile and childlike.

'I have made that onion soup you enjoy so much and a tomato tarte.'

There is a delicious, comforting aroma wafting from the Aga. (I had taken the precaution of preparing everything before I left.)

He pats me on the shoulder. 'Thank you, Françoise. It would float my boat, as I believe you young people say.'

'Float your boat?' I repeat. 'We are going sailing?'

He laughs. 'No. It is an expression that means one likes something very much.'

The English language is so strange!

'Write it down,' he instructs. 'It might come in useful some time.'

He's back to his old self. But his outburst about the Germans had frightened me. He genuinely hadn't known who I was just now. My mother had become like that when the drugs confused her. So too had Maurice.

'I want to call Emily first,' he announces. 'I tried before but it rang off.'

'Let me repeat for you,' I suggest. 'What is the number?'

You would think that Emilee might have given it to me if she cared at all for her father.

'*Hi. This is Emily. Please leave a message . . .*'

Hah! What good is that! I need to speak to Emilee herself. Not a machine.

'This is Françoise,' I say. 'Your father needs to speak to you. Please call urgently.'

I think of that official letter that had arrived for Emilee. Did that have something to do with her sudden absence?

'Perhaps she has business,' I suggest to Harold when I put down the phone. 'I am sure she will call us back now.'

'I do hope she's all right,' he says.

Of course she will be, I want to say. Women like Emilee will always look out for themselves.

'I need her back to sign that paperwork at the lawyer's,' he says.

'But it is already done,' I remind him. 'I was your witness. Remember?'

'No. I don't. Where *is* she?'

'She will be home soon,' I say soothingly.

'But what if she isn't? She's been away for months at a time before.'

I have to stop myself from tutting with disapproval. That woman's behaviour amounts to total neglect.

'Come, Harold. Let us not worry. If there was something wrong, the police would tell us. Why do we not do some meditation instead? Now sit down in your favourite chair. That's right.' I place his tartan rug over his knees. 'Close your eyes, and listen to the sounds. Do you hear that birdsong? Beautiful, isn't it? Fancy them singing at this time of year. And can you hear the gentle breeze outside? Let it wash over you and . . .'

Within minutes he is asleep. It is so good for him.

So you see. It is just as well that I am here instead. An old man like this should not be left alone.

Anything could happen.

France, 1944

We drive on. The men are silent. But we each know what the other is thinking.

That Jerry could have got us.

We might never have seen our families again. I could visualize my mother's eyes. Feel her arms around me. Smell the leg of lamb she used to roast every Sunday before the bloody war started.

'I'm hungry,' someone says.

'If I close my eyes, I can see the missus cooking up a dinner in the oven,' says another dreamily. 'I can taste the tatties and all. Crisp and golden, they are.'

'Fuck off,' snaps someone else.

'I could do with one of those and all.'

I am not used to language like this. My father would have flayed me alive for using such coarse words. But I was curious, like any boy my age. What would it be like to kiss a girl? There was one in our street I always liked. She had long blonde plaits that would swing as she played skipping games with her friends.

Last year, I put a Valentine's card through her door.

When I saw her again, she smiled at me. But that's as far as it had got.

'Hold on tight, boys,' barks the sarge, 'and we'll get something hot in your bellies before the end of the day.'

'How's that, then?'

'There's a farmhouse along here. They're waiting for us.'

'How do we know they're not going to hand us in, then?' asks someone.

'They've been checked out like the last lot.'

We drive on, rifles at the ready in case we pass an enemy truck. Constantly scouring the sky in case a plane flies overhead. Pissing over the side of the lorry.

'Should be nearly here now,' says the sarge, looking at his map. 'Right down this track and then . . . Fuck!'

There's a farmhouse all right. But it's ruined. Charred. Razed to the ground with only a wisp of smoke left drifting.

'The bastards must have got here before us,' mutters the sarge.

'Did they get them because they knew we were coming?' I ask.

'Maybe, lad,' says one Tommy.

'What do we do now?' pipes up another.

'We just keep going,' says the sarge.

The driver swings round. As he does so, there's the sound of splitting metal as the side of the lorry cab tears open like a tin can.

'Heads down,' roars the sarge. 'The bastards are still here. Put your foot on the bloody accelerator, will you!'

A bullet cracks off the metal next to me. By some miracle it whizzes past me but hits the head of the man on the opposite side. Albert. The one who had given me a slug of whisky. He slumps to the ground. I stared with horror at the muck spilling from the back of his head. Blood. Grey and white stuff.

He doesn't even make a sound.

'Faster,' the sarge is shouting.

'Someone's been hit here,' I yell.

'He's a goner. Just cover him up. Not with your jacket, you daft prick. You'll need that.'

'What with, then?' I ask tearfully. The lorry is swaying from side to side but the bullets are no longer coming. No one is behind us. Perhaps the snipers were locals, on the Germans' side.

'Let's put him under the seat, shall we lad?' suggests someone else.

As I do so, a photograph falls out of his pocket. A woman stares up at me with a child in her arms. His wife and son? He'd been a father? How would they manage now without him?

I watch over Albert for the rest of the journey. 'It's all right,' I say, patting his uniform, stiff now with dried blood. 'I'll bury you when we next stop. I promise.'

18

It's been two days now and Emilee still has not returned.

'Has she rung you?' I ask Harold.

We are in what the English call 'the sitting room' after breakfast. I have been reading the newspaper to him because Harold's cloudy, watery eyes are failing, despite the strong glasses he wears.

'No,' he says, sounding like a lost child. 'She hasn't.'

I click my tongue. I cannot help it; I am angry now.

This woman does not deserve a father who cares. I would have given anything for one like this. The one I got was not kind. My mind went back.

'*What about Françoise?*' my mother had sobbed when Papa was halfway through the door.

'*She has you, doesn't she?*' he had yelled back over his shoulder, not even turning to see me one last time.

I remember that as clearly as if it was yesterday, even though I was only six years old. The fear still lives with me. No child should ever have to see their parent cry.

Emilee has so much! Not just a father who loves her but also a beautiful home. She should have seen what my mother and I endured. A pokey apartment in the wrong side of the village where our neighbours would argue or make love, and sometimes both, on the other side of the wall. Often, we could not afford our bills and lit our tiny rooms by candlelight. I did not go to a good school like

Harold's daughter. I had to leave early to earn money. By then, the cancer had started. And so young! She could barely feed herself, let alone paint any more.

'How will we manage?' she had wept.

'Do not worry, Maman,' I had assured her. 'I will find something.'

And I did. I walked to the old people's home on the other side of the river and told them I was happy to do anything. They took me at my word. I was given the worst jobs. Scrubbing the toilets. Wiping elderly wrinkled, saggy bodies. Cooking their meals. Cleaning up after them if they were sick. Soothing them when they cried out for sons and daughters who didn't visit. Holding them when it was their time to pass over to the other side. And, of course, playing the piano to those who were still there.

The piano saved my soul. My mother had not been able to find anyone to teach me. How could she? We did not have enough money.

But there was a piano in the community lounge at the old people's home. And there was Maurice.

Maurice was eighty-two when I met him. He told me this every day as if it was something to be proud of. I see now that it was. He held up his age like a badge of honour. 'You should have seen the chicks who followed our band! Almost as lovely as you, Françoise!'

One day, when I had come in to vacuum the room, I found Maurice at the piano. His head was down, over the keyboard. For one terrible moment, I feared he was dead.

Then his head jerked upwards as if he had just been dozing. His fingers began to move. Never had I heard anything like it. It reminded me of my mother's playing, but this was different. This had an energy that pulled you to your feet like a magnetic force and made you dance around the room. I could not help it!

'Buddy Holly,' he said, grinning. 'Do you like it?'

'It's great!'

But then he stopped.

'Please,' I said. 'Go on.'

'No,' he said, moving along the seat so I could sit next to him. 'It is your turn.'

'But I cannot play.'

'Then I will help you.'

Initially, Maurice taught me to learn by ear. I rattled through tunes like 'Johnny B. Goode' and 'Sweet Little Sixteen'. 'I like the American rock and roll kings,' he would say.

Often, we would play together: on the same wide stool at either end of the piano. As I became more experienced, I learned to recognize certain notes.

We became an 'attraction', as the matron would say. Our impromptu concerts brought smiles to the faces of the residents. And then . . .

'Françoise!' Harold's voice cuts into my memories. 'Play for me. Please.'

I get up slowly, feeling as if I have been woken from a dream. I sit at the beautiful walnut piano that Emilee seems to take so much for granted, and my fingers start to have a life of their own. The keyboard brings back a comforting familiarity; all the keys in the same place as the piano on which Maurice had taught me.

Maurice had also introduced me to waltzes by Chopin. This went down well with the more traditional residents, who would try to perform the steps of their youth, their arms supporting one another.

I am not here. I am back in the old people's home. Maurice is still alive. So is my mother. I am in love with Jean-Luc . . .

'NO!'

There is a shout behind me. 'Not that tune. NOT THAT!'

'I am sorry,' I say, stopping. 'What would you like me to play instead?'

'Something with LIFE,' he roars. 'Chuck Berry. Bill Haley. But not *that*!'

So I do. But tears are running down his face. He has gone from being angry to sad. Emotions run rampant at that age. I know all about that. My mother had been the same.

'It is all right,' I say, leaving the piano and holding him to me. He clings like a child.

'Emily,' he sobs. 'Emily.'

He wants his daughter. The woman who shows him no respect. If she did, she would not have gone to London. 'On business,' she said. Hah! More likely she was bored with her father and had run away back to her exciting city life. She never seemed happy when she was here.

'Shall I ring her again?' I ask.

'Yes,' he sobs, pointing to his mobile, which is lying next to a large notebook in the basket at the front of his walker. (I got him this from a local shop because he is unsteady on his feet. We had frames like this in the home in France.) I have noticed that he jots down names of films he wants to watch on television. As I say, there are times when he is lucid and times when he is not. I have seen many like him at this age.

'Isn't she answering?' Harold's anxious eyes are on me.

'No,' I say. My heart aches for him. 'I'm sure she will soon,' I add.

'You said that last time,' he snaps, as if I am responsible.

I know I did. But how else can I reassure him?

Inside, I am worried too. I think once more of that official-looking letter that she had received. Is Emilee in trouble? London is a very dangerous place, or so I have heard. What if she does not come back?

What shall I do then?

That's when the phone rings.

19

It stops before I can get there.

'Dial 1471,' says Harold. I do, but the recorded voice says 'The caller withheld their number'.

Was it Emilee?

If it was, surely she will call again. I hope so. I feel abandoned here in a strange country with a man who does not have all his mind. I need to do something!

So that afternoon, I go to the pub. Pubs are very English, aren't they? And such a pretty sign over the door with a basket of trailing geraniums next to it.

'What can I get you?' says the man at the bar.

There is no carpet. My shoes are sticky on the floor. And there is a strong smell of sweat and ale. There are only two customers inside. They are staring at me as if I have landed from the moon.

'A bottle of fizzy water, please,' I say.

He makes a noise like a pig. 'Really? I thought you French only drank dry Martini.'

'And I thought you English only drank beer from the bottle,' I retort, eyeing the glass next to him. Then I put my hands on my waist and my head flirtatiously on one side. If he wants to stereotype me, then I will act the part. 'Isn't that a sign of a *real* man in this country?'

He stares at me as if I am 'taking the piss' (a phrase I have heard teenagers shouting to each other in the street).

Then he grins. 'I heard you had a tongue in your head,' he says.

Tongue in my head? I want to ask him what this means but I do not want to look stupid.

'You work for Mr Gentle, don't you?' he goes on.

'That's right.'

'Find him all right, do you?'

'I like him very much.'

'Is that so?'

I do not like what the barman is insinuating, or his leer. His breath smells of alcohol and I take a step back.

'His daughter is here too,' I say.

'I heard she had gone back to London.'

News travels fast here.

'Only for a short time,' I say. 'On second thoughts, forget that drink, thank you.'

'But I've already opened it.'

I put two pound coins on the bar. 'Keep it for yourself. It might water down all that beer you drink. Then you might have a smaller belly.'

The two men laugh. 'Asked for that one, didn't you, mate! That girl is smarter than she looks. Good on her!'

I leave with my head high. But inside, I feel shaky.

It is hard being accepted in another country. Yet I have to stay. Harold needs me. And I need him.

Two days later, Emilee's mobile is still going through to voicemail.

Harold is beside himself. (This is a phrase I remember from English lessons at school. My classmates and I could not understand how someone could be standing next to themselves.)

'Where can she be?' Harold keeps saying over and over again, as if this might bring back his daughter.

He is not able to sleep and refuses to eat. I try to distract him by asking him about his past. Most of the people I've looked after enjoy this. It seems to give them comfort. They recall the old days more clearly than yesterday or today. It is the mind's way of compensating for the gaps. ('Compensating' is a word I have recently learned from my dictionary.)

'Tell me what your life was like as a young man,' I ask.

But this makes it worse. 'I told you before – I *do not* want to talk about it!' he yells.

Then he picks up a glass and hurls it against the wall. It only just misses me.

Never have I seen Harold violent before. It shakes me.

'I'm sorry,' I say, gathering up the broken pieces. 'I didn't mean to upset you. But you cannot throw things, Harold. You might have hurt me.'

'I don't bloody care!' he yells, sweeping his hand across the table and sending plates flying. It is lucky I have not served the onion soup yet or we might have been scalded.

There is a yelp. 'Zorro's paw is bleeding,' says Harold.

His voice is completely different now. It is shocked. He stares at me accusingly. 'There is broken glass on the floor. How did that happen?'

'It was an accident,' I say quickly. I lift up Zorro's right paw. A sharp sliver is poking out. I try to pull it out but he won't let me.

'We need to get him to the vet,' I say. 'What is the number?'

Harold shakes his head. 'I don't know. But my daughter will.' He staggers to his feet, gripping the handles of the walker, and makes his way into the hall. 'Emily,' he yells up the stairs. 'Come down, will you? We need help.'

I am trying to hold Zorro back to stop him limping and making it worse. 'Harold,' I say, as calmly as I can. 'Emilee isn't here. She's in London.'

'Why? What is she doing there?'

I need to get him to see the doctor. These memory lapses are getting worse. But right now, I have to find the vet. I do a search on the internet while trying to keep Zorro still but the connection is blinking on and off. Perhaps it is the wind outside, which is beginning to howl.

Then I remember. The card the lawyer had given me when Harold and I had visited him. Maybe he will know. I do not like this man but I cannot think of anyone else to ask.

'Nick speaking.'

I had hoped the receptionist would answer but it is him.

'This is Françoise Alarie,' I say, swallowing my pride. 'We have a problem. Please could you help us?'

20

Luckily, the cut is not too bad. The vet (the one Nick recommended) removes the glass while I soothe Zorro. 'Shh, boy,' I say. 'It is all right.'

'You did the right thing in bringing him here,' says the vet. 'How did it happen again?'

'Françoise threw a glass at the wall,' says Harold, who had insisted on coming in with us.

How can he lie?

'That isn't correct . . .' I start to say.

He cuts in. 'Yes it is. You were angry.'

The vet is not so friendly now. 'Well, however it happened, be careful. Animals can get some serious injuries from treading on sharp things. Make sure he keeps this bandage on for forty-eight hours. I've given you a plastic collar, which might help to stop him worrying at it. Then I'd like to see him again to check it's healing. Go easy on the treats too. I've already mentioned that before to Miss Gentle. He's put on too much weight.'

So that is why Emilee is strict. I feel a little bad about that.

We drive back unsteadily. I am not happy with Harold at the wheel. He does not always notice bicycles and he is forever criticizing others on the road. 'Just look at that idiot turning right without an indicator!'

But I cannot drive myself. We had no money for lessons when Maman was alive.

'Why did you say I threw the glass?' I ask him.

'Because you did.'

'I didn't, Harold. It was you. You were upset because Emilee hadn't come home.'

His hand wobbles and we swerve to the left before he corrects the car. The van behind us hoots. 'Was it? I'm sorry.'

His voice is repentant and childish.

Once more, I feel a spike of fear. Not because his mood changed so fast from being aggressive to passive. I have seen all this at the nursing home. No. I am more scared in case he loses control of the car.

'It's all right. But you must not lie, Harold. And as for Emilee, I am sure she will be back soon.'

'Can you try to ring her again?'

'There is no reception because of the wind. I will do so later.'

I make the call when we are home and Harold is resting *'Hi. This is Emily . . .'*

I need to get her attention. If she isn't interested in her father, perhaps she might like to know what her 'friend' Nick is up to.

'Your father is worried about you,' I say. 'I also have something else I think you should know. I saw Nick with his wife. They were kissing. I think they must be back together.'

Then the machine clicks. I have run out of space. I was going to add that she is better off without a man like that. But it's too late – and either way it will hopefully make her call back.

*

Another day passes. Still Emilee hasn't called. 'Where is she?' Harold keeps saying, looking around the house as if she might be hiding somewhere.

I am torn between being angry and worried. I will give her one more day, I tell myself, and then suggest that Harold rings the police.

Meanwhile, Zorro is chewing the bandage off his paw, despite the big plastic collar the vet has given us. I cannot walk him far because of his injury, so we can only take short 'comfort breaks' in the garden.

I am going crazy in this place, in a foreign country with only an old man for company. I do not like leaving Harold alone for long but I have to get out. So, during his after-noon nap, I walk into the village and pass a charity shop. Second-hand shopping is one of my favourite pastimes in France. One of my best finds is my suede jacket, which I noticed Emilee admiring before she left. There is a stun-ning long purple coat in the window for five pounds.

'You are so slim,' says the shop lady. 'That is far too big for you.'

'Thank you!' I say. 'But I'll buy it for the beautiful col-our and then alter it at home.' I have already found Mrs Gentle's sewing box. I'm sure she would not have minded me using it if she was still here.

'What is your secret to your lovely figure?' asks the assistant admiringly.

'Chocolate!' I say.

'But doesn't that make you fat?'

'Non. I have one little square a day of ninety-per-cent-cocoa chocolate. It is good for you.'

'Well, I never. I will try that myself. Thank you!'

Of course, I have other tricks too. I never eat between meals. And if I eat a lot, I will cut down the next day. Certainly, I would not gobble a packet of crisps as I walk down the street, as I have seen so many of the English do!

Bon Dieu, it is getting dark. I must prepare Harold's dinner. Tonight, I'll make beef goulash. It is not just the ingredients that comprise a meal. It is the presentation too. I take care to make it look beautiful. When I arrived at this job, Harold was living off fish fingers with a pile of baked beans on top.

But as I walk back towards the house, I see a light going on. In my bedroom!

Harold's walker is at the bottom of the stairs. He must have gone up without it, gripping the handrail, without any help. My heart quickens. I rush up the stairs.

I'm right. My door is wide open. Harold has opened all my drawers. How dare he! The wardrobe door is open too. And my shabby, large, brown suitcase, which is under the bed, is out on the floor. Open.

My heart pounds.

He seems so frail, yet he seems to have mustered the strength to haul my heavy suitcase out. How? But as I know all too well, determination can help you do the impossible.

Harold's face is shining. Then he says something that chills me to the bone.

'Look,' he says. 'I have found my Emily!'

21

I did not want Harold to find out this way.

I had hidden her, until the time was right for me to tell him myself.

But now, as I stare at Emilee's auburn hair, I am reminded of that painting by Renoir. The one where the girl with the red bonnet dances with the man. I saw it once at an exhibition with Jean-Luc. 'Wow,' my old love had said. 'She is beautiful, isn't she?'

I had felt a twinge of jealousy. Had Jean-Luc been seeing someone else then or had it started later?

I shut the thought out of my mind to concentrate on what is happening now.

It is not fair. Emilee had everything I had been entitled to. We should have shared it all. This grand house. Not having to worry about how to pay the bills or where the next meal was coming from.

But above all, we should have shared Harold.

Maman had been in the final stages of the cancer when I found the portrait at the back of her wardrobe.

'Who is this?' I had asked, looking at the face, which might have suggested a certain jollity if it were not for the doleful expression in her eyes. The background was not finished and the shoulders seemed to fade away into the background, yet my mother's signature was at the bottom.

'No one,' she had murmured, trying to turn over in bed. It was so hard for her to find a comfortable position.

But something in the way she said it, made me certain that she was not telling the truth. Maman was a good person. I knew that. Yet there were times when we had to bend the facts a little in order to survive.

My throat thickens as I recall easing her onto a pillow. Her face was yellow. The disease had got to her liver now, the doctor said during his last visit.

'It must be someone,' I said. 'Did I ever meet her?'

'No.' Maman's voice was sharp. It had become increasingly so because of the pain. 'You did not. It was before you were born.'

'Did you paint it in France?'

She hesitated slightly. It was enough for me to know she was lying. 'Yes,' she said.

'Are you sure?' I pressed.

'Please, Françoise, do not talk of this any more. It is not important. You are upsetting me.'

When I looked again, the portrait had disappeared.

After Maman had died, I went through her possessions to try and find anything that would give me a clue. But there was nothing. Then came the funeral. The bank manager, who had been at school with her, attended. My mother had been popular, with her kind manner and her beautiful paintings. She had even been chosen by a local dignitary to paint his portrait at a special rate. But where had these people been when we ran out of money to pay for our medical insurance?

I managed to hold back my tears until everyone left. Only then did I let them pour out as I sat at her freshly dug grave. I was conscious afterwards of a presence behind me. It was the bank manager. He was a round man who never went anywhere without a black hat, whatever the weather. But now he was holding it under his arm as a mark of respect.

'I am so sorry for your loss,' he said.

I could tell his voice was thick with grief. 'May I ask if you could meet me in my office this afternoon?'

To my surprise, he gave me a savings book. It was in my mother's name. There was not a great deal of money but it was enough. 'How did she have this?' I ask. 'We were always struggling.'

'Your mother kept all the money she made from her paintings. She wanted you to have it when she went.'

'I could have used this for her treatment,' I wept.

'She hoped you would be able to live well once she was gone. There is something else too.'

He gave me a sealed envelope. Inside was a letter and a birth certificate.

'Who is Harold Gentle?' I asked shakily.

He blushed. 'I do not know. Your mother kept her private business to herself. Just one more thing.'

Another?

I did not expect this. It was the missing portrait of the girl with the chestnut hair. And on the back was an address. Willowmead House, Willowmead, Cornwall.

What was all this about?

I went back to the little apartment that, until so recently, I had shared with Maman. Now it was just me. I made coffee and drank it from her mug. I wrapped one of her shawls around me: a soft pink woollen one I had bought her with my first wages. I sat in her chair with the high back near the fire. I read and reread my mother's letter. It made me stiffen with anger. With fury.

It was clear what Maman meant me to do. She wanted me to go to England and meet my real father.

And then I left. I terminated the rental agreement. I took my birth certificate as well as the portrait (which she had also mentioned in her letter). I caught a train to Paris and then another to London. After that, I took a third train to Cornwall. I did not know Harold had advertised for a companion. I simply turned up, full of indignation, prepared for a big disagreement.

But when I knocked at the door, I was taken aback by my father's warmth and obvious loneliness. 'You saw my advertisement!' he beamed. 'That was quick. Please! Come on in.'

'What advertisement?' I almost said. But I held my tongue while he gabbled in the way people do when they do not see others often. He did not ask me why I had not made an appointment. After a little time, I realized he had been looking for help. I also guessed he might be in the early stages of dementia. The heat of my fury was extinguished. Underneath it all, he was a lonely, lost old man.

I would make myself indispensable. I would be the daughter he should have had. And when the time was right, I would reveal myself.

Even so, I did not mean him any harm. On the contrary. I found myself warming to Harold. I wanted to look after him in the way that any decent person would do. And despite what he did, I grew to genuinely care for him.

And then Emilee turned up! I knew instantly from the portrait who she was. When my mother had painted it, she was not to know this child would be my half-sister.

But I do not care for her. What kind of woman leaves her ninety-four-year-old papa all alone? If she really loved her father, she'd be here now, by his side. Like me. A truly good daughter.

Now Emilee is looking up at Harold and me from her portrait.

'Why do you have this?' he demands.

'Because she is my sister,' I say.

'What? Are you mad?'

I take the birth certificate out of my pocket. I carry it everywhere so no one could discover it accidentally. The time had to be right.

Now that time has arrived.

'Look at this,' I say gently.

'My name is on this,' he says incredulously.

My voice trembles. 'That's right.'

'You think you are *my* daughter?' he questions, as if this cannot be clear from the evidence in his hand.

Only a few minutes ago, he was confused. Now he is lucid.

'Yes.'

He is still studying the certificate. 'Céleste,' he says. 'Who is she?'

'You must remember her! Please!' A pleading note enters my voice. 'She was one of your au pairs when Emilee was growing up.'

He snorts. 'I have no memory of her.'

'I did a DNA test when I arrived,' I say. 'I took hair from your hairbrush and sent it off with a strand of my hair. I have the result. Look!'

I wave the piece of paper in front of him.

His face remains scornful.

'Pah! Tests can be made up. Papers can be forged. I'm a lawyer, don't forget – I know a con when I see one.'

I will not allow him to get out of it this easily.

'My mother is dead! You and Emilee are the only family I have left,' I yell. I make it a rule of mine never to lose my temper with those I care for. But this is different. This is personal.

'I'm sorry about your mother,' he replies. 'Truly I am. But it doesn't give you an excuse to come here and claim I am your father.'

'But you are! And she never got over you. How could you have behaved so badly? You were an elderly married man with a young daughter who seduced a seventeen year-old girl who was far from home and vulnerable. It's disgusting.'

His face turns dark. 'That's not true. As far as I am concerned, you are not my daughter. And if you take this any further, I promise that you will be sorry. I have many friends in high places. I wouldn't push me, if I were you.'

How can an infirm man suddenly become so menacing?

There is a furious barking from downstairs. Zorro. He needs a walk. Then the sound of the front door opening and a voice calling out.

'Dad!'

Emilee is back?

135

'If you tell your lies to my daughter,' hisses Harold, 'you will regret it.'

Maybe I misjudged him. Where is the kind man I thought I knew? Harold might be old. Yet he is dangerous.

And I get the feeling that he would do anything to keep me quiet.

France, 1944

Albert's eyes stare glassily up at me as the lorry continues to bump along the road.

'He's beginning to smell,' says one of the men.

'Reckon we should just stop and lob him out,' says another.

'You can't do that,' I plead. 'He deserves a decent grave.'

'What's going to happen when we get to the next place, then? There isn't exactly going to be a burial committee waiting for us, is there?'

The first man stands up. 'That stink is making me sick. Stop the truck now and I'll put him on the roadside.'

There's the click of a rifle.

They all stare at me.

'If you so much as lay a hand on him,' I say quietly, 'I will shoot you.'

'Hold on, Gentle,' says the sergeant. 'Watch what you're saying.'

'And you watch what you're saying too, Sarge,' I reply.

'I could have you court-martialled for this.'

'And what would that look like? Allowing one of your men to be chucked out of a truck like a dead rabbit.'

'This is war.'

'Exactly. We have to look after each other. We have little else but our dignity.'

'Maybe he's right,' mumbles someone.

But inside I am shitting bricks. I could have got into real trouble then with the sarge. But this poor bloke had given me kind words and a swig of his whisky when I'd been scared. I owed him a decent burial at the least.

No one says any more. The conversation moves on to their empty stomachs. Mine was rumbling too, even though I couldn't eat a mouthful after Albert's death.

Where are we going? The sergeant isn't meant to say in case we get captured. But rumour has it that we're heading for another 'safe place'.

We arrive after the moon has been in the sky for some hours. 'Out,' instructs the sarge. 'Run straight to the farmhouse.'

'What if it's booby trapped?'

'Then we're all fucked.'

I begin to drag the body in. 'I'll give you a hand with that,' offers one of the men.

'No,' I say. 'I'll do it. We needn't lose more of us than necessary. If I'm spotted, I'll take the hit.'

'That one's stronger than he looks,' I hear one of them muttering.

Albert's heavy, even though he had been short. It takes every ounce of my strength to drag him towards some trees.

Then I see a pair of eyes in the thicket. I freeze.

'N'aie pas peur,' says someone. 'Je suis un ami.'

I can remember enough of my schoolboy French to understand.

It's a light voice. Like an adolescent just before his voice cracks. I see a boy in breeches looking out at me. 'Il est mort?' he asks.

'Yes.'

'Attendez ici,' he says, and disappears.

I wait, as he asked, shivering, wondering what the fuck I had done. You heard of some Frenchies who would grass you to the Jerries. What if this was a trap?

But then he returns with two shovels. 'Allez.'

Together we dig a shallow grave. The boy takes the feet and I take the shoulders.

'May God bless your soul, Albert,' I say, as we cover him up.

Then I begin to shake with cold, terror and sorrow.

'Allez,' said the boy again, beckoning me towards the house. 'Nous avons de la soupe, du pain et du fromage.'

Soup, bread and cheese sounds like a banquet to me.

'You're a good lad,' I say, slapping his back. 'Comment vous appelez-vous?'

'Je m'appelle André. Et vous?'

'I'm Harold. Harold Gentle. Pleased to meet you.'

22

'Where have you been?' I demand.

'Work,' replies Emilee, shortly. She speaks to me as if I am a fool.

'Your father has got worse since you left.'

'What? In a few days?'

'It happens,' I say, thinking of patients who I had cared for. Maurice in particular comes to mind. One day he had been playing 'Reelin' and Rockin''. The next he was in bed, complaining of chest pains. The day after that, his bed was occupied by someone else. My own chest still aches from his loss.

'Harold is losing his balance now. I buy him a walking frame with money he gives me And he is getting confused. His memory is going.'

I need to protect myself in case Harold tells Emilee that I revealed he was my father. They might both throw me out of the house before I can make them see the truth.

'Then why didn't you ring me?' she says harshly.

'I tried, but it goes through to voicemail.'

'It *went* through to voicemail,' she corrects me. 'As I said, I was busy.'

'I left messages.'

'I didn't get them.'

Emilee is lying. She has to be. She would have got the

one about Nick and his wife. Maybe she is angry with me for telling her. Or embarrassed.

'Is my father all right now?'

Our father, I almost say. But I hold myself back. Now is not the time for such a revelation. I must choose it carefully or else her reaction will be as bad as Harold's.

'You can ask him yourself.'

We are having this conversation briefly at the foot of the stairs while Harold is trying to make his way down. I rush back up to help him. Emilee does the same. We are on either side of the old man, each trying to outdo the other with our assistance. I am still his carer, after all. Besides, there is no way I am going home to France until he admits what he has done. Françoise Alarie is not beaten that easily. I owe that to my mother.

'I'm sorry I had to leave you for a while, Dad,' she is saying.

His voice quivers. 'I was frightened. There was no one here to look after me.'

What?

'I was here, Harold,' I say defensively.

'But you were always out.'

Emilee is sending me furious, accusing glances.

'That is not true,' I protest. 'I only left the house when you asked me to go shopping for you or to walk Zorro.'

'Well, I don't remember that. You threw a glass against the wall and hurt Zorro's paw.'

'That was *you*!'

'And you would not ring my daughter for me.'

'I left messages for her!'

I try to calm myself. Old people often forget things. But there have been times when I wonder if this is a convenient excuse. The elderly can be manipulative. As if their age gives them permission to lie. Or to erase a wrongdoing which they had made in their youth. My mother had been little more than a child. He had ruined her life. And her pain had become mine.

'I can look after my father now,' says Emilee when we get him into the sitting room and sit him in his favourite chair overlooking the garden. 'You can have some time off if you want. It sounds as if you deserve it.'

My English is good enough to know she is being sarcastic.

I want to tell this stuck-up woman that she has no right to speak to me like this because *I* was the one who got up in the night when Harold needed his bedsheets changed after soiling them. *I* am the one who has provided company and made him laugh, when reading out amusing pieces from magazines because his failing eyesight will not allow him to do that himself.

But instead, I take myself off for a walk with Zorro along the clifftop (his paw seems much better now). Walking has always been my way of releasing the tension inside. As I look down at the fierce high waves, I shudder. I prefer the safety of the land. The sea is unpredictable. Like love. Like human relationships. Harold knows I am his daughter now. But I am shocked by his cruel denial of me.

When I get back, there is a smell of burning.

Mon Dieu! Emilee has left the kettle on the Aga. It is boiled dry.

'What have you done?' says a voice behind me.

'What do you mean, what have I done?' I say.

'The kettle is black at the bottom,' says Emilee accusingly. 'You left it on when you went for a walk.'

'No I didn't.'

'Are you calling me a liar?'

I am. But I cannot say that or she might go to Harold. What if he fires me? I will have lost my chance to make him acknowledge me.

'I think you might have got confused,' I say quietly.

'And I think you've got it wrong.'

'Well, it wasn't me. And who else but you could have put it on? Your father he sleeps in his chair.'

'Well don't mention it to him. I don't want him to get upset.'

I leave it at that. Yet I am not convinced. Something is not right with Emilee. She is more stressed than usual. She is on the edge. Something must have happened in London.

I need to know what. My future might depend on it.

23

It is a week since Emilee returned, and Harold is getting weaker and weaker. I wonder if this is an act to make me feel sorry for him. Then – or so he might think – I will be less likely to tell Emilee his dark secret in case it makes him worse. Like I say, the elderly can be very manipulative and cunning.

But no. It is real. I see this as he struggles to climb the stairs to his room at night. And even though I am furious with him, my compassionate side takes over. 'We should make him a bed in the sitting room,' I suggest.

'I've already got that organized,' snaps Emilee. 'If you don't mind, I'd like some time with my father on his own. I am going to play the piano to him. *My* piano.'

'The one you gave up?' I cannot resist saying.

She looks at me with what seems like genuine bewilderment. 'What do you mean?'

'Your father said you stopped playing because you did not care for it any more.'

She makes a 'pah' face, so like Harold's. 'That's nonsense! He wouldn't have said that. In fact, he told me not to spend so much time practising because I needed to study for my exams instead.'

It is hard to know which one is lying. I do not trust either of them any more.

*

A delivery van turns up that very afternoon with one of those electric beds where you can raise the top and bottom. I am impressed by Emilee's choice. We had a similar design in the home and they were very good. It is big but there is plenty of room for it in le salon.

I sign for it with the tortoiseshell fountain pen Harold gave me, right before our argument.

'Where did you get that?' Emilee demands.

'Your father presented it to me.'

'I don't believe you. My mother gave it to him one Christmas.'

'Ask him yourself if you don't believe me.'

So she marches into the sitting room where Harold is in his chair. 'Did you give Françoise the pen Mum gave you?' she demands.

'Yes. She needed one to write down her English sayings,' he says.

'How *could* you?' she says.

'Don't nag me,' he moans. 'I'm in pain.'

'Where does it hurt, Harold?' I ask, kneeling by his side.

'Everywhere.'

How I wish I could do something more. It is not right that anyone should suffer. Even someone who has made many mistakes, like my father. How lovely it is to say that word!

'We need to call the doctor,' says Emilee.

If only I could tell her the truth about my birth.

'What can she do?' growls Harold.

'She might be able to give you a different painkiller for your arthritis, Dad.'

'Arthritis? Is that what you think it is?'

'Isn't it? That's what you've always told us.'

'Then I'm right, aren't I?'

None of this makes sense. Something tells me that this is more than elderly confusion. He is trying to cover something up.

'I think you should definitely call the doctor, even if he doesn't want you to,' I tell Emilee when we are in the kitchen together. I am getting down a mug. She is making his coffee in the percolator. Anyone watching might think we are working together. But we are in fierce competition.

'I've already done that,' she says. 'You don't have to worry. He is my father, even if he insists on giving away things you have no right to accept.'

To be honest, I had been thinking of returning the pen but now her anger is such that I change my mind.

I think back to Maman on her deathbed. There had been no sign that she had wanted to tell me her secret then. Perhaps our parents' generation had got it right, the way they shovel the difficult past to the next generation to deal with once they're dead and gone. Maybe my generation talks too much.

'Thank you,' Harold says, when I take the tray into him.

There is a yellow tinge to his complexion. 'You look after me so well, Emily.'

'I am Françoise,' I say under my breath. 'Your other daughter.'

But he is asleep now.

*

146

The doctor comes. Emilee takes her into the sitting room, where Harold lies in his new bed, unable to get up now. I wait in the kitchen.

I do not have a good feeling about this.

When I hear the doctor leaving, I come out into the hall. Emilee is leaning against the door after seeing her out. She is crying.

'What is it?' I ask.

'Cancer. He's had it for three months but didn't tell me.'

A cold fear shoots through me.

'What kind of cancer?'

'Pancreatic. Now it's everywhere. Even his liver.'

I think of that jaundiced tone to his skin.

'Have they done scans?'

'Yes. Weeks ago. Before you arrived, when I was in London. But he kept it quiet . . .'

Her voice tails away.

I want to cry but it is caught in my throat. 'I am so sorry, Emilee.'

'Why are *you* upset? He's not *your* father.'

I bite my tongue. 'But I care for him.'

'You've certainly given that impression.'

'What do you mean by that?'

'I mean,' hisses Emilee, 'that I know what you are doing. I've seen it before in the hospital. Sick people are suddenly befriended by neighbours or "well-wishers"' – she makes a quote in the air with her fingers – 'towards the end of their life and then they end up with a nice bequest or even the house.'

'That is *not* why I am here,' I say truthfully. All I want is recognition but I cannot tell her that yet.

'Well . . . not any more. I am back. I can look after Dad on my own. We don't need you.'

No! I have not finished what I came here to do.

Somehow, I have to get Harold to acknowledge me as his daughter.

But I must be quick. He might not have much time left.

24

I have to find an opportunity to speak to Harold and persuade him to let me stay. Despite everything, I want to be
with my father for as long as I can, before he departs this
earth.

I am owed this, surely, having been deprived of his
company all my life?

I cannot really explain this. It is not as if Harold
Gentle is a purely good man. He behaved appallingly to
my mother. He denies that he is my father. And although
he can be oh so charming, he has a quick and fierce
temper.

But maybe I was silly to be scared of him before. What
can an old, ill, dying man do to me?

Besides, against my better judgement, I have grown to
care deeply for him. We have the same love of books. I
too admire Dickens and Shakespeare. We share the same
fault too: that conviction that we are always right in our
opinions.

The next day, he seems a little brighter and wants to get
up. I help him dress and go to the kitchen to make him a
coffee. I don't know where Emilee is. I only hope she
hasn't said anything yet to Harold about me leaving.

'When will you tell Emilee you are my father?' I ask. He
is sitting in le salon. There is a glass of whisky by his side.
He must have helped himself just now even though it is

early in the day. I consider taking it away and then remind myself that when you are old, you are surely entitled to have some treats before the end.

'I've told you,' he says. 'I am not your father.'

'I could go to a lawyer with the birth certificate and my DNA result,' I say.

'Pah! And I could tell you exactly how that would fall down in court right now.'

'Fine,' I answer, taking a deep breath. 'But who will look after you when Emilee takes off for London next, leaving you all alone?'

A look of fear crosses his face momentarily. 'I'll get someone from an agency,' he growls.

'No one will put up with you,' I say. 'No one like a daughter. I might be upset with you, Papa, but I still want to take care of you.'

'Why? Are you after my money?'

'Actually, I want something far more precious.'

'Ha! The house. I knew it.'

'Not that either. I want to get to know *you*. I want to know more about who my father really is. What is behind this front you show to others? You see, I think there is more to Harold Gentle than the rest of the world knows. Not even your other daughter.'

Am I imagining it, or does a fearful look alight on his face pour un moment?

'I have no idea what you're talking about. Now get me another whisky, will you?'

Of course, I am lying. I don't *just* want to know my father.

I want something far more important that money can't buy.

His love. His recognition.

I want the whole world to know I am Harold Gentle's daughter, whether Emilee likes it or not.

25

I cannot bear the suspense any more.

'Have you told your father you want me to leave?' I ask.

'Not yet,' she says.

'Why not? Won't you need someone if you have to go up to London again?'

Emilee visibly flinches. There is something that scares her about London. If only I knew what.

'I can manage,' she says.

But she doesn't sound certain.

'You've tried to find a replacement for me, haven't you?' I probe.

'I might have done.'

'Let me guess. None of the local people will help because your father is not easy. And you are concerned about hiring just anyone from an agency. So instead you have me. Better the devil you know than the devil you don't. Isn't that what you English say?'

She still says silent. So I am right, then.

We are in the conservatory. There are plants everywhere, surrounding two wicker seats. Emilee is perched on the edge of one, staring out across the lawn. I would like to take the other but she does not invite me so I stand by it instead. Officially, I am on duty, but Harold is napping.

It is one of those sharp, bright, English autumn

mornings that pretends to be summer. That glowing orange sun hanging over the cliff that looks so inviting but freezes you to the bone when you go outside.

'You know,' I continue, 'if Harold was my father, I would not wish for a stranger to be here either.'

'Really?' she asks.

'It's what you call an invasion of privacy, n'est-ce pas?'

She nods.

'You are wrong about me wanting material things,' I say. 'I don't. I just enjoy looking after the elderly and sometimes I get too attached to them.'

She makes a snorting sound. 'Enough to send them on their way before their time?'

I give a start. 'What are you talking about?'

Emilee fixes her eyes on me. I force myself to hold her gaze. Françoise Alaric is not scared of anyone.

'I checked your references by ringing the nursing home where you worked last,' she says. 'The matron told me you were a valued member of staff. She said you were "wonderful at easing our residents through the final part of their journey".'

Emilee makes those irritating finger quotes again.

I feel myself blushing. 'I did what I could. I just try to make them comfortable.'

'That's one way of interpreting it.' Her voice becomes brisker. 'But now I am here so, as I said, I can manage Dad on my own.'

Somehow I need to make her give me an extension.

'Could I ask one favour before I leave?' I say, stroking the leaves of a palm next to me. (It had been turning brown and dry with neglect when I arrived. The gardener appeared to have forgotten the conservatory, but I took it on myself to revive the plant. Greenery is so good for the health.)

Emilee's eyes harden. 'That depends on what the favour is.'

'I would like to give your father my resignation personally, on my own.'

The surprise on her face is exceedingly satisfactory.

'All right. When?'

'This afternoon. That will give me time to pack my bags so I can leave tomorrow.'

'Good.'

There is the tinkle of Harold's bell, demanding our attention.

'Sounds as if he is awake,' says Emilee. 'Why don't you go in now and tell him?'

My heart is thudding. This is a big gamble.

Harold has managed to get out of bed. There are times when I wonder if he can do more than he makes out, like when he fetched himself that glass of whisky. He motions towards his lips. They look parched. I have already brought in fresh water, anticipating this. I help him back into bed and hold the cup to his mouth. He sips noisily.

'Thank you, Emily.'

I've noticed that his voice is getting louder, his hearing failing him.

'It's Françoise,' I say, hurt.

'That's what I said.'

I have been here long enough to know that Harold cannot bear to be wrong. So I don't correct him. Instead, I potter around, tidying up. Then I start humming softly. It is the Chopin waltz that he had not liked before. One of Maman's favourites.

'Please. No,' he says.

'Why not?'

I feel bad pushing him, but he is coming to the end of his time. I am sure this holds the key to something. This might be my last chance. So I carry on humming.

There is a moan from the bed.

'My love. I miss you so much. It has been so long. I am so sorry for what I did . . .'

So he *did* love Maman!

I go back and kneel by his side. I try to speak loudly, hoping Emilee can hear. She is, I am sure, listening, on the other side of the door, which I have deliberately left ajar. I would be eavesdropping too if I was her.

But she is not me. I have one up on her even though no one else can know this yet. It is my trump card. How tempting it has been to drop little hints to Emilee! But part of me feels sorry for her.

'You have such lovely hair,' he whispers, reaching out and stroking my head. I want to cringe. Yet at the same time, I want to hold his hand there for ever.

I need to bring him back. 'And what about my mother, Céleste?' I say. 'She had lovely hair too. When she was dying, it all fell out because of the treatment.'

'She's dead?'

Had he really forgotten I'd told him this or is he pretending?

'Yes. But she was beautiful right to the end. And she kept saying your name.'

I expect him to deny everything again but he visibly deflates.

'Stop,' he whimpers.

'How could you have seduced her?' I hiss. 'She was only seventeen. You were an old married man.'

'You wouldn't understand.'

My blood is beginning to boil. 'Try me.'

'I can't,' he croaks. 'I'm too scared you will tell Emily.'

I have him.

'I won't if you allow me to stay on so I can get to know you better.'

'Why?'

'Because you are my father,' I say. 'Aren't you?'

Go on, I want to shout. *Just say it.*

But instead, he ignores my question. Despite his frailty, he is now struggling to sit up.

'Hand me my cheque book,' he demands. 'It's in that drawer.'

I did not expect this. It's not why I am here. But it might help me achieve my goal. So I do as I am told.

He writes a figure and passes it to me. 'Is that enough?' he asks.

'Maybe an extra zero,' I say.

His crinkled eyes narrow. 'You drive a hard bargain.'

'Like father, like daughter,' I reply. I stare at the cheque. It's more than I'd ever dreamed of. Of course, it's not the money that matters. It's the gesture behind it. 'Thank you, Papa.'

His eyes narrow. 'And you won't tell Emily that you are my daughter?'

At last! The words I came here for. But what if she hadn't heard?

'I cannot hear you, Harold. Can you repeat that?'

'DON'T TELL EMILY THAT YOU ARE MY DAUGHTER,' he booms.

I breathe a sigh of relief. 'No, Papa. Of course I won't.'

26

Emilee is outside the door. She doesn't even pretend she wasn't listening. I admire her for that. For my part, I don't pretend to hide the cheque. In fact, I wave it in the air. I want her to see it. It is surely proof that Harold recognizes his paternity.

'How *dare* you extort money out of him?' she says. Her eyes are wild with fury. It suits her.

'I didn't. He offered. Why shouldn't a man give money to his daughter? Don't look so surprised. You must have heard.'

'He's too ill to know what he's saying,' she splutters. 'He just gave you the money to stop you lying.'

'Let's go into the kitchen to talk,' I hiss. My feelings are mixed towards Harold. Sometimes I hate him. Sometimes I love him. But the 'professional carer' side of me knows it would be cruel to deprive an old man of peace in his final hours.

Emilee takes her father's chair at the head of the table. She is making a point. In a strange way, I am beginning to admire her more. She is a fighter after all, like me.

'Do you remember having an au pair when you were a child?' I ask.

Her brow furrows.

'We had a few over the years,' she says suspiciously. Then she becomes defensive. 'My mother was always busy with her charitable work and this is a big house. She needed help.'

'*My* mother played the piano,' I say.

Her face goes still. 'I remember one who did that. I'm not sure what she was called but I liked listening to her.'

'Céleste,' I say. 'That was my mother's name.'

She actually laughs. 'Are you seriously trying to tell me that my father got her pregnant?'

'You heard me through the door, didn't you? And if you didn't, let me tell you again. I have a DNA test with my hair and your father's. The results are here. Look.'

I hold up the document, which I carry everywhere for safety. A reminder of what I'm here to do. As if I need it . . .

'And,' I add. 'Here is my birth certificate with your father's name on it.'

Emilee looks away.

'I don't need to see a "result" from some test that I don't believe for a second is reliable,' she spits. 'And as for that birth certificate, I wouldn't mind betting that your mother just wrote down my father's name to hide the real man who fathered you.'

'Then do your own test!' I grab a pair of scissors from the cutlery drawer and snip off a small strand of my hair and push it across the table to her. 'All you have to do is take some from your father too and have the test done. Then you will see I tell the truth.'

She ignores the hair. 'It's all a lie. It has to be. My parents were so in love; so happy.'

'Marriages can seem good on the outside,' I point out, 'but might be rotten at the core.'

She makes a snorting sound like a pig. 'You don't know anything about my mother, so don't make assumptions.'

'You don't know anything about mine, either.'

To my surprise, Emilee's face begins to crumple. 'But I do. I liked her. It's coming back to me now. Céleste was so *nice* and so young. How could she have done that?'

'How could our father have done it, you mean,' I snap back.

'If you are right – and only *if* – your mother must have thrown herself at him.'

'Thrown herself? What do you mean?'

'She must have seduced him. My father is a good man, an honourable man.'

I will not let her go on. 'How dare you!'

Then I think of the letter my mother had left with the bank manager.

I am not the kind of woman who has an affair with a married man, chérie. You must believe that. So I am going to tell you how it happened . . .

Emilee's face is bright red now, her features inflamed and her sneer a gash across her face. 'I'm not stupid, Françoise. I can see what you are doing. I know you went with my father to the lawyer's about his will.'

I am taken aback. 'Nick told you? But that was confidential.'

'No. It wasn't Nick.'

'Then who?'

'I can't say.'

'Actually,' I say firmly, 'I was witnessing something.'

'I don't believe you. You think you've got it all sewn up, don't you? Well, I don't care. Even if he was unfaithful to my mother – and I'm not saying he was – it was a long time ago. He's dying now.'

'Exactement,' I reply. 'We have to work together to help his pain.'

Emilee makes a snorting noise of disbelief in her throat. 'How?'

'By looking after him side by side, of course. What else?' My voice softens. I have to convince her. 'So don't send me away, Emilee. Please. You need me to help. What is it going to be like for you when he is about to . . . to go.' My eyes fill with tears. 'I nursed my maman. I know what it is like. How I wished there was someone else to watch while I went to the bathroom or fetch her some water. It is not easy to do this alone.'

I see her hesitating.

'All right. You can stay until he . . . until it is no longer necessary. But after that, Françoise, I never want to see you again. Got it?'

'Just so long as I can spend time with our father,' I plead.

Her voice turns hard. 'So you can get more money?'

I shake my head in denial. 'That's not what I want.'

'What *do* you want, then?'

'Recognition,' I say. 'And an apology for what he did. I loved my mother with all my heart, but now I have met Harold, I realize something else. Deep down, all I'd ever wanted was someone to protect me like your father protected you. He would do anything for you, Emilee.'

For a minute, I feel like I have struck a nerve. Something gives in her eyes.

'Françoise,' she says. 'I am sorry you did not have a

161

father when you were growing up. Yet don't you see? It's too late for that.'

But she's wrong.

I'm going to prove that. No matter what it takes.

And Emilee will help me. She has not left the hair on the table. She has taken it with her. When she gets the results, there will be no doubt.

27

The pain gets worse. I cannot bear to see Harold writhe in agony. His skin is yellow. His bones are standing out like a skeleton.

We take it in turns to sit by him. 'Where is Emily?' he groans when I hold his hand.

Then, when she takes my place, he calls out for me.

Is it confusion caused by the pain or is he playing a sadistic game?

One night when he's in bed, he demands a steak. 'I am hungry!' he roars. 'Bring it to me. Now.'

'But Harold,' I say. 'You cannot swallow.'

'COOK ME ONE!' he roars again.

So I do as he says. The way he likes it. Tender. Juicy. I bring it up.

'What's this?' he asks.

'You said you wanted a steak.'

His face turns grotesque, twisted like one of the stone gargoyles on the church roof back home. 'You *stupid* woman. You know I cannot swallow. You are taunting me.'

I am used to behaviour like this. *'Providing the patient is safe, it can be best to go out of the room for a short time, take a deep breath and then go back in again,'* the matron would tell me in the home where I worked.

I take the steak down to the kitchen.

'You are in luck,' I say to Zorro, who is waiting

expectantly. I cut it up and put it in his bowl. He wolfs it down. Then I go back up to Harold again. He is asleep.

Another time, I make some parsnip-and-carrot soup; blending it finely so he can swallow.

'What's that yellow powder?' asks Emilee suspiciously, as she watches me add a tablespoon to the soup.

'Turmeric,' I say. 'It is good for the joints and inflammation. It helps his arthritis. But you have to be careful. It stains your fingers yellow.'

Emilee looks as though she is going to say something else, but doesn't.

The doctor suggests a hospice nurse. 'No!' thunders Harold. 'I do not want a stranger with me at the end.'

'It's all right, Dad,' says Emilee, stroking his brow. 'I'll be here.'

He cannot move from his bed now.

'Have you told him that you know he's my father?' I ask her.

'No,' she snaps. 'I don't want to upset him.'

'Nor do I.'

'You could have fooled me.'

'He loves me, Emilee. And he loves you too. Can't you see that? It's why he wants us both here with him.'

'You are deluding yourself about the first part.'

Perhaps. Am I crazy to hope that my father will learn to love me as much as my sister?

But Harold *does* want us both close to him.

'Emilee,' he says. 'Tell Françoise she must not go back to France. Françoise, tell Emilee she must not return to London. I do not want either of you even leaving the house. If something were to happen to either of you, what will become of me?'

My mother was the same when she was ill and I had to go to the shops.

'*Don't leave me, Françoise! What if something happens to me when you are gone?*'

'*But I won't be long, Maman.*'

'*I am scared of being on my own. Can't you ask someone else to get the shopping?*'

The truth was that I craved fresh air. But how could I leave Maman? I was a prisoner in our own home. So many other carers are the same. And now, it is happening again. Except this time, there are two of us. Emilee and me.

'Are you sure, Dad?' asks Emilee. 'Don't you want me, your daughter, to be with you?'

She glares at me challengingly as she says this.

But what will Harold say when he realizes she knows his secret?

'I want Françoise too. Give me my medicine.'

I reach for the bottle at the same time as Emilee. We keep it high up in a kitchen cupboard, on the other side of the room from the Aga, but I had brought it out earlier, ready for the next dose.

She snatches it from me.

'I'll do it,' she says.

Then we sit by him, waiting for the morphine to have its effect. The doctor has put him on the liquid form, now that he finds it hard to swallow tablets.

'It still hurts,' he moans, moving from one side to another.

'I can't give you any more, Dad.'

I have seen this so many times before at the home. Distraction, I have learned, can help.

'Why don't I read to you?' I say. 'Some poetry perhaps.'

Poems are short. Their rhythm is also soothing.

'Pooh sticks,' murmurs Harold.

What is he saying?

But Emilee is jumping up and fetching a book from the shelf behind him. It is the book she found me reading to Harold when she arrived.

'You used to read *Winnie the Pooh* to me every night, didn't you, Daddy?' She shoots me a triumphant look.

He nods.

'Remember our favourite line?' she continues. '"You're braver than you believe, stronger than you seem, and smarter than you think."'

He nods again.

'That used to help me, Daddy. And it's true about you too.'

She starts to read. Harold closes his eyes, but when she pauses, he opens them again.

'Go on,' he commands.

I am back in France. Listening to my mother reading. Her soft voice helps to ease the pain from the children at school who taunted me for not having a father after my mother's husband left us, or wearing old clothes that did not fit properly.

Emilee reaches the line Maman and I had liked best. 'Sometimes the smallest things take up the most room in your heart.'

There is a little sob. I look across our father to this

woman with the golden-red hair. For a split second, our eyes meet with shared pain. Then her hostility returns.

That's when I realize. Emilee will never accept me.

'Do you want to do the next shift?' I suggest. 'Then I'll take over.'

'All right,' she says.

28

Emily

Dad is sleeping fitfully. Why is death so hard? Just like birth. We don't arrive on this earth or leave it without pain.

No one really knows what might happen when a baby is born or when someone dies.

It's the final adventure into the unknown.

Daddy is talking now.

'Please, Albert. Give me a fag.'

I stroke his forehead. 'Who is Albert, Daddy?'

'Just one puff. It will help the nerves.'

But he has never smoked! He must be rambling.

'Emily,' he whispers.

'Yes, Daddy.' I am kneeling by the side of his bed, holding his hand.

'There is something I need to tell you.'

My heart almost stops. 'What?'

'I should have told you before but . . .'

He starts to cough.

I give him some water.

He takes a small sip.

'What should you have told me before?' I ask gently.

'I've always loved you,' he groans.

He had never been one to express emotions. Tears begin to run down my face.

'I've always loved you too, Daddy.'

'Not *you*.'

I feel hurt. But of course, he's talking to Mum again. 'Mummy knows you love her as well.'

He's thrashing around now. Cross. Distressed.

'Not her. The French woman. Such beautiful hair . . .'

Céleste?

Françoise's mother.

Anger wells up inside me.

How can he think of her at the end instead of us? It's not just that she was so young – although that makes me retch to think of it. It's the betrayal.

He is quiet for a bit. Then he begins to sob. My heart aches at the gasping sound he's making.

'Please,' he begs. 'Give me more morphine.'

'I can't. Not for a bit.'

He scowls at me. I am a child again. I see the father who expected me to do what he said. 'If you loved me, you would,' he growls.

'It isn't good for you – the doctor would . . .'

Then he says something I will never forget. Something so cruel that I feel as if my heart is being ripped right out of my chest.

'Please stop!' I say, getting up. 'You win. I'll do it.'

'Thank you,' he says. 'There's just one other thing.'

He stops.

'What?' I say crossly.

He closes his eyes. 'It doesn't matter.'

29

Françoise

I take over from Emilee just after midnight.

'My turn now,' I say gently.

She is very sleepy. Clearly she had nodded off. Watching someone die doesn't just tear your mind apart. It is also exhausting.

'Thank you,' she says.

I am on my own now. It is very quiet. I can hear my own breath.

For three hours, I sit and watch him. This man who could have made our lives so different. Despite Harold's earlier declaration that he couldn't hurt his wife or Emily, I begin to fantasize. He might have welcomed us in, Maman and me. Maybe Mrs Gentle would have accepted us too. Perhaps she wasn't as naive as it seems. There are people who accept mistresses and lovers in their marriage. We could all have been happy together without jealousy or deceit, poverty and pain.

What if Mrs Gentle knew about my mother all along? Was that why Maman had to leave here?

But he didn't love us enough to come to France and see us in secret. (I'm not sure I believe him when he says he didn't know Maman had had a child.) Then I would have had a real father, and Maman would have had the man she'd loved, even for part of the time. Mrs Gentle and Emilee could have remained blissfully ignorant. No one would have been hurt.

It would have been a solution – better than the way it has turned out. At least for Maman . . .

The next thing I know, the clock by the side of his bed says 2.49 a.m. I must have nodded off, just as Emilee had on the previous watch.

Harold's breath is much fainter. He is making little rasping sounds.

Not long now.

I kneel by his side.

'I love you, Papa,' I whisper. 'Despite what you did. I do not know why. I just do.'

A hand reaches out to me. I hold it. He is cold.

'Emily,' he murmurs.

I am about to tell him that it is me, Françoise. But then he says something that makes my skin prickle.

'There is something I must tell you.'

'What is it, Daddy?' I ask, trying to sound as much like Emilee as I can. I know it is naughty but I cannot stop myself. In my time, I have heard many deathbed confessions. This one is different. This is my father. I am sure that he is going to tell me (the woman he thinks is Emilee) that Françoise (the real me) is his child.

Again and again, I have seen men and women shed secrets that have weighed them down all their lives. If only they had done so earlier, they might have lived more happily.

So it is my duty to let him relieve himself.

'Emily,' he says. 'Please understand what I am about to say.'

His speech is suddenly clear. I have seen this too at the end of life.

But then he says something that makes me gasp out loud. I do not see this coming. I can barely breathe.

'You do forgive me for not telling you earlier, don't you?' he says when he has finished. His red eyes stare at me beseechingly. Then his expression changes. His voice rings out angrily. 'You are not Emily.'

'No,' I say, trembling. It is not that I am scared he might hit me. More than that, I do not want to upset a dying man.

'You are my Antoinette!' His voice sings into the air. It is joyous now. Not furious.

Once I had an old man in the home who went through all of his dead relatives and friends, convinced they were by his bedside. I allowed him to think they were there to give him closure.

'I can never forget you,' he gasps. 'I am so sorry.'

'Why are you sorry, Harold?' I ask.

His eyes stare at mine. 'Because you died for me, Antoinette. Don't you remember?'

'Get down,' he starts to scream. 'The Jerries are coming!'

'It's all right,' I soothe. 'You're safe. I promise.'

'Really?' he says.

'Really,' I say.

He gazes up at me, so trusting. Then his hand falls on the bed and his eyes go still.

I take his pulse. He's no longer breathing.

I stand up and open the window. '*To let the soul out*,' matron always said.

I am not sure if I believe this or not. Yet it seems the right thing to do.

He is no longer in pain. I am glad for that. Yet I am overwhelmed by a deep sadness too.

There is something else as well. My head is reeling from the confession he made to the woman he thought was Emilee.

Then I drop a kiss on his forehead – still warm – and make my way to Emilee's bedroom. I tap on the door. It takes a while for her to open it.

When she sees me, I know that she knows. But I say it anyway.

'It is over.'

France, 1944

I follow André into the farmhouse. It seems dark from the outside because of the blackout curtains. But inside, there is a roaring fire and the smell of something so good that my stomach churns. It has been empty for so long that I can barely remember the excitement of good food. Now a plate of meat – real pork! – is placed in front of me by a jolly-faced woman in an apron.

'Thank you,' I say.

Saliva dribbles down the inside of my cheeks as I bite into the crisp crackling. Yet I find I cannot chew.

I keep thinking of poor Albert, whom we'd just buried.

'No stomach for war,' scoffs the driver, who'd finished his off with half a baguette. 'That's your trouble, Gentle.'

André pipes up. 'One day, you might need someone to bury your body too.'

'That's enough, André,' says the woman. She gives me a sympathetic glance. 'I will keep your dinner for you until later.'

'Where did you learn to speak such good English, Madame?' asks our driver.

'It is thanks to my daughter,' says the woman. 'She is teacher until the war starts.'

'Where is she now?'

'Making your beds in the attic.'

Then there is a sound from the room next door. Music!

'Is that a piano?' I ask. I'd had an aunt who had played. As a child, I'd sat by her feet, mesmerized.

'My sister loves her piano,' says André solemnly. 'Her favourite composer is Chopin. Sometimes she lets me turn the pages.'

'That's nice.' I used to do the same with my aunt in her drawing room, with lace antimacassars on the backs of her elegant chairs to protect them from the grease of her friends' hair cream when they came to visit and listen. This image of a life before war, when everything was correct and safe, comforts me.

'What is your sister's name?' I ask.

'Antoinette,' he says.

PART THREE
Emily

30

Nothing feels real. How, I wonder as I look through the curtains, can the moon be shining so brightly? How can the waves have the effrontery to pound so loudly at the bottom of the cliff?

How can the world go on when my father has just died?

The man who had always been here for me. The only man I could rely on. Who had known me from the minute I'd been born. Who had held my hand each step of the way.

The man who had cheated on my mother.

The father who could be so brusque. Who sometimes treated me like a fool. When I was twelve and had left the keys in the front door by mistake, he had flown off in one of his tempers. 'You silly girl. We could have been burgled.'

He confiscated my door key for a whole year after that to teach me a lesson.

Yet, when I once came bottom in my chemistry exam, he was surprisingly sympathetic. 'Not to worry. We all have our off days. How about we sit down together and I'll go through the periodic table with you?'

The following year, I was top of my class.

Strange how the good bits make you forget the bad.

'Your father is prone to mood swings,' my mother would often say. *'We have to make allowances for him. The war affected him, you know.'*

She'd give a little sigh. '*If he'd only talk about it, it might help. But he won't. Not even to me.*'

And now it's too late.

I knew that from the minute Françoise had knocked on my door in the early hours of this morning.

'Did he say anything before he went?' I wept.

'Non.'

I'd followed her – dazed – into Dad's room. 'I want time to be with my father alone,' I said.

She'd looked at me with that coquettish questioning manner of hers. '*Our* father,' I expected her to say. But she didn't. Instead, she had the audacity to drop a kiss on his pale forehead and leave, closing the door silently behind her.

The kiss – so tender – made me cry even more. Zorro, who had slunk in, had jumped on his bed and tried to lick him awake. 'He's gone,' I said, burying my face in the dog's neck. 'It's too late.'

Zorro made little distressed whimpers.

'Talk to me, Daddy,' I said. Part of me expected him to open his eyes. To hold out his arms and hug me.

But he just lay there. I curled up next to him. Zorro too.

How I reproach myself. I should have stayed up all night next to my father instead of allowing that woman to share shifts, but I'd known I was too exhausted to look after him properly. It might not have been safe.

If only we knew in advance precisely when someone was going to die, it would be so much easier.

Just as it would if we knew exactly when someone was going to be born. My mind goes back to my recent trip to London, where I'd had to give a statement about what had happened at the Smith birth. The next step will be the hospital hearing, although I haven't got a date for that yet. What will happen if I'm not allowed to work as a midwife any more? I push the thought away. Not now. Not when my father has just died.

I trace those bushy grey eyebrows with my index finger. I drop a kiss on the top of his nose as I used to when I was a child. 'Don't be so soppy,' he would say.

The three of us stay huddled together. Dad. Zorro. Me. Outside, the day starts to dawn. I open the curtains. There's a flamingo pink streak across the sky. The sun is rising. The moon is on its way home.

I go back to the bed and hold his hand. Still cold. What else had I expected?

The door opens.

It's Françoise. 'I have called the doctor.'

'Why?' I am shocked. Angry too that she is taking over my role as daughter. 'You have no right.'

Her face is blotchy from tears, although she still manages to look irritatingly beautiful. 'We had to ring someone, Emilee. You cannot just sit there all day.'

But that's *exactly* what I want to do. I want to sit and howl and beat my arms up and down. There are some families who do that – I've seen them in the hospital, united in their vocal grief. It has always struck me as being therapeutic. So much better than bottling it up or putting on a brave face.

'Try to take comfort from the fact that he's not in pain any more,' says the doctor when she arrives.

Of course, it's too late for her to do anything. Yet a small part of me had hoped she might be able to perform a miracle. I've seen a few of those in my time. Once, when I was filling in on the cardiology ward during a bank shift, one of the elderly patients collapsed. His heart stopped during visiting time but I revived him. '*You saved his life,*' said his son. '*We can't thank you enough.*'

My thoughts turn dark as I remember the Smiths.

'When did your father have his last dose of morphine?' asks the doctor.

'During the night, when I was with him.'

'May I see the bottle?'

'Of course.' I fetch it from the kitchen cupboard and show her.

'Is the level the same as when you put it back?' she asks.

'It's hard to tell but I'd say it was . . . more or less.'

The doctor stands up. Faces me. Her expression is both puzzled and apologetic at the same time. 'I only examined your father yesterday. Pancreatic cancer is known for spreading quickly, but, to be honest, I expected him to last longer.'

She makes an awkward sound in her throat. I recognize it from the hospital. That sound when one of us has to give bad news to a patient or loved one.

'I'm sorry, Emily, but I can't write out a death certificate until we can be sure of the cause.'

'Surely you don't think there was some kind of foul . . .'

I can't finish the sentence. It feels like I'm on a television drama. But she says it for me.

'"Foul play"? No. I don't. I'm just following the rules. That's all.'

'So what happens now?' I ask.

'I'll need to report it to the coroner, who might want to order an autopsy. There could be an inquiry.'

My chest feels cold. 'And we can't bury him until then?'

'Well, a coroner might release a body after an autopsy, before the inquiry results.'

'How long might it take to do all this?'

'It partly depends on the toxicology reports.'

'Toxicology?' I breathe. 'Why do you need that?'

'As I said, Emily, we need to cover everything. It's just routine in cases like this.' She gives me a pat on my shoulder. 'I'm sorry for your loss.'

31

During the morning, a small, steady trickle of people come to the house to pay their respects.

Or to stick their noses in.

Nearly everyone in Willowmead knew my father. At some point in their lives, they or someone in their family will have been to his office on business.

There was, when I was growing up, an air of reverence for 'Mr Gentle who lived in the big house'; the man who used to swim across the bay early every morning until my mother's death. 'I just don't feel like it any more,' he had said after she died. 'The energy has gone out of me.'

I try to block the memory from my mind. I'm getting even better at compartmentalizing.

'Please come in,' I hear Françoise trill. She has the audacity to play the part of the gracious hostess, seeing in well-wishers and accepting their cards and posies of autumn flowers. (There's a plethora of chrysanthemums.) My rival looks stunning in a long, flowing purple velvet housecoat. It suits her and she knows it. Must have cost a fortune. Had that been one last gift from my father before he'd died?

I watch our guests glancing from me to her. I know what they are thinking: *That's the daughter who had stayed away for so long. That's the French woman who moved in to look after him.*

'There'll be no one like Mr Gentle again,' I hear someone say.

'You're right there. Mind, you wouldn't want to get on the wrong side of him. He couldn't hold a cleaner down after Jean died, thanks to that temper of his. Maybe that's why he had to get a French one instead.'

'I thought she was a carer, not a cleaner.'

'Both, according to some. And maybe a bit on the side.'

'At his age?'

'You know what they say about never being too old.'

I pretend I can't hear, but inside I am burning with shame.

I go upstairs to my room to take some deep breaths alone. I sit on the edge of the bed. All I want to hear is Dad's voice. Then I remember. He sometimes left messages on my phone when I was working. I hadn't listened to my voicemail lately in case there was a message from the hospital.

The recordings play in chronological order, starting with the oldest. The first is from Dad.

'*Emily,*' he says in that imposing grainy voice. '*Can you ring me?*'

It was when I'd gone to London to give my statement.

In fact I *had* called, but then hung up when Françoise had answered. I could have rung back but cowardice had taken over. I was too scared she would question me about my whereabouts.

I play it again and again.

'*Can you ring me? Can you ring me?*'

Each word breaks my heart. I hadn't. And I should have done.

The next message is from Françoise.

'*Your father is worried about you. I also have something else*

I think you should know. I saw Nick with his wife. They were kissing. I think they must be back together.'

I go downstairs in a daze.

'I'm so sorry for your loss, love,' says Sally from the post office. When I was younger, my mother would allow me to post a letter for her 'as a treat'. It made me feel so grown-up. Sally would always remark on what a good daughter I was for 'helping' her.

'Have you thought about a date for the funeral?' she asks.

'Not yet,' I say.

How can I tell her that, any minute now, undertakers will be coming to take his body to a mortuary? To test it. To reveal how he died.

How can I admit that we will have to wait to bury him until the coroner releases the body?

How can my father now be just 'a body'?

And how can Nick be such a bare-faced liar?

Then I see him, coming towards me.

For a minute I think he is going to give me a hug.

But he just holds out both hands and clasps mine firmly. 'This must be horrible for you,' he says quietly.

I step back.

'I've missed you,' he adds.

'Have you?' I say quietly, thinking about his lips on mine in the car and then Françoise's message about him kissing his wife. 'What about Sophie? I hear you have patched things up.'

A look of confusion crosses his face. 'What? I don't understand.'

I'm not having this conversation here. 'Thank you for your condolences,' I say loudly.

Then I turn my attention to the person behind him. It is David Wingett, a kind man who does a lot of good work for charity.

They are queuing up the drive now. 'It's hard to imagine that Mr Gentle has gone,' I hear someone say on the doorstep.

'I still can't quite believe that *Mrs* Gentle has gone,' says another. 'She was such a good woman, always running around after her husband. Must be four years now. If you ask me, he lost the will to live after she went.'

Hah! If only they knew! Even though I am grieving for dad, I also want to scream out the accusations running around in my head. According to Françoise, he had been a dirty old man who had seduced the young au pair.

No. I won't believe it. I can't. If it's true, it makes our lives a sham.

When the result of that second DNA test comes through, I know I will prove her wrong.

I have to.

Two men in black stand next to me. They have come to take Dad's body away. The mourners have gone now. It is just us. Him and me. And her.

'No,' I cry, standing in front of his bed. 'You can't. I won't let you.'

I am a child once more. I am afraid. My father is leaving me at the school gates on the first day of term. (My mother had not felt well.)

'*Come back, Dad*,' I'd cried in my stiff, new, green uniform. '*Please.*'

'Shhh,' says Françoise at my side. 'I know it's hard but we have to let these men take him.'

'*We?*' I scream. 'There is no "we" in this. You are just the hired help, Françoise.'

Her face crumples. The undertakers look shocked. Have I gone too far?

'He's my Dad,' I weep. 'I want to keep him here.'

I refuse to let him go. I kneel by his side. My arms are around him. I'm aware his body is beginning to smell. I do not care. I've seen dead bodies before.

I want to shake him. Slap him. Cuddle him. I collapse on the ground, screaming. Pummelling the floor with my hands.

The doctor comes again. Françoise must have called her. 'Let me give you something to help you through this, Emily.'

'No!' I wail. 'I just want Dad here.'

My father had already organized his funeral service. He did so after my mother died.

'I'm not having someone choosing a hymn or reading I don't enjoy,' he'd told me. '"Jerusalem". That's what I want. And make sure everyone belts it out, won't you, Emily?'

Always in charge, that was my father. Even in death.

But something doesn't feel right. I can't help thinking that Françoise is hiding something.

I don't know what.

But if she was capable of extorting money from Dad, what else might she be capable of?

32

The inquest opens the following week. 'This is good,' said Françoise when I told her. 'It will be sorted fast, yes, and then we can bury him.'

"We" again. This suggests a knowledge of my father that she has not had over the years. This woman cannot waltz in during the last few weeks of his life and take over.

There is a special court for inquests called the Coroner's Court. I'd no reason to have been in one before. Everything feels very formal. I recognize some people from the village in the gallery. I hadn't realized it would be open to the public.

'We are here to establish the following points: The identity of the deceased. The time, date, location . . .' The coroner pauses for a nanosecond '. . . and the cause of death.'

There is a hushed silence, but inside, my head is spinning. It occurs to me, as I listen to the coroner's solemn voice, that death is a five-letter word unlike any other. We live life as if it was our right. Yet it can strike out of the blue at any time.

It can arrive too soon, or it may be long overdue.

It can be a merciful release, or it might be a crime.

The darker side of me has often been shocked by the fact that according to statistics, the murderer is often known to the victim.

It might be a wife, a husband, a son. Or maybe a daughter.

A daughter who has turned up out of the blue . . .

I shiver. Nonsense, I tell myself. I am letting my imagination get the better of me. Dad had cancer. That's what had killed him.

The coroner continues. 'I must stress that this is not a criminal investigation. The police may be making their own inquiries.'

The police? There's a definite pricking up of ears, the shifting in their seats of people around me heightens the tension in the room.

'Various tests need to be carried out as part of the autopsy. This will take time.'

More stirring. Is this normal procedure?

But the coroner is continuing.

'Until then, I am adjourning the inquest until the autopsy results are ready. We will then resume, at which time I will ask questions of those who were with the deceased during the final hours.'

That's me. And Françoise.

I feel myself going red. Why? I have nothing to hide.

The question is, does she?

33

The children in the village have put out pumpkins in the windows.

My father used to help me carve mine every year. I did the same at the hospital one year when I was on the children's ward as part of my training.

'I don't want the ghosts to get me,' said one little boy, his pale face creased with worry lines.

'Don't worry,' I'd reassured him. 'They won't.'

It struck me then – as it does now – that we try to protect children from stranger danger yet, at the same time, we subject them to all kinds of horrors such as ghosts, ghouls and zombies, expecting them to accept it as fun.

Then again, I'm not a mother. How would I know what is right?

But I *am* a daughter.

Though not as good a daughter as I should have been.

I should have come down more often. I wasn't even by his side when my father took his last breath. *She* was. What would the autopsy reveal about that?

I receive a phone call from Nick. His warm voice, both familiar and also professional, is so all-consuming that it's as if he is right here next to me. But I can't be drawn in again.

'I'm very sorry about your father,' he says.

'You told me that when you visited.'

'I know. But I wanted to say it again.'

'Why are you ringing, Nick?'

He clears his throat. Nick has always done that. Even when he was a teenager. It generally comes before an awkward moment.

'Have you got time to come into the office today?'

Time? I have all the time in the world. My father is in storage, waiting to be opened up. The house feels like a mausoleum of silent rebuke. I am waiting as well – to hear from the hospital about my fate. The clock is counting down.

And to cap it all, the man I have been stupid enough to fall for again is back with his wife, if indeed they had ever been apart. History repeating itself over and over again. When will I learn?

'Why?' I ask.

'To discuss the will.'

It would have been easier if Dad had used another solicitor. Not the boy who had been the love of my life. Whom I've never been able to replace.

'I need to see Mademoiselle Alarie too,' he adds.

My heart starts to race. So she's been included in the will.

Yet hadn't I been expecting this? It's obvious that she'd got her claws into my father. But how can I make a fuss? Dad had the right to leave what he wanted to whoever he wanted. However much it might hurt.

Françoise affects surprise when I tell her that the solicitor has asked to see us at two o'clock in the afternoon.

'The solicitor?' She repeats. 'You mean your friend Nick?'

'That's right. The one you so kindly told me about on a recorded message. And, in case you wondered why I haven't mentioned it before, it's because I have only just discovered it. Just what I needed after the death of my father.'

'I am sorry. I thought you should know, though.'

'Thanks for that. And now Nick wants to see us about the will.'

I watch her face carefully. She goes pink. Then pale. Then coy. I have to hand it to her. I never can tell exactly what she's thinking.

Françoise presses her right hand against her chest, rather like a melodramatic heroine in one of those 1950s films that my parents used to love watching. They would snuggle up next to each other on the sofa. Sometimes, I'd almost felt like an intruder. How had it been possible for my father to put on such a front if he'd been shagging the au pair?

'Why should he want to see *me*?' Françoise asks.

'Why do you think?' I reply curtly.

From the kitchen window I can see that the waves are rough. Angry. The sea will be throwing itself onto the beach. I love it when it's like that. How many hours did Nick and I walk along that beach during our youth, arms slung around each other? Talking. Feeling the thrill of each other's warmth. Why is it that you never get quite that thrill again when you're older? What is it about first love that makes it more precious than any pearl in the sea?

'I do not know,' says Françoise, in reply to my question.

'Oh, come off it,' I snap. 'He's going to leave you money, isn't he? Or is it the house you were after?'

She shrugs. 'I do not ask for anything.'

'Really?' I laugh. 'What about that cheque I saw you holding when you came out of his study right before he died?'

Her eyes widen. 'That was a present. I do not ask for it. He insists.'

'Insisted,' I correct. 'But the point is that you didn't have to cash it.'

'I haven't,' she says.

I hadn't expected this. 'Really? Why not?'

'Because I do not feel right about it. Look.'

Then she puts her hand in her pocket and brings it out. Slowly and deliberately, she rips up the cheque before my eyes.

Then I get it. It's all part of the act. Just like my mother's earrings and the tortoiseshell pen. But why should she worry about the cheque? It will be small change compared to the money my father has probably left her.

'We're off for our walk,' I say briskly. 'You and I need to leave here at one thirty to give us time. Come on, boy.'

Then I turn on my heel and go.

It's only a few seconds later that I realize Zorro isn't with me. He's sitting next to Françoise, as if bewitched.

'Come on,' I repeat firmly. He throws an apologetic look up at the woman and then grudgingly follows.

Every now and then – like now – I am reminded of the power in nature. Just look at the rage of the sea. It's rolling and gasping and screaming and writhing. The waves whip round like whirlpools smashing against the rocks. I've always swum all the year round and found great calm in the salt water. But today it's clearly dangerous. It's alive with fury.

'Not today,' I tell Zorro as he heads towards the water. I marvel that such a huge force, stretching as far as the eye can see, is capable of pure serenity one minute and total ferocity the next.

I throw a ball along the shingle. Zorro chases after it.

Then he stands still and stares ahead. 'What are you looking at?' I ask.

He continues staring. It's as if he can see something. The hairs on my arm begin to prickle. My father? Don't be so daft, I tell myself. When someone has gone, they've gone.

It was why I chose to be a midwife. I wanted to bring people *into* the world. Not see them out.

Then I see a flash of pink.

Françoise had been wearing a soft-looking pink jumper that morning with a roll neck.

It's gone.

Had she been watching me?

And if so, why?

France, 1944

It is on the second day of hiding that I meet Antoinette. We are under instructions to stay hidden in the attic and not move.

'The farmer is risking his life to help us, lads,' the sarge tells us.

So we do as we're told. But it's not easy. After all, we're here to 'wipe the German bastards out'. The news is that the tables have been turned and the Allies have gone on the offensive.

But how can we do our bit if we're hiding away like a bunch of cowards? I'm the kind who needs something to do. I want to be fighting to save my country.

Then the piano starts again. It's a waltz by Chopin. I only know because my aunt used to play it. The sound makes me feel at home.

'I wish she'd shut the flaming heck up,' says one of the lads.

'It's beautiful,' I say.

'Got the hots for her, have you?'

'I don't know what you mean. I haven't even seen her and nor have you.'

'Doesn't matter, does it? She's a bit of skirt, ain't she?'

'Fuck off,' I snap. I rarely swear. But this oaf is making my blood boil. Besides, the music is calming. It reminds me of family and normality.

I squat on the bare wooden floorboards in the attic, fantasizing about the pianist. What does she look like? Why is she playing when there must be so many jobs to do on the farm?

And then, one day, there is a knock on the loft door. Usually it is André who brings us thick slabs of bread with cheese or empties the bins where we do our business.

But this time it is a young woman with dark curls and shining eyes. Instantly I know this must be André's sister. Antoinette. The piano player. She looks older than me — mid-twenties at a guess — but even so, I feel my cheeks flushing. She is the most beautiful woman I have ever seen.

'Vite,' she says. 'My father says the enemy is searching the farms. You need to hide somewhere else.'

Where?

'Bloody French,' says the idiot who had criticized Antoinette's playing earlier on. 'Bleeding chucking us out.'

'No,' she retorts, those black eyes flashing. 'We are not abandoning you. My father has found a safer place. Follow me.'

'What if it's a trap?'

This last question is addressed to the sarge from another man. I have to say that the same thought is crossing my mind too. We've heard stories about the locals betraying us to save their own skins.

'I don't know,' he says hesitatingly.

'We have no time,' urges Antoinette. 'Follow me.'

No one moves. Her dark eyes turn to me beseechingly. 'I would not let you die,' she says. 'Please trust me.'

My feet begin to move. That look! Saviour or siren? Who knows?

All I can say is that right now, I would follow this woman to the end of the earth.

And beyond.

34

When I return, Françoise is cleaning. Rubbing away at the mirrors with some vinegary stuff that makes my nose tickle.

She's no longer wearing the pink jumper.

'Were you on the beach?' I demand.

She looks as if I've asked her a very stupid question.

'No. I am here. All the time.'

'I don't believe you,' I mutter.

'What do you say?'

'Nothing.'

She shrugs.

'Why did you change?' I ask.

'Change?' A red spot appears on each cheek. 'What do you mean?'

'You're wearing a blue jumper. It was pink this morning.'

'I got it wet,' she says, as if she's amused.

'With the sea?'

'No. I have not been out. With the water from the sink.'

I turn to storm up to my room, the only place where I can be truly alone.

'How can you be cleaning at this time? Do you not feel any emotion at all?' I add over my shoulder.

'Because,' she says delicately, 'it is my way of coping when things go wrong.'

'Wrong?' I stop. 'You're getting what you want, aren't

you? Nick has asked you to come in about the will. You and I know that means he's left you something.'

'No, Emilee.' Her voice comes out like a cry. Her face is crinkled with her effort to sound genuine. 'My father is gone. Just before I have got to know him.'

'We don't know he's your father until I get the result of that DNA test,' I point out.

'You know I already did one for your father,' she retorts. 'It showed I was his daughter.'

'So you say,' I fire back. 'But you organized that one, didn't you? This one will show the truth.'

'Fine,' she says, tossing those dark curls. 'You will see.'

She is almost belligerent now. I knew it. She's scared. Fear often makes people angry. I saw that enough times in the delivery suite. *'It's all right to be frightened,'* I would tell my patients. *'But if you can, try and feel calm. Your baby will feel calm too.'*

That seemed to help.

If only I could do the same for myself.

'By the way,' she adds, 'you left the electric heater on in the bathroom.'

Did I? I don't remember turning it on.

'Are you sure?'

'Absolument. It overheated and now it doesn't work. Luckily it had an emergency cut-off device or it could have caused serious damage.'

I don't believe her. She's just trying to undermine me. It's verging on gaslighting and I don't like it.

'There is something else too, Emilee.'

What now?

'The post has arrived. It's on the hall table.'

My heart starts to beat. There are several envelopes. All for me. Most are sympathy cards.

Apart from the two I have been waiting for. The first has a bright red official stamp marking it out, like a blood-stain. And the second is from the DNA people with the results of the test I ordered.

We have lunch separately, by unspoken agreement. I take my hastily cobbled-together cheese sandwich into the dining room, leaving Françoise with hers in the kitchen.

'You do not want a slice?' she asks, indicating the savoury tarte she's made herself.

'No thanks.'

How can she bother to cook or arrange the food so prettily on her plate when Dad has just died? She can't care like I do; I can barely bring myself to eat.

I sit down but I can't swallow.

I have to say, grudgingly, that there is a pleasant lemon smell of furniture polish in the dining room. Gone too is the dust that had settled on the window sills since the cleaner left, along with Zorro's dog hair on the wooden floors. I'd done my best to tidy up when I'd come down during fleeting breaks from work, but I'd never been here long enough to make a lasting impression.

Yes. Françoise is certainly thorough when it comes to wielding a duster. But what else is she thorough about? Murder, perhaps?

She is waiting for me by the front door at one thirty promptly.

What a picture of innocence! Françoise is wearing a jaunty little hat and a coat with a fur trim. 'It is not real,' she says, as if reading my mind. 'I buy it from a charity shop.'

I wouldn't be surprised if some sugar daddy in France gave it to her. In fact, she probably left a trail of older men behind, claiming each of them as her father. I can see it now.

Together we walk to my father's old office. It still feels weird that Nick is working there. If things had gone differently, we would be married. We might have had children. We could even have lived at Willowmead House with my father and taken care of him. None of this would have happened.

My phone pings with an email as we walk in. There is just time to glance at it briefly. It's about the Smith case. I cannot say I am surprised. But I am still shaken.

'Thank you for coming,' says Nick.

I try to concentrate but I can't help thinking about the email. I can't pretend any more now. It's so easy to get stuck in the past. The what-might-have-beens. How I wish I could be one of those people who manage to live one day at a time. If I'd done this during the Smith birth, it would have been all right.

Nick indicates that we should take a seat. His desk is very tidy. It used to be a mess at school, but I suppose he's grown up now. There's a picture of his lovely little boy, but not one of his wife. Maybe he placed it in a drawer before we arrived.

He puts his hands together, intertwining the fingers, and looks at me. 'I'm going to come straight to the point,' he says. 'There is a bequest to Joe of ten thousand pounds.'

'I know about that,' says Françoise.

'How?' I ask.

Her voice sounds smug. 'Your father asked me to come here before you came home. He wanted me to witness his gift to the gardener.'

She'd been a *witness*? So that's why she went there with Dad. Perhaps I'd read her wrong and he hadn't signed over the house or money to her after all.

'There is also a bequest to the village school.'

My father had been a governor there. He had taken his duties very seriously.

'In addition,' continues Nick, 'there is his life history, which Harold wrote down. He was very insistent that you should both share this and read it together.'

'Vraiment?' says Françoise. 'But I ask him to do this and he says he will not.'

'My father would never talk about the past,' I say, remembering how I had sometimes asked him to tell me about the war. This had always angered him. 'What do you want to know?' he would snap. 'It's been and gone.'

'His memories are written in a notebook which he handed to me,' says Nick. 'He wanted me to keep them for safety until his death.'

Hah! More like Dad was too scared to tell me how badly he'd behaved until he could no longer be blamed. It was his way of confessing. Of getting off the hook. As for the notebook, I remember how he used to carry it round in the basket of his walker along with scrunched-up tissues. Before his death, when I'd tried to tidy it up, he'd snapped at me, telling me to 'leave my stuff alone'. After that, the notebook had disappeared. I hadn't given it a second thought. I certainly hadn't thought he'd give it to Nick.

Nick turns over a page. 'And now to the main part of this business. You will see from the dates of the codicils, that Harold has recently made changes to the will.'

I stiffen. I sense Françoise doing the same.

'Harold wanted to make a special gift to you, Françoise.'

I hold my breath.

'He wishes you to have all of Mrs Gentle's sewing boxes and also her cookery dishes because, in his words, you are a "good homemaker".'

A red colour rises in Françoise's face. Also in mine. My father has managed to slight me, at the same time as complimenting this woman.

'Now for the final part.'

There is a quietness in the air that reminds me of my father's last hours.

'Your father has left all his money and the house to you, Emily.'

I glance at Françoise. She is staring straight ahead but there is something in her eyes that says 'What else did I expect?'

'Actually,' I hear myself say, 'that's not fair.'

They both look at me with a 'what?' expression. But no one could be more surprised than I am. It's not until the words come out of my mouth that I know I mean them.

I stand up, falling clumsily against the side of my chair. My balance has been a bit shaky at times since the bike accident. Quickly, I right myself. 'I want to give Willowmead House to Françoise.'

Her eyes widen. 'You do not mean that?'

'I do, actually.'

Nick leans forward, looking at me with what I call his

'lawyer face'. 'I have to say, Emily, that I think you should give this some time before deciding.'

'I don't need it,' I say firmly, thinking of the letter and the email, which had given me the date for the hospital hearing.

My head begins to ache again. The sooner I'm out of this office, the better. 'Just give me what you need me to sign when you're ready,' I say.

I can tell that Nick is not happy. Of course, he doesn't know about the birth certificate or the DNA.

'Thank you,' she says outside the office, when it is just the two of us. 'I presume you give me the house because you have the results of the DNA test which you did.'

I can't argue with that.

'When things go wrong,' I say, 'it's important to put them right.'

She holds her head high in that haughty way of hers. 'I am glad you think that way.'

But she doesn't know the real reason for my actions.

No one does. Apart from me.

35

I walk back through the village. One or two people nod as I pass and express condolences. But they are seeing the old Emily Gentle. Not the new one.

Could I be sent to prison for what happened at the hospital?

I don't think so, but then again, it's not the first mistake I've made. They'll use that against me at the hearing. I know they will.

If I was jailed, I'd never be able to live here. Not even when I got out. The gossip would be too terrible.

Then there's my father.

Each painting, each carpet, each rug, each little china ornament screams neglect. If I'd come down more often – or found a job near here – Dad's last few years would have been more comfortable. I might even have realized he was ill and helped him get treatment earlier.

Instead, he'd had to resort to advertising for help.

I have been a bad daughter.

I do not deserve to inherit a house that will constantly remind me of my wrongdoings.

The autopsy results have still not come back, so the body – such a bland word for a once living, breathing father – cannot be released.

Françoise and I do not talk any more about my decision to give her Willowmead House. Maybe she is being polite. Or perhaps she is scared I will change my mind.

I won't.

Everyone in the village keeps asking me when the funeral is going to be held. I have to explain there is a delay. 'Do you think something is wrong?' asks Françoise.

'Why should there be?' I reply.

But inside, I feel unsettled too. I just want to put my father to rest.

Then Nick calls. 'I wondered if you'd like to come out for a drive?' he asks.

'No thank you,' I say curtly.

'Please. There are a few things I think we ought to talk about.'

I should tell him it's too late. That I'm not a fool. But I find myself agreeing.

Nick has a natty yellow two-seater Audi: the kind we'd have both ogled when we were teenagers.

'I don't often get a chance to drive it,' he tells me. 'Sophie doesn't like me having Billy in the front seat. And there isn't room for anyone in the back.'

He speaks about Sophie without any embarrassment. How can he be so two-faced? *Françoise saw you kissing*, I want to say.

But now doesn't seem the right time. Or maybe I'm just being a coward. Sometimes it's easier to pretend that everything is all right.

Hadn't I been doing that for most of my adult life? But I've lost the ability to fool myself.

It's another stunningly bright, crisp day. 'You don't mind the top being down, do you?' he yells.

'No,' I call back. Just as well I've brought a scarf. My hair is going all over the place! But it feels so good to be out of the house and away from the phone and, above all, to be away from that woman.

We're coming into Fowey now. I've always loved it here. The little streets criss-crossing between tall, white houses. The art shops. The ferry that once Nick and I, as lovesick teenagers, had taken across the river and strolled past Daphne du Maurier's old house, arm in arm.

He swings into a car park as if he knows it well. A pregnant woman is walking past. He slows right down. I wonder how far gone she is. Maybe six months.

He seems to notice my stare.

'Do you miss your job?'

'Yes,' I say briefly.

He appears to take my cue by changing the subject.

'Shall we take the ferry?' he asks.

'Why?'

'Because it's a nice walk.'

'I mean, why are we having a walk at all? Why am I with you?'

'Because you enjoy my company, I hope,' he says. 'I certainly enjoy yours.'

He must be a very good liar. I feel myself getting hot with embarrassment and anger and disappointment. Not just with him but with myself for being such an idiot.

'You're giving out all these mixed messages, Nick. First, you kiss me. OK. Not properly but well . . . enough.'

I'm flushing beetroot now.

'Then Françoise sees you snogging your wife and –'

'Whoa,' he says in a half-laugh. 'What are you talking about?'

'She saw the two of you in the car park. Billy was there.' He flushes too. So it's true.

'We weren't exactly kissing,' he says. 'It was on the cheek.' Then he rubs his neck as if he's sweating. 'Look, Emily. We were together a long time, Sophie and me, even before Billy came along. We have a child together. We have history. Yes, we've split up. But it's not as clean cut as that. I still care for her and she cares for me. Yet at the same time, we know we're not right for each other.'

I get that. I've also seen the bond that a child creates between a couple. How can *I* compete with that?

I've witnessed that magic spark between parents when they look at each other with a gaze that says *look what we've made*.

And I've also seen the awkwardness between some new parents. There have been fathers who have been stiff, uncomfortable. As if they don't want anything to do with the baby.

It wasn't hard to guess which couples would last the course.

'But,' adds Nick now, 'I have feelings for you too.'

'Don't,' I say, walking on. 'I'm not doing this.'

'Doing what?'

'Getting involved with a man who isn't over his marriage.'

'I didn't say that.'

'Yes you did.'

He catches up with me. We're queuing for the ferry now. It's looks a bit like a floating platform.

'Please, Emily. Don't shut me out. I know this is a difficult time for you, but I can help.'

'Hah! By playing around with my feelings?'

'I don't want to do that. Actually, I wanted to have some time with you to talk about your father's will.'

'Isn't that rather unprofessional, outside the office?' I ask.

'Probably. But I'm talking as both a friend and a solicitor.'

And I'd thought this was a date . . .

'I don't think you should give Willowmead House to Françoise,' he says, holding out his hand to help me onto the ferry.

The touch of his skin scorches me. Then he lets go and I feel ice-cold.

'Really? And what gives you the right to interfere? You don't know me any more.'

'That's true.' His voice drops. 'But we used to be very close, didn't we?'

Please, I want to cry. *Please don't say things like that.*

He places a hand on my arm. So briefly that I don't have a chance to shake it off. 'And even if we hadn't, Emily, I would still be advising you, as a client, to take some time before making a rash decision. I've seen all kinds of scenarios when it comes to wills. I usually get people fighting for a bigger share. But I did have one client who insisted on giving her portion to her brother because she felt he'd been treated badly by their parents all his life. She regretted it later when she was down at heel and he refused to help her. I just don't want to see you in financial trouble.'

He has a point. Dad's 'estate' – the legal term – wasn't as large as I'd thought it would be.

But considering the legal case against me, the amount pales in significance.

'What about work?' he says, as if picking up on my thoughts. 'When are you going back?'

'I'm having a career break,' I say quickly.

'Why?'

'I just felt like it.'

We're on the other side now. It's greener. Quieter. *Wind in the Willows* country. Kenneth Grahame had stayed at one of the hotels near here and excerpts of his inky handwriting and sketches are still hanging there on the walls.

We walk on in silence. If we were on the other side, I'd have turned round and gone back, but the ferry isn't due to return for a while. I am marooned.

'I'm sorry,' he says after a while. 'I spoke out of turn about Willowmead House. You're right. It is your decision.'

'Thank you,' I say. I almost trip over a root on the footpath. He puts out a hand to steady me. I pretend to ignore it and manage to steady myself by grabbing a tree branch. *See?* I want to say. *I can manage on my own. I've done that ever since you left me.*

'There's just one thing I want to suggest,' he says gently.

I wouldn't have come if I'd known there was going to be a pep talk. 'Honestly, Nick. I've had enough of talking.'

'No, please, hear me out. There's something about Françoise that I don't trust. I see a lot of people in my line of work and you get a feeling. No more. Just a feeling. But it does seem odd to me – and to some in the village – that she was only here a short time before your father began lavishing attention on her. He bought her clothes from that expensive new boutique you know.'

I hadn't.

'And he ordered in parcels from London shops too.'

Is that right?

'And now you're giving her the house. How much do you know about Françoise's past?'

I'm tired of hiding things.

'Only that her mother died and that she found her birth certificate with my father's name in her mother's papers.'

'What?'

'Céleste – her mother – was our au pair when I was a child. When Françoise got here, she did a DNA test which apparently proved Dad was her father.'

He lets out a whistle. 'How do you know it's genuine?'

'I had one done too, using hair from each of them. The results arrived the same day you read the will. Apparently, Dad never knew her mother was pregnant. Or so he claimed to Françoise. At least, that's what she told me.'

He shakes his head.

'I also know that before she came here, Françoise worked as a carer in an old people's home in France. I rang them, asking for a reference. I was told she was very good at helping end-of-life patients.'

'I see,' he says slowly. 'The firm sometimes uses a private investigator to do some work for us. How would you feel if we got her to look into Françoise's past a bit more?'

'How much will that cost?'

'We'll sort that out later. I just want to be sure you're doing the right thing. That's all.'

'Why?'

Because I care for you. That's what I want him to say. Or is it? I feel so confused.

'It's what I'd do for any friend,' he replies.

There you are, I tell myself. A friend. You asked for that.

'And now,' he says, 'let's put all this to the back of our minds and enjoy the walk.'

To my surprise, we do. We walk for miles. I stumble on some more tree roots and this time I allow him to help me up. We stop at a cosy pub and have the most delicious pea soup with big slabs of seed bread. Nick is so easy to talk to, providing we avoid subjects like my job. In fact, he spends most of the time talking about his son. What Billy's doing at school. How he's obsessed with facts about marine life. How Nick hopes he isn't too upset by the separation.

'Billy and I are going to a firework display on Saturday,' he says. 'Remember the parties on the beach?'

How could I forget?

A crowd of us had always gone down after school. We'd light a bonfire and toast marshmallows. Then we'd dance, walk along the sand, kiss, snuggle up . . .

'Would you like to come with us?' he says suddenly.

'I'd love to.'

Despite my grief, I get a feeling that things might be picking up after all.

36

Every November there was a firework display at the hospital. When I was training, it had been a chance to find a boyfriend. In my first year, a medical student had asked me to go with him, but the relationship had fizzled out. He was so boring compared with Nick. Everyone was. My young heart had ached for him.

As the years went by, invitations to go to firework displays or parties or other social events seemed to dry up. Instead, a surge of friends' wedding invitations poured in.

November the fifth became one of those days when I would volunteer to do an extra shift. The same went for Christmas Day or any other time of year when I might be even more aware of my single status.

Anything to avoid the 'Found anyone special yet?' remarks from my parents or the locals when I went back to Willowmead.

But this is different, I tell myself as I take in the excited chatter of the children, their glowing faces, the parents making sure that their little ones don't get too near the bonfire, the mug of mulled wine that Nick has given me (now cupped in my hand) and the excitement in little Billy's eyes as the first rush of pink and silver shoots up in the sky with all those oohs and aahs.

'Wow,' says Nick. 'That's loud.'

'Did you know that the speed of sound in water is more

than four times faster than the speed of sound in air?' pipes up Billy.

'Where do you learn these things!' chuckles Nick.

'On YouTube. Can I have a hot dog please?'

What a polite little boy. He didn't even seem to mind that I was here.

'Sure,' says Nick. 'Would you like one, Emily?'

'I'm fine, thanks.'

He puts his arm around Billy, who looks up at his dad with adoration shining in his eyes. A pang of longing claws at my chest.

'We won't be long.'

I sit down on the cushions Nick has thoughtfully brought, taking it all in. There are quite a lot of people here I don't know; people I didn't grow up with. New families who have moved in since I lived here full-time. That's a relief. No questions.

I begin to shiver, even though I am all tucked up in my cosy Puffa coat, sipping the warm mulled wine.

What am I doing here? Kidding myself, like I always do. It's crazy. I could go back to the house. I could even pack up and run away. I could . . .

'We're back!' chirps a little voice. 'I brought you a marshmallow stick. Dad says you loved them when you were younger.'

I am on my feet, about to make my hasty getaway. But how can I, with this sweet little boy holding up his gift? 'That's so kind of you,' I say.

Then I look up at Nick. 'I'm surprised you remembered.'

'I remember a lot,' he says quietly.

For a minute, I am back at school. Just eleven or twelve

perhaps. At the end of the day, a crowd of us would sometimes go to the sweet shop. Mrs Michaels would weigh
out the sweets. My favourites were marshmallows. The
pink ones. 'Don't you like the white?' Nick had asked one
day, when we found ourselves walking back side by side.

'No,' I said. 'Here. You have them.'

It had become a tradition between us.

'They're really special when you toast them,' says Billy
now. 'Look, I've got some too!'

So I can see. They've dribbled down his cheek. I resist
the temptation to clean his little face. He's not mine. But
Nick is doing it. Billy grins. 'Don't fuss, Dad!'

'Well we can't have you looking like a marshmallow
monster, can we?'

'But we *like* marshmallow monsters!'

Nick turns to me. 'It's one of our stories.'

'Dad makes them up,' pipes Billy. 'Mummy says he'll
frighten me but he won't 'cause I know they're not real.'

Mummy. Marshmallow monsters. A window into a life
I've not been part of. Another language. Another world.
This isn't a date between two old lovers. It's a *Let's take
Emily out to take her mind off everything* outing.

So get real, I tell myself. Just try and loosen up for once.
Enjoy the friendship. Stop thinking about what might
have been.

Whoosh. A rocket explodes overhead, showering down
gold and silver rain. 'Wow, Dad, did you see that!'

'I did!'

'And did you, Emily?'

This little boy is almost too perfect.

'It was lovely, wasn't it?'

There's another whizzing noise. Then a pop.

'But nothing happened,' says Billy, disappointedly.

'Sometimes they don't work,' says Nick.

'Why not?'

'It's just one of those things,' he continues. 'The spark dies or maybe the people who bought it didn't look after it carefully enough.'

Nick is looking at me. It's as though he's trying to tell me something. Or is that my imagination?

We hold each other's eyes. I've no idea how long for. Seconds. Minutes. Hours. A lifetime.

Then there's a bang. Followed by an explosion. And a scream. 'Where's Billy?' Nick shouts, turning this way and that, scanning the crowd for that shock of blond hair.

'He was here just now,' I blurt out. How stupid had we been!

I run after Nick. He's heading for the crowd, which is gathering around someone.

'Dad!' calls out a voice. It's Billy. Thank God. Nick is scooping him up, holding him to his chest.

'Why did you run off like that?'

'I wanted to see where the dead rocket was going to land.'

'Quick!' yells another voice. 'Someone's hurt here.'

I'm diving into the centre. 'I'm a nurse,' I say.

I'm there. Back in my uniform; at least in my head. Slung around my shoulder is my bag, which has the basic essentials for most emergencies. I rarely go anywhere without it.

I'm kneeling next to a woman who's clutching her left arm.

'It's all right,' I reassure her. 'You're lucky. It's a burn but not a bad one.'

'It hurts so much,' she says. I can see she's trying not to cry. Her children are hovering near her, worried, scared that their universe might be ripped away from them.

'I was just standing there with my kids,' she says. 'This thing landed and then exploded.' She's shaking now with shock.

I grab my bottle of cold water from my bag and pour it over the burn.

She calls out in pain.

'I'm sorry,' I say. 'Has anyone got any clingfilm?'

'I've got my sandwiches wrapped in the stuff,' a lady in the crowd says.

Luckily, she's used several layers. I'm able to use the clean bits to wrap around the burn.

She starts to shiver. 'I need a blanket,' I say. 'And someone to give her a lift to the hospital.'

There's a chorus of offers around us. One of her friends is going to take the children back with them. 'It's all right,' I tell her. 'You'll be fine.'

Her eyes hold mine. 'Thank you.'

I feel that old glow of knowing I have helped someone. After the Smiths, it feels so good.

'You were amazing,' says Nick.

'I wasn't,' I reply, embarrassed. 'I didn't do much.'

'But you did. You were so calm.'

'And you did that magic stuff with her arm!' adds Billy.

I find myself laughing. 'You're right, Billy. Medicine *is* magic because it makes people better.'

'Is that why you became a nurse?' he asks.

We're walking back to the car now.

'Yes,' I say.

But that's not the whole truth.

Nick drops me back at the house. He touches me briefly on my arm as he opens the car door for me. 'Thanks for coming,' he says.

He'd been quiet on the way back. I can tell he's still shaken after Billy running off like that. So am I. I don't even want to think about what could have happened. That sweet little boy could so easily have been hit by the rocket.

I look up at him as I step out. Something gives in his eyes. He pulls me to him. I sink into his warmth. 'It's so good to have you back, Emily,' he murmurs.

'It's good to be back,' I gulp.

But my head is all over the place. I want to tell Nick exactly what's been going on in my life.

Yet I can't. I don't want to lose him a second time. I'm not even sure if I have him now.

'I'll call you tomorrow,' he says, letting me go.

Disappointment wafts over me. For a moment, I thought he was going to kiss me. 'That would be lovely,' I say.

'Just one more thing.'

My heart starts to race.

'I know I said it wasn't my business before, but please don't sign over the house to Françoise until our investigator has reported back.' His eyes are troubled.

I shiver again. 'All right,' I say.

Françoise is not up and her bedroom door is closed. For a minute, I stand outside, listening. There is nothing. Is she too standing on the other side, listening keenly?

I take Zorro out for his evening walk and then go to

bed. But I cannot settle. Something is about to happen. I sense it.

Eventually, I drop off. But when I do, I have such terrible dreams that I wake myself, screaming out loud.

On Monday morning I open my eyes at nine – much later than usual – to the sound of my mobile ringing.

'Miss Gentle?' asks an official voice.

'Speaking,' I say. My heart is thudding madly.

'This is the Coroner's Office. We have the results of the autopsy.'

37

Françoise comes into the house just as I put the phone down. She has Zorro with her.

He bounds up to me.

I bury my head in his fur.

'What is wrong?' asks Françoise.

I hate the fact that she is so good at reading my moods.

'We need to talk,' I say abruptly.

'What is it?'

'The Coroner's Office has just rung. They gave me the results on the phone.'

Her face goes still. I watch every muscle, searching for every twitch. But her face is smooth.

'And what do they say?'

I stare at the purple beret and the bright red lipstick. I look at the gloves she is taking off, to reveal those hands with the long fingers that had enchanted my father when she'd played the piano. I want to strangle the swanlike neck and rip out every hair on her head for what she has done.

'There was a high level of toxicity in his blood,' I say slowly.

She gives a little gasp, with one of those infuriating 'How can it be?' gestures of hers.

'I don't understand.'

'Then let me spell it out for you,' I say. 'There was more

morphine than there should have been in his blood. Far more.'

Her eyes are wide. 'How did it get there?'

'You did the last shift with him, Françoise.' I am having to clench my own fists to stop myself flying at her.

Her eyes are hard now. Furious. 'Are you accusing *me* of killing my own father?'

'Well, did you?'

'Of course not. You're the one who gave him the last dose.' Her voice turns softer. 'You are upset, Emilee. It is understandable. But mistakes can be made. Perhaps they have got it wrong.'

'That's rubbish. You're just trying to get out of it.'

'Then let us see what the coroner says at the inquest, shall we?'

She goes upstairs to her room. Is she going to do a runner? If so, I need to act fast.

I think of the morphine bottle in the kitchen cupboard.

'*Is the level the same as when you put it back?*' the doctor had asked.

'*It's hard to tell but I'd say it was . . . more or less.*'

I'd thought, at the time, this was true because I had no reason to be suspicious. Now, with the toxicology results, everything has changed. This is such strong stuff that only a little more could have constituted an overdose.

But Françoise is right. I *was* the one who had given him the last dose. Hang on. I'd fallen sleep afterwards, hadn't I? What if she'd come in then and given it to him? In fact, thinking about it, she could have dosed him up any time after I went to bed.

I think of the cheque my father had given her. Maybe

he had promised her more on his deathbed. She wasn't satisfied with just the house that I'd foolishly said she could have. What's to stop her from going to court with that birth certificate and DNA result, claiming half the money too?

Or is there more to it than that?

Perhaps Françoise is furious with him for having destroyed her mother's life and this is her revenge.

What was it the French matron had said? '*She was wonderful at easing our residents through the final part of their journey.*'

Had Françoise had taken it upon herself to administer 'justice'? She'd had the perfect cover. Dad was dying anyway.

Then my mobile goes. It's Nick. 'Can you talk?' he asks.

'Give me a minute,' I say.

I go into the garden for privacy, just in case that woman comes down again.

'Our investigator has reported back.'

'That was quick.'

'It only took a few phone calls to find out something rather interesting.'

My blood goes cold.

'What?'

'Did you know that Françoise nursed her mother through a long illness, which turned out to be terminal?'

'Yes. I did.'

'But did you also know that Céleste's death was sooner than expected? And that's not all. There was a patient called Maurice. His relatives were concerned that Françoise was getting too close to him. They were about to move him to another home before he died because he kept talking about leaving her money in his will. Then there was an old lady who gave her a sapphire necklace.'

I listen, disbelievingly, as Nick tells me the rest. Then I dial 999, my fingers fumbling.

'I want to report a murder.'

France, 1944

'*Quick,*' *Antoinette says. 'We have no time. Follow me.*'

   At first, I assume the others are behind me as we run softly over the wet grass towards one of the barns. But when I look back we are alone. I am the only one to trust her.

   '*There is not room for all of you anyway,*' *calls out Antoinette, pulling me in.*

   '*I can't leave them,*' *I say, turning to go back.*

   '*Do not be so stupid.*' *She catches me by my wrists. Her grasp is surprisingly strong. 'What is the point of you all dying?*'

   We have been using the 'death' word so often during the war that it almost seems too common to be real. But right now it seems a distinct, terrifying possibility. To my shame, I feel the urge to empty my bowels. I have to use every ounce of inner strength to make sure I hold everything in. This means standing still for a moment.

   As I do so, I hear voices shouting from the distance in German.

   '*If you don't do what I say,*' *hisses Antoinette, 'they will kill me too.*'

   How could I live with that? So I follow her, up the wooden steps and through a trapdoor into the roof space.

   '*Now stay there,*' *she says, pointing to the bales of straw. 'I will bring you food when I can.' She crosses herself. 'And for the love of God, stay quiet. Even if they find you. Say my family had nothing to do with this. That you took shelter without telling anyone. Swear on your life?*'

   '*I swear on my life,*' *I say.*

PART FOUR
Françoise

38

'Françoise,' says Emilee, knocking on my door. 'Are you there?'

I am packing, throwing clothes into my suitcase in any old order, instead of folding neatly as I normally do. I am not going to stay here with a woman who suspects me of killing my own father.

'Yes,' I call out. 'Entres.'

She looks at the suitcase on my bed.

'I knew it,' she says. 'You're doing a bunk?'

'What is this word?'

'You're running away.'

'No. I am not. I am going home to France, where people do not accuse me of terrible things.'

She is glaring at me. 'You can't leave. A policeman is here to see you.'

I stop. My mouth is dry. 'Why?' I say, even though I am surprised they have not been here before. Did not the coroner say that the police might be making their own investigations?

'They have taken away the morphine bottle for examination. They need to go over the house and also talk to you.'

She emphasizes the 'you'. What was it that Harold (I try to call him Papa but it does not always come naturally) had said to me once when he was telling me about one of his law cases? 'Guilty people usually respond by attacking someone else.'

· Emilee is the guilty one. I know that. All I have to do is tell the police what I discover when I came in to find her asleep on her watch with Harold. I should have done so before. But fool that I was, I felt sorry for her. Maybe even protective. It is hard to watch someone you love suffer. But now, if the police suspect me, I will come clean, as the English say.

Yet what if they don't believe me? Suppose I end up by taking the blame? I could face years in prison. I must think fast.

The policeman is waiting downstairs. He is very young, with a shiny red forehead. We go into the sitting room and sit on one of the faded pink-and-blue sofas.

'I believe you were Mr Gentle's carer,' he says.

'Yes.' I want to tell him that I am his daughter too but I suspect this might confuse things. Then again, has Emilee mentioned it? If she has and I don't, it will look as though I'm hiding my true motive.

'How would you describe him?'

Impossible. Kind. Generous. Mean. A mixture of contradictions. But I feel this would not help my case either.

'He was a nice man, Mr Gentle. A real gentleman.'

'Like his name, eh?' asks the policeman. He makes a little laugh at his own joke. Then his face turns serious. I steel myself.

'Can you recount exactly what happened on Mr Gentle's last night?' he says.

I close my eyes briefly. I can see it now. My father. Frail. In pain.

Angry. Pleading. Shouting. Crying. Furious.

I try to find my voice. 'Emilee and I had been taking it in turns to sit with him.'

'What kind of state of mind was he in?'

'He was in much pain.'

'Was he on medication?'

'Yes. Morphine. He'd already had his evening dose.'

'Who gave him that?'

'Emilee. Then I took over.'

'How long was it after that when he died?'

Died.

Surely there is a kinder, more humane word than that? I begin to shake. 'About three hours.'

'And as far as you know, she gave him the right dosage?'

'She should have done,' I say forcefully. 'After all, she is a nurse.'

'Indeed.'

'And you didn't give him any medication?'

'Of course not. He wasn't due to have more until later.'

'So you didn't touch the morphine bottle?'

'No. Why should I have?'

'Did anyone else come into the room while you were with him in the night?'

'No.'

'Were you awake for all that time?'

'I fell asleep briefly.'

His boyish face takes on a keener look. 'Then surely you can't be certain that no one came in?'

'I'm a light sleeper. I wake at everything.'

'What happened when you woke up?'

'I found Harold's breathing was fainter.'

'Did you call his daughter?'

'I was about to . . . but then he just stopped breathing. It was very peaceful.'

'Like your mother's death?'

My breath catches in my throat. What does he know? Who has he been talking to? I will not give him the pleasure of asking.

'Yes,' I say quietly. 'Just like my mother.'

'Is there anything else you'd like to tell me?'

I think of what Harold had said towards the end. *Antoinette*. But how could that help? It might just muddle things. It's why I had not told Emilee either. I thought it might distress her even more. I do have some heart.

'No.'

'Thank you. That's all for now.'

'You are going?'

'Not yet. We will be talking again to Miss Gentle.'

So they will tell her about what I have said and try to catch me out. It is Emilee they should be investigating.

'Just one more thing,' says the policeman. 'Do not leave the area until we have finished our investigations.'

'I cannot go back to France?'

His face is stern. 'Definitely not. In fact, we require your passport.'

'Is that an order?'

'Yes.'

'We also have a warrant to search the house,' he adds.

'You will go into my bedroom?'

'Yes. Is that a problem?'

'No,' I say.

*

I am frantic as I walk down to the beach. The sea is dashing against the rocks. The wind whips my hair. I taste the salt on my tongue. The police suspect me. I can feel it. It's always the hired help, n'est-ce pas? In films, the 'carer' is often the one who kills the wealthy old man to get the money.

And what will happen when they find out that Emilee wants to give me the house? At the time, I was moved. It showed, I thought, that she was a decent person.

But maybe it's so I'll keep my mouth shut about my suspicions.

There is something else too. What is to stop Emilee from lying to the police? Telling them that I blackmailed her to give me the house, otherwise I would tell the village that Harold was my real father. Some might even say that I am the special daughter.

Who will they believe? The daughter of the most important man in the village who has lived here most of her life? Or the French stranger? The outsider?

That is it. I am not going to protect her any more. I will reveal what I found. I am a fool for not having done so before.

That woman Emilee deserves to be locked up for her father's death.

39

Harold Gentle's handsome face is looking up at me from the order of service in my hand.

It is a younger Harold than the one I cared for. He is standing on the beach, with his arm around a woman, who I know is his wife from the pictures in the silver frames I dust. His other arm is around Emilee. How old would she have been then? Late teens, perhaps? She does not have that wistful expression that I have come to know so well. The one on the service sheet has a sunny smile instead.

It is she who chose the picture for the funeral service sheet. Naturally, there are no cosy family photographs of my mother and me. We do not belong to the Gentle family. Or so people think.

The church is packed. The coroner has given permission to 'release the deceased back to the family', even though we do not know yet when the inquest will resume.

Is this a good sign or not?

I cannot work it out. And I do not want to ask. I have to watch every word I say.

I am standing in the second row, behind Emilee. My rightful place is next to her but I do not want to make a scene.

As I glance across to the opposite aisle, I am aware of nosy faces peeking sideways at me. Goodness knows how many others are doing the same behind me but I will not give them the satisfaction of looking. 'That's the French girl who got presents out of Mr Gentle,' whispered one. 'I heard Joe the gardener says so.'

How dare he? Yet I've lived here long enough to know that rumours can fly thick and fast (as they say here) when someone leaves this earth.

It was the same after my mother died.

I glance up again from under my hat at the people on the right of me in the pew. There are no other relatives left, apparently. 'The village is our family,' Emilee had said haughtily when I'd asked.

Some are standing in the aisle because there is no room to sit. My father – how wonderful it is to say that, even just to myself – was well known around here. He was, I believe, 'an eccentric'. I had plenty of time to study that when I looked after him. When you are living with each other, day by day, almost minute by minute, you get to see someone as they truly are.

Not just the physical form, which in Harold's case was beginning to deteriorate. But the inner part as well.

'It is not until the end that the soul really takes shape,' my mother used to say. 'It is because we are too scared to reveal it before.'

Pain takes its toll too. The pain of the body that is wearing out. And the mental pain from having lived through too much, ready for it all to be over.

So where does that leave those who remain behind?

It is hard to stand close to a loved one who is about to go. Sometimes it is easier to walk away. I saw this in the nursing home. Old people begging me to give them something so they could pass over to the other side without any more pain.

'Please,' I would say. 'Do not ask this of me.'

'But Françoise,' they would beg, 'if you really cared, you would help.'

Of course I cared. But some things are simply wrong.

I look at Emilee. She is sitting down, her head bowed. What is she thinking? Part of me wants to lean over the dividing pew and take her hand in comfort. We are together in our grief, after all.

'I saw a police car outside their house,' I hear someone whisper. 'Bit odd, don't you think?'

Now there is a stirring. Emilee is walking up to the pulpit where the vicar usually stands. She looks very elegant in black. Her face is pale. She starts to speak.

'My father was a very special man.'

Tears start to run down my face. I do not ask for them. But I cannot stop. I am fed up with pretence. Let everyone know. I do not care!

He was not just your Papa! I want to stand up and shout. *He was mine too.*

'He was strong and good and kind,' continues Emilee.

Yes. He could be. But not all the time. This woman might have had the advantage of knowing him all her life. I knew him when that inevitable blackness was coming towards him. Fear of death can distil the soul and the mind. Show it for what it really is.

'I had a wonderful childhood thanks to him and Mum.'

Jealousy slithers through my blood. I should have been the daughter to enjoy that. I would have been if Harold had known about me from the start. I am sure of that. He had honour about him. He would have acknowledged me to his wife and daughter.

But did he really not know that your mother was pregnant? whispers a little voice inside me.

My mother had denied this in her letter to me. However, was this the naivety of a woman in love?

Yet, if there is one thing I can say for sure about Harold Gentle, it is that he was not who he seemed.

Then again, nor are any of us. Not Emilee, or that Nick who she loves (I can tell this from her face), or me, or even Maman.

'My father was always there for me,' Emilee is now saying. 'If I had a problem, I would go to him.'

More tears are running down my face now. Tears of loss and tears of anger. I had no one to go to. I had to protect my mother. I understood this, from the day that the man I knew as my father left. I had to be a big girl. I had to help earn money so we could eat and pay the rent. I had to be strong. I had to lose Jean-Luc in order to put Maman first.

My linen handkerchief (which I made myself) is soaking wet. I open my bag for another but there is none.

'Here, love,' says a voice next to me. 'Take this.'

A woman passes me a tissue. I have seen her somewhere. Ah yes. She is the wife of the gardener. Sometimes she brings him sandwiches and a drink when he is working.

'Thank you,' I whisper.

She touches my arm briefly. 'I know what it is like to lose someone,' she says quietly. 'I would have cared for Harold myself, if it weren't for the fact that I have had my own family commitments.'

Then I glance at her husband. He gives me what the English call a stony look.

He does not like me. Harold knew that.

'*Joe thinks you're after my money,*' he would joke.

'*And you, do you think that?*' I had asked.

Harold and I had that kind of relationship. He appreciated my honesty.

'*I think you are lonely, like me,*' he said.

I almost have to stuff the tissue in my mouth to stop myself crying now.

Because it was true.

'*Why does your daughter Emilee not come down to see you?*' I'd asked in the early days.

His lips had tightened. '*Do not think too badly of her,*' he had said, without answering the question. '*She has had her troubles.*'

I could see this from that letter with the hospital mark. Her face had looked 'thunderstruck' when it had arrived. Yet how I wish I knew what was inside.

'My father will remain in my heart for ever,' Emilee is saying now to the church.

As she speaks, I see her eye catching Nick's, the handsome solicitor. I bet Emilee had asked him to pry into my life in France.

But then, I think of something so simple, that I wonder why I do not consider it before.

Emilee had investigated my past.

Now it is time for me to investigate hers.

It might give me something to fight back with.

I am certain there is more to Emilee than I can see.

France, 1944

I am ashamed to say that after Antoinette leaves me, I can hold myself no longer. I squat in a corner like a dog and open my bowels.

It is not just the fear.

It is the shame of having abandoned my unit.

I should have stayed with the others — not allowed myself to be led to safety like a kid.

What will they say when I go back to them? I might be court-martialled. Shot. At the least, sent back in disgrace.

But there had been no time to argue, I reason. If I had, she might have been caught.

I try to clean myself down with the straw in the loft.

And then I hear it.

The crack of a pistol.

Standing on a bale of straw, I open the skylight and look through. What I see makes my body go cold. The sergeant and the rest of my unit are racing up a hill. The Germans are behind them.

Getting closer.

Another crack of gunfire.

Someone falls. They are too far away for me to see who. Was it the sergeant? Or the driver?

The matchstick figures don't seem real. Yet only a few hours ago, we had all been pressed together, side by side on the boat; on the lorry. We had come out from England together, determined to fight for king and country.

And now we are dying.

Or rather, they are.

One by one, I watch in silent horror as each of my companions slumps to the earth. Dead. Lost. In a foreign field far from home.

Then I too fall, but on the straw, my head in my hands.

They will come for me next.

I deserve it. A traitor. A white-livered traitor.

That's what I am.

But Antoinette and her family must not be allowed to die as a consequence. I have to get out of here.

40

After the funeral, the mourners gather at the local community centre, where Emilee has arranged for refreshments to be provided. I listen with interest as they reminisce about my 'father's' life. I am lucky. My English is better than many of my friends' because, after my father left, my mother and I slept in le salon so she could sublet our bedroom to a teacher. He came from a place called Gloster even though it is spelled with many more letters.

'The English language has many difficult rules,' our lodger told me. 'But they are worth learning. It has a beautiful cadence and will help you to go far.'

'Thank you, Mr Montague,' I said, making a mental note to look up the word 'cadence'.

'Please. Call me Brian.'

The neighbours gossiped, of course. A good-looking young man living with my recently abandoned beautiful mother was bound to cause some finger pointing. At school, I was taunted. *Is he warming your mother's bed yet?*

'Take no notice,' my mother had told me, tossing her wonderful dark curls. 'He pays the rent. Besides, he is too young for me.' Her eyes had gone dreamy. 'There is nothing quite like an older man for treating you like a queen.'

I'd thought at the time she meant my 'father', who was a few years older than her.

Now I realize she'd meant Harold. My real papa.

Brian had stayed with us for some time. I don't know exactly how long because, when you are a child, the days and weeks go by at a different pace. But I do know that when he eventually moved on to teach in Paris, we went back to having meat once a week instead of every day.

'Can't you find another lodger?' I'd asked Maman.

She'd given one of her tinkly laughs. 'There is more competition now. People are paying less. But do not worry. We will manage.'

We did, but it was not as comfortable as before. The demand for Maman's paintings decreased along with the standard of our tenants. My mother had to ask one to leave when he 'mistakenly' thought our bed was his.

I often wondered what happened to Brian. I will always be grateful to him for my English. His tuition didn't merely help me achieve good grades at school. It also helped me get my job with Harold.

And now, it is going to be très utile for looking into Emilee's past.

I plan to start my investigation straight away. In fact, I will leave the reception early to do so. I do not wish to be here, watching Emilee talk to these people in this village hall, which hums with the stench of mothballed suits and gossip. Can she not see that behind their 'I'm so sorrys', they are eager to find out more? They wish to know what his pain was like at the end. They want to go into detail, as if it will somehow protect them when it is their time to go.

But most of all, they want to know about me. 'What about the French carer?' I hear one of them say. 'Will she be leaving now?'

'She's going to stay on for a while to help me sort out

the house,' I hear Emilee reply. Hah! If they knew I was his daughter too, they might be kinder. Instead, they look at me like I am no one important.

'When is the inquest starting again?' I hear someone else ask.

'We haven't got a date yet.' Emilee's voice has grown terse.

'I'm surprised you're allowed to have a funeral before the inquest is over,' persists the woman.

Emilee is looking flushed. 'We're just following the rules,' she says. Then she moves on to speak to someone else.

If I leave now, I can use Harold's computer while Emilee is still here. It is my only opportunity. I do not have a smartphone. I could afford one if I wanted. But I do not wish to be traced.

What a relief to be alone in the house. All that talk. All those thoughts of his final night that keep coming back into my head.

And yet, I do not feel alone. When I go into the sitting room, I expect to see Harold there on one of the sofas, waiting for his evening glass of whisky or for me to join him in a game of chess.

Often, when there was just the two of us in the house, he would talk to me about my day and then tell me things about his life.

'You are easy to chat to, Françoise. You do not know me so you will not judge. And besides, I am an old man. I need to let this out.' His eyes would water then. 'I could not talk about the past to my wife, or even Emily. I still don't because I can't upset my daughter. Yet now my

241

life is almost at an end, I feel a burning need to tell someone.'

I often heard such requests when I was working in France at the nursing home. But I was particularly flattered because Harold wanted to tell me and not Emilee. So I listened carefully.

'Why don't you write these stories down, Harold?' I asked him.

'No. I am too tired. I prefer to talk.'

And I would listen, spellbound. Sometimes he told me the same story from the war. Over and over. But then it would be a new one. Every now and then he declared that he did not want to talk about the past at all and that I should not pester him – even though it was his choice to speak. But when he did, his tales were better than any television drama. He went through so much at such a young age! How lucky he was not to be blown up on the beach when his troop landed in France. It made me understand why Harold is the man he is. The things that built him.

'Do you think it is possible to love two people at the same time?' Harold asked me.

'I do not know,' I shrugged. 'I have never been in love.'

'Never been in love?' he demanded. 'But you are a beautiful woman. How can that be?'

'Perhaps,' I said, 'it is because I do not trust men. The man I thought was my father left us.'

'Ah,' he said. His hand patted mine. 'I see. If I had known you existed, it would be very different. You do know that, don't you?'

'But then what would Emilee and your wife have said about that?' I asked.

He'd shaken his head. 'I don't know, Françoise. I couldn't have hurt them. I loved them too much.'

I remember this particular conversation so clearly. Harold would not have left Emilee and his wife for me and my mother. Maman and I would always have been second-best. The thought fills me with jealousy as I now sit down at the computer and type in his password.

Password not recognized. Try again.

How can this be? I used it only yesterday.

Then I realize. Emilee has changed it.

I can have two more attempts at getting the right password. What would Emilee have put in?

'G . . . E . . . N . . . T . . . L . . . E'.

Password not recognized. Try again. Of course, too obvious.

I feel sweat gathering at the nape of my neck. Think, I tell myself. If you were Emilee, what would you put? What is important to her?

The name of the house perhaps? Maybe Willowmead House is the most beautiful home I have ever seen. But Emilee doesn't seem as attached to it as I would have thought. Otherwise, why would she offer to give it to me?

One more go. What else is important to this woman?

Then I get it.

Me.

That's who.

She is jealous of me.

She does not want to be a sister.

She is used to being an only child.

She only wants one of her.

I type in each letter, my fingers shaking.

DAUGHTER.

I'm in!

Then I type in 'Emily Gentle' followed by the name of the hospital that was on the front of the envelope she received.

I click on the first search result. Instantly, the words HOSPITAL INVESTIGATION MIDWIFE SUSPENDED flash up on the screen, followed by a news report.

I read the first paragraph and gasp. That poor family!

So that's why Emilee had come running home!

Not to see her father – our father – but to hide.

There is a noise. She is back. Swiftly, I turn off the computer.

41

Mon Dieu! That was a big wave. I duck as it rears its head over the railings and showers down onto the promenade.

I am trying to get yesterday's funeral out of my mind, to clear my head. Walking is the best way. I begin to think about Emilee's suspension. I need to know more. But then my mind starts to turn back on itself. It is churning, bringing all the dirt rushing to the top. I cannot get my mother's face out of my head. The way she would cry with pain. *Do something, Françoise. Please.*

I would take her in my arms, her ravaged body, and hold the cup of water against her dry lips for her to sip from. Soothe her with the old nursery rhymes she would sing to me as a child.

Sometimes it worked and she would fall asleep. Sometimes it didn't and she would scream at me.

She does not mean it, I would tell myself.

But it hurt.

And then one day, she said his name.

'Harold.'

'Harold?' I repeated. 'Who is he?'

'Harold will come and find us,' she murmured. 'I know he will.'

I rack my brains. I do not remember any other Englishman apart from Brian.

Yet she would repeat his name over and over again in those final weeks.

Each time I would ask the same question. 'Who is Harold?'

Each time she would ignore me.

The sea is roaring now. It is like looking at foaming mountains, higher than a house.

A towering wave soars over the railings and drenches me in icy water. Brings me back to my senses. I need to go home and change. By now, Emilee will be out. She said she had an appointment in the village.

It will be safe to use the computer again. To see what else I can find out.

The house is empty. Her shoes have gone but Zorro is still here.

I switch on the desktop.

For a second, I fear she may have changed the password. But DAUGHTER still works.

I type Emilee's name and that of the hospital, just as I did before. There isn't much more to read in the original text I found – it's just a listing amongst hospital disputes which are either happening or about to take place. So I type in 'Smith' to Facebook.

There are several by that name. But then I add some other search words and I find him!

Quelle horreur! There are so many angry words jumping up before me about a midwife and her 'incompetence', followed by a string of comments below.

Good on you, mate. These things need to be out in the open. Damn both of them.

Then another.

The inquiry is still happening, isn't it? I don't think you're meant to comment about something that hasn't been decided yet.

I work there, said someone else, *and was told that the midwife had the hots for the consultant. Maybe she wasn't concentrating. She's been suspended now. There's going to be a big hearing at a high level. She could be struck off.*

I read it again twice, making notes. So that's what it's all about.

I'd noticed, ever since I met Emilee, that her head was always in another place.

Do the police know she is being investigated by the hospital?

If not, it is surely my duty to tell them.

Then another thought comes to me. It is so terrible that I can hardly voice it even to myself. But I have to. If Emilee is struck off, she will need money to survive.

Is it possible that she hastened our father's death?

42

The next day the sea is calmer. The mood of the house is not. It is tight. Like a coil about to unravel.

Emilee is keeping her distance. She is very quiet. I do not talk or attempt to make small conversation. I am still trying to work out what to do. Last night it seemed so clear. Now, I am not so sure.

'We all need a second chance, don't you think?' Maman once said to me.

'Not all,' I replied. 'But maybe some of us.'

'You are too hard for your years, Françoise,' she joked.

'Not hard,' I teased back. 'Merely practical.'

But perhaps Maman had been right.

I jog down to the shore, wearing my ear muffs. It is cold. But bracing too.

Zorro is so excited. He is burying his nose in the sand, digging out a large stone. I have forgotten to bring the ball and he thinks a stone will do instead.

'You silly thing,' I say.

And then I see it.

A huge wave that comes out of nowhere.

Zorro lets out a terrible yelp. It sounds almost human. Then he is pulled into the water.

'Come back!' I shout. But the current is too strong and he is being carried away.

What can I do? I do not swim but I cannot let poor

Zorro go. I wade out, grabbing his collar. My fingers slip off with the force of the waves, but then they mercifully close around his collar again.

Another wave is coming. I feel fear rise in my throat as it gets closer. The water goes over my head and smashes me down on the rocks. I lose my grip. The water is taking me. Blinding me. Gushing into my mouth. I am choking. My legs are kicking but I cannot stay upright. I go down.

I am drowning. This is it. My life comes before my eyes. Maman. The piano. Jean-Luc. Harold. Emilee.

Then I feel a firm hand seizing me.

I am on my back. Someone's hand is under my chin and I am being dragged back towards the shore, gasping with fear and choking from the salty water in my mouth and throat.

It is only when I am lying on the beach, shaking with cold and fear, that I see who my rescuer is.

Emilee.

'What were you doing in the sea?' she yells. 'It's freezing and rough. Are you insane?'

'Zorro,' I try to say.

As I say his name, he bounds over, licking me feverishly. Shaking his wet fur all over me.

'He went in,' I gasp. 'I tried to rescue him.'

'He can swim. You clearly can't.'

'He didn't look like he was swimming. A wave took him. I thought he was going to drown.'

'So you risked your life for my dog?' she demands.

I nod. It was instinct. No more than that. It felt like the right thing to do.

I am weeping now.

249

'And you risked your life for me,' I say to her.

Emilee makes an 'it was nothing' face. 'I was fine. I've been swimming here all my life.'

But we both look out at the sea. In the space of a few moments, the waves have become even higher. Pounding onto the shore, like a madman out to get us. I have a picture of Harold on his deathbed. Leaning out to me. Desperately trying to tell me something. '*Antoinette . . . died for me.*'

Shivers rack my body.

'Come on,' she says briskly. 'We had better go home.'

Home.

Willowmead House, which she has offered to me. Maybe there is another reason for this. Perhaps she thinks that it will stop me from pursuing my suspicions about Harold's death. Rescuing me just now makes me more obliged to her. But she did not arrange that. She had been able to take advantage of the situation. Wasn't that why she had dived in after me? But wouldn't it be better for her if I had perished? Then there would have been no 'loose ends', as the English say.

As we make our way back, dripping wet and shaking with cold, I begin to wonder if I have misjudged this woman. She's smart.

Like me.

Full of contradictions.

Like me.

Yet there is also a kindness to her.

Like me too.

We are partly bad. And partly good.

But only one of us killed our father.

Which means one of us is lying.

43

'What would you do, Harold?'

I am standing by his grave. The earth is freshly dug. There is no headstone yet. It is not ready. When it does come, I have been told it will be made of marble. I can tell you what the words will be without asking: HAROLD GENTLE, BELOVED HUSBAND OF JEAN AND FATHER OF EMILY.

There will be no mention of me. The daughter who was there when he needed someone.

'I would like some advice,' I say now.

Harold had been good at giving advice. He'd never been slow to express his views. We would talk for hours in those weeks before Emilee came home. Politics, books, music, everything. He'd been particularly interested in France. Where had I grown up? *Lyon.* Had I ever visited the Normandy beaches? *No.* What French literature had I read? *Camus. Françoise Sagan. Voltaire. Paris Match. Whatever I could borrow from the library.*

There are some people for whom age does not matter. Whether they are fifty years older or fifty years younger. What *does* matter is that unknown bond that draws them to one another. A sort of recognition that suggests you might have met before in a previous life.

My mother used to believe in that. Me, I am not so sure. But I do think we are drawn to certain people. This is not always for the good. I think of Jean-Luc with his cheeky smile, denim jacket, floppy fringe and hot, determined kisses – and then throw him out of my head.

'All I want,' I say to Harold, 'is to know whether or not I should tell the police about Emilee's investigation by the hospital. They ought to know, surely? Perhaps I should also tell them about her forgetfulness.'

Why? What good would it do? my conscience seems to say to me. *Do you want to kick someone when they are down? Clearly she is not herself. She needs help. Not someone to stab her in the back. Besides, people like us who care for others – whether it is bringing them into the world or easing them out – are under such strain. It is so easy to make a mistake.*

I kneel by the grave and place a sprig of holly from the garden on the upturned earth. But as I turn to go, I hear a voice, so powerful in my head that I could almost swear it is Harold. I can hear our conversation as clearly as if he is on the sofa and I am next to him.

'She is trying to make it right by giving you Willowmead House. She saved your life in the sea. She is your sister.'

'I'm not going to accept,' I say.

'Have you told her that?'

'No. I want to see if she changes her mind.'

'Isn't that rather childish?'

'Maybe.'

'Françoise, my child. What exactly do you want?'

I want people to look at me and say, 'That's Harold Gentle's daughter.'

I even look a bit like him. I am tall, like he was. I have a nose with a strong bridge. So did he. My brown eyes have flecks of green in them. His too.

I want the security of knowing that I had a papa. A good one. A respectable one. To be a part of something. To fit in. To be less alone.

I need those roots that I never had in my life, and that my mother never had either. Her parents had died of natural causes within a few months of each other when I was five, leaving her with no emotional or financial support.

Yet, I have a terrible feeling that my paternity won't help me when the police come to visit again. Could they even twist it as evidence against me?

I can see the headlines now: 'French woman killed father in revenge . . .'

Who would believe me? I might not believe myself if I read my own story in the newspapers.

As I walk back from the churchyard, I see a little boy on the swings in the village playground. A man is pushing him. I draw closer and see that it's Nick. There is no sign of a wife.

It is too late to pretend I have not seen him.

'Did you receive my letter?' he asks.

'Yes,' I say, thinking of its request to sign my formal acceptance of Willowmead House.

'I'm still considering it.'

His face is stern. I can tell he does not care for me. That is good. For I do not care for him either.

'It is none of my business, but –'

'You're right,' I say. 'It is none of your business.'

'Dad! Dad! Push me!'

I glance at the little boy on the swing.

'Shouldn't you be minding your son instead of giving me advice?' I say.

'I don't need lessons on how to bring up my child, thank you very much,' he retorts.

Then he turns to his son – but not before giving me a look that suggests I am no more than dirt in his eyes.

If only he really knew me.

44

When I return to Willowmead House, I stand for a moment and look up at it. I often do this. It is so beautiful with that old red brickwork and tall chimneys, the winter jasmine climbing up the walls and the line of wallflowers neatly planted by Joe.

The gardener is weeding now. He looks up briefly, frowns and then continues digging.

The house is quiet when I go in. There is a pleasant smell of lemon furniture polish left over from my house-work earlier.

'Emilee,' I call out.

She is not here. But her coat and shoes are present.

I go up to my bedroom and read Nick's legal letter again. It is long and complicated, with a section at the end for me to sign. Then I tear it into little bits, just as I had done with Harold's cheque.

What are you doing? I ask myself. Haven't you always dreamed of living in such a house?

Yes. But not like this.

There is a noise. At first I think it is Emilee. But it is Zorro, looking for me. 'Come in, you old softie,' I say.

He is nudging me with his nose now. Making little barking noises. Taking me towards the door. Across the corridor. Towards Harold's old room.

The door is locked.

Zorro barks.

What is going on?

I knock. 'Emilee? Are you there?'

There is no answer.

Zorro barks again.

I begin to feel silly. It is perfectly possible that Emilee has locked it to stop me going in. Or that she's inside, sorting out her father's things – *our* father's things – and doesn't want anyone to disturb her.

But Zorro is getting frantic.

I rattle the door handle. 'Please. Open.' Then I run downstairs and out into the garden.

Joe is still there.

'I need help,' I gasp.

He looks up with ill-disguised contempt.

'It is Emilee,' I say. 'I think she has locked herself in Harold's room.'

His mouth sets. 'Maybe,' he says grimly, 'she wants time to herself.'

'But Zorro is upset,' I protest. 'He keeps whining outside the door like there is something wrong.'

The gardener gets to his feet unsteadily. 'All right,' he says gruffly. 'We'll take a look.'

Together, we knock at the door again. 'Miss Emily?' he calls out.

No answer.

Then he takes out a piece of wire from his tool belt and picks the lock.

It still won't open.

'There are bolts at the top,' he says. 'Someone's pulled

them across. I'll get the ladder and go up from the outside. See if I can get in that way. You stay there.'

I am really scared now. Something is wrong. I feel it in my gut.

Zorro is whining by my side.

'It's all right,' I say. But we both know I am just trying to comfort him.

I hear the window being drawn up. At least she didn't bolt that.

Then a gasp.

'Sweet Jesus.'

'What's happened?' I cry.

I hear hasty footsteps on the other side of the door.

The sound of bolts being drawn at the top and bottom.

I burst in. Emilee is on the floor. Her eyes are closed.

I lean over her. Her pulse is still there. But it is faint. Yet there are no cuts. No blood. No sign of tablets suggesting an overdose.

'Ring for the ambulance,' I shout.

Joe runs down the stairs to the phone.

I hold Emilee in my arms. There are documents everywhere. She must have been going through Harold's things.

Then I see it. Right by her side as if it had dropped out of her hand.

The official words glare out at me.

It is a certificate of adoption.

45

'How do you feel?' I ask her.

Emilee is sitting up in bed. The paramedics have been and gone.

There was no need to go to hospital.

She had had a 'dizzy spell'.

'Your obs seem steady,' they told her. 'It would be a good idea to get yourself checked out with the doctor in a day or so, just to be sure.'

She nodded meekly.

Joe had fussed around, bringing her sweet tea. But now he has gone and it is just her and me.

'Why do you think you fainted?' I ask.

Of course, I suspect it's because of the adoption certificate, but I feel it would be better if she told me in her own words.

She shrugs. 'I've been under a lot of pressure.'

'Because of the hospital investigation that is coming up?'

Her eyes widen. 'So you *did* open my letter?'

'I do not open letters unless they are addressed to me,' I say stiffly.

'I don't believe you.'

'That's up to you,' I shrug. 'I found out about the investigation because I checked you out. I just looked you up on Google, it wasn't hard. It led me to a Facebook page belonging to some man called Smith. He was ranting about you. Is it true that you won't be allowed to work as a midwife if the investigation goes against you?'

'I don't know. It depends.'

'I'm sorry.'

She stiffens. 'I don't want to talk about it.'

'But that is not all, is it?' I say softly. 'You are upset because of the papers you found in Mr Gentle's room.'

She gives a start, as if she has only just remembered them. 'Where have you put them?'

'Back in the box that they presumably came from. It was by your side too.'

'Did you read them?'

I'm not going to lie. 'Some.'

There is a silence.

'So you know I am adopted,' she says flatly.

'I have done for some time,' I say.

'What? How?'

My mind goes back – not just to the night of Harold's confession to 'Emilee', but to much earlier than that.

'Your father told me,' I say. I don't feel as triumphant in telling her this as I thought I might. Before, I had prided myself on being 'one up' on her. But now I feel pity. I would have been devastated if I had discovered Maman was not my birth mother.

Her face is getting red. Angry. 'Why didn't he tell me?'

'He did. He thought I was you when he was dying and he confessed everything. He told you – me – that he was sorry for not telling you earlier.'

'But I want to know when you first knew.'

I take a deep breath.

'All right. If you are sure.'

'I am.'

So I begin.

But all the time, I cannot stop my thoughts from circling. Is this a trick to put us off the scent? Harold's mind had not been his own in the weeks leading to his death. Supposing he – or maybe someone else – had already told Emilee she was not his blood daughter. What if she was pretending to have just discovered the adoption certificate to cover her tracks?

If my suspicions are right, Emilee would have been furious when she'd first found out.

Furious enough to have killed him?

46

The more I think about it, the more it makes sense.

If Emilee had discovered the truth, she might well have felt vengeful towards her father. You hear about children being shattered when they discover their parents are not who they thought.

'It was before you had come home for the first time, Emilee,' I say. 'Before your father knew who I really was.'

Harold and I had fallen into a comfortable evening routine. He had his glass of whisky. I had my glass of white wine.

Then he had a second glass. That was when he first began to ramble about the war . . .

'The fighting,' he said. 'It was so vicious, inhuman.'

'I am sorry, Harold. Do you want to tell me about it?'

'I've never told anyone before,' he said.

'I had a friend called Maurice,' I said slowly, 'who had been in the French resistance movement. He told me things that he had never told anyone before. He said it helped him. That it was as if I had taken a thorn out of his side.'

'Maybe I'll give it a go, then,' he replied. 'It's not like I've got long to go anyway.'

I swallow the lump in my throat as I recount this. 'That's when he told me about landing in France and seeing people blown up on the beach. He –'

'Why did he tell you about it and not me?' Emilee interrupts. 'He always refused to discuss it with me and Mummy.'

'Sometimes,' I say soothingly, 'it's easier to share secrets with people we don't know well.'

When I had asked him what happened after that, he had looked so sad that I'd tried to cheer him up by moving forward. 'What happened after the war?' I asked. 'How did you meet your wife?'

His face brightened. 'I decided I wanted to be a lawyer when I returned. I wanted to put things right, to do some good. To impose order on the chaos. I was single for many years and then I met a young girl in the office called Jean. She was one of the secretaries at the firm and had lost her parents when she was a baby. Our loneliness drew us together and we got married quite quickly, intending to start a family of our own.'

His voice sounded a little hoarse.

'Do you want to rest?' I asked.

He shook his head and took a third glass. I tried to stop him but he brushed my hand away. 'No. I need this to talk. It feels right after keeping it in for so long.

'We tried for a baby. But nothing happened. There weren't the tests or the treatments that there are now. So we resigned ourselves to being childless. But then one day, a young woman was brought into the hospital where a friend worked as a surgeon. She was seven months pregnant. A car had knocked her off her bicycle. Tragically, she died soon after she got there but through some miracle, he managed to save the baby.'

I gave a little gasp.

'Extraordinary, isn't it?' said Harold.

For a minute, I saw the kindness in his face, that warmth which made me want to hold him. To feel his arms around me. That was the strange thing about Harold. He was a conundrum. So hard one minute. And so kind the next.

'No one seemed to know who the father was. She wasn't married. The adoption people were going to step in, so my friend told them about us and asked if we could be considered. It all sounds very informal but there weren't the same rules and regulations that there are now.'

It is like a fairy story.

'So Emilee is adopted,' I gasped.

'She doesn't know. I wanted to tell her when she was little but Jean didn't. The longer it went on, the more difficult it was to tell her the truth.'

Then he gave a little start, as if he had just realized his indiscretion. 'You must not tell her.' He seized my wrists. His hold tightened. 'You promise me that.'

'Yes. Of course. Please. You are hurting me.'

'I am sorry.'

I rubbed my wrists. 'Why are you telling me all this, Harold?'

He smiled, as if he hadn't hurt me – even though red marks were coming up. 'I do not know. Maybe it is because you are a good listener. Maybe it is because I am coming to the end of my life.'

'You must not say that.'

'But it is true. I have pancreatic cancer. The doctor has told me. She's the one who advised me to advertise for a carer to help me at the end.' He gave a hoarse laugh. 'No one local wanted the job after the cleaner left – my reputation for being crabby and demanding put everyone off. So I decided to try advertising in magazines instead.' Then his face turned serious again. 'But you must not tell Emily. Promise me?'

'I promise,' I said. I knew better than to argue with a dying man.

How wonderful it must be to have a father who cares about your feelings, I thought, jealousy rising up inside.

'We loved Emily as our own daughter,' he murmured. 'Yet I do sometimes wonder what it would be like to have a child of my own flesh and blood.'

As I recount all this, she makes a little cry. I stop. This cannot be easy for her.

Emilee's eyes are flashing. 'But he did have a child of his own, didn't he? He had *you*! He even confided in you about his cancer but not me. You pretended you didn't know when I told you what the prognosis was. You let me nurse him, thinking it was *just* old age and arthritis. You let me leave.'

'He asked me not to tell you. He was protecting you.'

'I don't believe you. You wanted to keep me in the dark. You wanted to be the only one there when he died.'

This isn't true, although I admit I did feel a slight gratification at being the daughter who knew.

'Like I said earlier, he did try to tell you on his deathbed,' I point out. 'It's just that he mistook me for you.'

'That makes it even worse,' she cries. 'You should have gone to get me. I would have asked him so many questions and now I can't.'

'He was confused and dying – it would have upset him.'

'Too bad. I am entitled to know!'

I can see her point.

'I wish you had never come here, Françoise,' Emilee screams. 'You have ruined our lives. I could have gone on in blissful ignorance. Now I have no idea what my real parents were like. I could have happily continued my life without knowing you existed; without knowing I wasn't really theirs; without . . .'

So maybe she hadn't known she was adopted? That spoils my theory for thinking she killed Harold in revenge. Or perhaps she's simply a good actress.

Zorro starts barking. There is someone at the door.

'I will get it,' I say, grateful to get away.

It's Nick.

'I heard about Emilee,' he says. 'Is she all right?'

'Physically she is fine. But she is a little upset at the moment.'

I feel strangely protective, holding the door slightly ajar. Not wanting to let him in, in case he upsets her even more.

His blond hair is ruffled. His eyes are steady, focused on me. His gaze intense. Pleading. 'Please, Françoise. I'd like to see her.'

'I'll ask what she wants,' I say stiffly.

'Actually, I need to see you too.' He shuffles awkwardly from one foot to the other. 'I've just heard something through the grapevine. No doubt you'll hear soon, but I wanted to tell you first. The Coroner's Office has set a date for the inquest to resume. You are both required to give evidence.'

I had been fearing this.

'There's something else,' says Nick. 'I probably shouldn't

be telling you but a contact of mine in the police says they found something in Emily's workbag when they were searching the house.'

'But that was a few days ago.'

'There was some delay in the lab about checking it for fingerprints.'

'What?' asks Emilee. She is coming down the stairs, looking very pale. 'What did they find?'

Nick's voice is serious. 'An empty morphine bottle.'

I gasp. She makes a bleating noise that sounds like 'No'.

At the same time, there is a knock on the door. It is the baby-faced policeman. He looks straight at Emilee who is almost at the bottom of the stairs now.

'Miss Gentle, I would like you to accompany me to the police station for further questioning.'

She stands on the first step. She wobbles. And then she crashes to the floor.

'Emily!' screams Nick.

France, 1944

I only get as far as the barn door before Antoinette arrives. She is breathless and flushed.

'Where are you going?' she hisses, shoving me back into the barn.

'I cannot stay here.' Tears are running down my face. 'The bastards shot them. I saw them through the skylight. They will come for me now. They'll search the buildings and then they'll get you and then —'

'Shh,' she says, almost harshly. 'Or they'll hear you.'

She pulls me back up the ladder.

'Why are you doing this for me?' I choke.

'I like you.'

We are crouching between hay bales.

She cups her hands around my face. 'You're sweet, Harold.'

No one had ever called me sweet before. Then again, I hadn't had any experience of girls, let alone women.

'How old are you?' I whisper.

'Twenty-one. You?'

'Fifteen.'

She laughs. 'You look older. Is that how you got away with joining up?'

I nod. Then her face turns serious. 'People are dying all the time, Harold. You saw that just now. I have witnessed it myself in the streets. Sometimes, you have to take a chance in life. We don't know if we are going to be here tomorrow. So we have to make the most of it.'

And then she kisses me.

PART FIVE

Emily and Françoise

47

Emily

Maybe I was being too dramatic when I told the police I wanted to 'report a murder'.

After all, I had no actual proof against Françoise.

But they came round fast enough to investigate – and now it's rebounded on me. I am the suspect.

'Can you explain why this empty morphine bottle is in your bag?' asks the policewoman.

She's not the baby-faced young constable from before.

This is a DI whose face suggests she takes no prisoners. Her eyes are hard. They bore through me. I steel myself not to look away. It's not easy. I still feel wobbly after my faint. And that headache from the bike accident continues to come back every now and then.

'No,' I say.

'Come on, Emily,' she says, as if she knows me. 'Your father has died of an overdose. Our investigation has strong evidence that it's unlikely to have come from the bottle you kept in the kitchen.'

My fingers clench into my palms.

'But now a second bottle has turned up. Did you get hold of that from your job at the hospital and overdose your father?'

'No!' I blurt out.

Her voice turns soft, the way the police do on TV dramas, when they're about to go in for the kill. 'Your father was in pain, Emily. He was dying anyway of cancer. It would be understandable to be tempted to bring his agony to an end.'

I shake my head, unable to speak.

'My client is very distressed,' says Nick. He is sitting beside me as my solicitor. I know from my father that a lawyer does not have to believe clients in order to represent them. Maybe he doubts me just like the police seem to. I wouldn't blame him.

'Miss Gentle,' he says, 'has just recovered after a collapse. Yet she still insists on helping you with your inquiries, which shows she wants to assist. Do you have any evidence for your accusations? Are there fingerprints?'

The DI turns her steely gaze to him. 'No.'

'Then all this is pure speculation, isn't it?' says Nick firmly.

The DI remains silent.

'I'll take that as a yes,' he says. 'My client and I are finished here.'

'For the time being, maybe,' she says curtly. 'We will be in touch.'

Nick has parked outside. I get into his car quickly, hoping no one from the village sees us.

'Do you think I was telling the truth?' I ask.

He sighs. 'I believe you loved your father. And I have often wondered what I would do if someone I loved was in pain, and was probably going to die anyway.'

How many times did I ask myself that during Dad's final days?

'What happens now?' I ask.

'The inquest will go ahead. You and Françoise will be asked to give evidence, along with the doctor. But at the same time, the police will continue their investigations.'

'Are they looking into Françoise too?'

'I expect so.'

'Good. They should.'

We're outside Willowmead House now. Nick turns off the engine and faces me. His eyes hold mine. I try not to look away. 'Do you honestly think she is capable of murder?' he says.

'Do you?' I ask, deflecting the question. I have not grown up with a lawyer for nothing.

'I think we all are, deep down,' he says. 'Don't you?'

He is looking at me with a slightly harder expression.

My skin is crawling. 'I don't know,' I say. Then I try to sound light-hearted. 'You don't mean you suspect *me*, do you?'

'I'm just saying that sometimes we do things we don't mean to in life.' His voice is a bit softer now. 'And I want you to know that if you ever need to confide in someone, I'm here.'

'Thanks,' I say, opening the car door to get out. 'I'll remember that.'

48

Emily

The inquest is continuing in the same modern courtroom as before.

I feel like a criminal.

Françoise and I are sitting next to each other at the front, ready to give evidence. I glance at her. Her posture is very stiff and upright.

I look down at the ground.

How could my father's life have come to this? Except he is not my father, is he? Not my real one.

My mind goes back to the night he died. When he said he had something to tell me.

Something so cruel that I felt my heart was being ripped right out of my chest. Then, after I said 'You win,' it seemed he was about to tell me something else. But he stopped.

Was he, in fact, about to reveal that I was adopted?

My instinct tells me this. But I won't ever know. Instead, he had chosen to confide in Françoise, a total stranger. If I'd come back from London sooner, I would have cared for him. My father would not have had to advertise for help. Françoise would never have disrupted our lives.

And what about my real parents? Was that story about a young single mother who had died in a road accident really true? If so, how tragic. And then there was my real father, whom no one knew anything about.

Did the two people I called Mummy and Daddy really love me? Mum had. I'm pretty sure of that. But Dad had expected so much of me. Was that his nature or was it because I wasn't his? Either way, it had affected my life. Made me the person I am today.

'Please be seated, everyone.'

The coroner's voice breaks into my thoughts. It's the same one as before. She is a short woman with a sharply styled bob and a no-nonsense expression. She reminds me of one of my tutors from my midwifery training. The type you wouldn't want to fall out with.

Nick is in the adjacent row. He glances across and gives me an 'it will be all right' smile. But he doesn't know that. None of us do.

'We are here today to determine the cause of Harold Gentle's death,' says the coroner.

My mind is all over the place. I am back, walking through the woods with my father. I'm ten. Maybe eleven. We are gathering hazelnuts. I stand on a twig. It snaps. The sound is unexpectedly loud.

My father is on the ground. His hands over his face. He is whimpering like a baby.

'Dad,' I say. 'What's wrong?'

'They're coming for us.' He pulls me down next to him. 'Don't you see? We have to hide.'

'Hide from who?'

Then, my mother catches us up.

'It's all right, Harold,' she says, taking him into her arms.

'No!' he shouts. He is pushing her away. She falls against a tree. Blood is trickling down her face.

'You've hurt Mummy!' I scream.

'It's all right, darling. Daddy's just having a funny turn.'

Somehow she manages to calm him down. We walk back to the car. We go into the house. We sit down and have Sunday lunch. We don't talk about what has just happened.

The coroner continues.

'The pathology results show that Harold Gentle had advanced pancreatic cancer.'

I still can't believe he'd confided this in Françoise over me. I would have come home sooner. Our final weeks together could have been nostalgic, instead of poisoned by Françoise's interference.

'Toxicology tests showed a high level of morphine in his blood, a level that was significantly greater than would have been present from the dosage prescribed by his doctor.'

Even though I already know this, my body begins to shake as the facts are laid out so baldly. I glance at Françoise. Her face is staring straight ahead. There is no emotion.

'I will now call Emily Gentle, daughter of the deceased, to recount her father's final hours.'

My legs are wobbly as I go up to the stand.

But I am not his daughter, I want to say. *I am his adoptive daughter. That's the real daughter. There! Françoise. The pretty one. The younger one. Watching me. Her fingers clasped together. That's what her hard stare reminds me of. It is the same as my father's.*

I hear my own voice ring out, as if it belongs to someone else's. 'My father's carer, Françoise Alarie, and I took it in turns to sit with him on that last night. She took over from me just after midnight. His breathing was slow but steady.'

'Did you give him a dose of morphine before you left?'

'Yes.'

'Was it from the bottle in the kitchen?'

'Yes.'

'Yet I gather that there was another bottle found in your medical bag?'

I feel myself burn. 'The police told me this but I didn't know anything about it.'

'Are you sure you gave him the correct dosage?'

'I am a midwife. I am used to giving medication.'

'I gather that you had a bicycle accident in September and injured your head?'

How did they know that? I don't remember telling anyone else. It had to be Nick. But why would he give them ammunition they could use against me?

'Is that true, Miss Gentle?' probed the coroner.

'Yes,' I say reluctantly.

'Did you have a medical examination afterwards?'

'No.'

'Have you been forgetful recently about other things?'

'Once or twice.'

'You forgot to lock the car when on holiday in Cornwall, I believe.'

I glance across at Françoise. Her expression is very still. She is the only living person who knows this. Had she blabbed? If so, to who?

Maybe I shouldn't have signed away the house to her. My mind had been confused by guilt over the father she had missed out on.

But she hadn't known Dad. Not like I did. She hadn't seen the tempers and the outbursts Mum and I had had to put up with over the years.

'How can you stand it?' I'd asked her.

'Because, darling,' she'd said, giving me a warm, reassuring cuddle, 'he's not himself when he behaves like that. He is a scared fifteen-year-old boy who has seen and done things that no one should ever have to do. Promise me that, if by any chance I go first, you will look after him, Emily?'

'Of course.'

No one expected Mum to die before Dad. She was so much younger. She was just being overprotective.

But when this did happen, I had broken my promise. I had stayed away.

Why? Not just because of the distance or my unsocial hours. But because I was angry with him.

If it hadn't been for his stern, moralistic upbringing, I might have had the courage to keep Nick's child. *Our child.* And yes. I am still furious with my father for that.

Really furious.

But enough to kill him?

Not in my right mind. Of course not.

But the truth is that my head hasn't felt the same since the accident.

Is it possible that I did something awful without knowing?

49

Françoise

'Françoise Alarie. Can you please tell us what happened during the evening of Harold Gentle's death?'

I stand upright, the way my mother taught me. '*Never slouch, Françoise. It suggests weakness and it is not flattering for a woman's body. Pretend your spine is made of steel. Flaunt your height. And always dress well.*'

I toss my flouncy skirt, one I made myself from a blue-and-pink spotted cotton remnant I found in the market. Then I speak. It's now or never.

'Do you mean my father?'

There is a ripple through the court. There are locals here. An inquest is held in an open court for anyone to attend. The news will be all round Willowmead in minutes. Emilee's face is white.

The coroner's voice is crystal clear. 'Are you telling me that Harold Gentle was your father?'

'That is correct. I have the results of a DNA test to prove it. My mother was the family au pair. Mr Gentle had an affair with her when she was a young woman.'

The whispers are becoming louder. Sally from the post office is here. She is talking excitedly to the man next to her who owns the pub.

'May I remind everyone that this is a court of law,' says the coroner. 'Please be silent.'

Then she looks at me. 'Can you describe your relationship with Mr Gentle?'

'I cared for him very much. He loved me too. He was surprised to discover I was his daughter at first, but then he is pleased.'

He didn't exactly say those words, I remind myself, but I know he had cared for me.

'I looked after him when my sister was in London and then I continued to care for him when she returned.'

I intentionally use the word 'sister', to show I am not ashamed of my mother's role in this. Yet inside I am flustered. I must calm myself. My life depends on this. I take a deep breath, still my mind.

'As Emilee has said, I took over from her just after midnight.'

'So you did not give him any morphine?'

'He was not due to have any until the early morning. But I did give him a dose earlier that day, in the afternoon.'

'Are you sure you gave him the correct amount?'

'Of course I am sure. I look after old people for many years. I know my job.'

'Did you use the bottle from the kitchen?'

'Bien sûr.'

'And did Emily Gentle take the bottle of morphine from that cupboard for the night-time dose?'

'I suppose so.'

'Did she put it back?'

'I do not know. But again, I suppose so.'

'If she did, is it possible, in your opinion, that Mr Gentle could have got out of bed and retrieved the bottle himself after it had been put back?'

They've asked me this before. If they hope for a different answer, they are wrong. I make a 'pah' sound. 'How can he? He is an old man. He could barely walk. He was not mobile enough.'

'Do you know how an empty morphine bottle ended up in Miss Gentle's workbag?'

'No.'

There are no more questions.

I am glad to go back to my seat.

What will happen now?

Emilee's shoulders are stiff. Nick seems worried too, twisting his hands constantly.

The coroner shuffles her papers. I hold my breath as she speaks.

'The evidence supports the conclusion that Mr Gentle died from an overdose of morphine. However, it is unclear as to whether he took it himself or if someone else gave it to him. I am therefore unable to reach a conclusion, so I will be adjourning the inquest and referring the matter to the police while they continue their investigations.'

We leave the room. I wait until we are outside, where no one else can hear us. 'Over there,' I hiss, pointing to a park.

Only when we are out of earshot of anyone, do I speak.

'What did you do, Emilee?' I whisper. 'What did you do to our father?'

She is staring back at me, as if genuinely confused by my accusation. 'Nothing,' she says.

Then her eyes turn fierce. 'What did *you* do, *sister*?'

50

Emily

I am too embarrassed to go out the next day. Everyone now knows, from her little speech in court, that Françoise is my half-sister.

'Did you have to tell them that?' I say. We are in the kitchen. I've made myself a cup of tea but am unable to have my usual slice of toast. Françoise, on the other hand, is eating her way through a bowl of home-made muesli quite calmly.

'It is the truth,' she says.

I can't argue with that. Besides, what does it matter? I'll be moving on shortly. I have to. After all, I have given away my family home to this woman. No job, no house, no real family. Alone. Yet none of this is as bad as the terrible mistake I made on the maternity unit.

Then Zorro begins to bark madly, rushing towards the door. Moments later, there is a knock.

It's the police.

'Miss Gentle? We would like you to come down to the station.'

Again?

Françoise has a smug look on her face.

'And you too, Ms Alarie.'

*

I want to reach out for Nick in the police interview room. Instead, I clasp my hands tightly together as I sit opposite the two detectives.

I expect them to start gently enough, as they did in the investigation. To ease me in. To soften me. But they drop a bombshell.

'You are a nurse and a midwife, I believe?' says the DI.

I stiffen. 'I'm a midwife, yes.'

'But you're not working at the moment.'

'No.'

'Why is that?'

I hesitate. 'I'm taking some time off.'

She gives me a hard stare. 'Our investigations show that you have been suspended while an internal inquiry takes place into a serious incident that occurred while you were on duty on 30 September this year.'

I freeze.

Nick sends me a '*What?*' look.

'Did you not think of telling us this earlier?'

'I didn't think it was relevant,' I say.

'I agree,' says Nick, coming in quickly. 'I fail to see what this has to do with Mr Gentle's death.'

The DI doesn't reply. There is no need. Her point has been made. I am no longer to be trusted.

'Did you get on with your father?' she asks.

'Yes.'

'But he is not your natural father, is he?'

So Françoise has told them. Of course she has.

'I was adopted when I was a baby.'

Nick turns to me. 'I never knew that,' he murmurs.

'I only found out recently,' I say.

'How?'

My voice comes out as if it doesn't belong to me. 'I found the documents in my father's possessions after he died.'

'Does anyone else know?'

'Françoise, his blood daughter.' I choke.

'How did she discover this?'

'My father had already told her.' I'm aware my voice is rising.

'Do you feel angry with your father now?'

I turn on her. 'What do you think? My parents had kept this from me. And then, I discover my father had confided in a virtual stranger.'

Nick is shooting me warning signs. But it's too late. I've lost my temper. I can see in the DI's eyes that the damage is done.

'Was she close to your father?'

It's not difficult to see where this is going.

'They got on well.'

She is making notes all the time I am talking.

'When did you find out that Françoise was your father's natural daughter?'

'Shortly before my father's death,' I mumble.

She tilts her head slightly, her interest piqued.

'Did that upset you?' she asks.

'Yes.'

No point in lying.

'Enough to harm your father?'

'No. Certainly not.'

But my words don't sound genuine, even to me.

'What kind of father was Mr Gentle?'

How can I put this diplomatically and also be truthful?

I hesitate. 'Firm but kind,' I say at last.

'Would you say you had a happy childhood?'

I think of my pony. The swims in the sea. The homework advice. The unexpected angry outbursts. His determination that I should live up to our family reputation.

'More or less.'

'Can you describe some times when he showed what kind of father he was?'

'He could lose his temper,' I hear myself say.

Her eyes sharpen. *Like me.* Is that what's she's thinking?

'But there was a reason for that,' I add hastily. 'He had a bad experience in the war.'

'Which war?'

How old is this woman? She must think I'm referring to a more recent conflict. 'The Second World War.'

'But he would have been too young to fight, wouldn't he?'

'He joined up at fifteen, after lying about his age.'

'What happened?'

I'm losing patience now. 'He saw people die. That's what happens in wars, isn't it?'

Her voice is steady. 'Did he hurt you when he lost his temper?'

'No.'

I think of my mother's red wrists from his tight grip, when she did something he didn't like. I should have said something. I ought to have got help. But she had begged me not to. *'He doesn't mean it, Emily. He doesn't know what he's doing.'*

My mother was a good, caring woman. Too good. Too caring. Too forgiving. *'If we don't forgive others,'* she would say to me, *'how can we expect to be forgiven ourselves?'*

'He'd raise his voice at us if we did something he didn't like,' I continue.

'Such as what?'

'They could be small things like tidying up after him – he hated it if his things were moved around.'

The policewoman's eyes sharpen with interest. 'Bit of a control freak, was he?'

'He belonged to a time when the man of the household was also the master. But he could also be very kind.'

That's the part of Dad I want to remember. Not his dark side.

'He wasn't always very understanding,' I say.

'What do you mean by that?'

'He just wasn't.'

'Can you give me an example?'

I rack my brains but there's only one thing that stands out. The thing I've been burying for so long. And now it's emerging. I can't stop the words.

'It was because I was scared of upsetting him that I had an abortion.'

Nick makes a strange sound. I cannot look at him. My head is hurting. Too late, I realize I should have kept quiet.

But I can't stop now. My mouth is pouring it all out. I am vomiting up the past.

'When I was eighteen, my boyfriend broke up with me. I was devastated. Hysterical. Then I found out I was pregnant. I didn't tell him because I didn't want him to think he had to marry me.'

I cannot look at Nick so I have no idea how he is reacting.

'I knew my father would be furious. He expected me to

have a career. And he was very conscious of his position in the community. There was no way he would have tolerated an unmarried, pregnant daughter. And it would have finished off my mother.'

I shiver as I recall looking up the phone number of a clinic in a telephone box. 'So I found a clinic and . . . and I had it done without telling anyone.'

I think of the child I had got rid of. Of my friends who have babies now. Of the yearning inside me to hold a little bundle, breathe him in, hold her face against mine . . .

I glance at Nick. He is ashen. 'Only later did I realize that I should have told my ex-boyfriend too.'

'I see,' says the DI. Her voice is kinder now. 'So . . . let me rephrase my earlier question, Emily. Did you feel angry with your father?'

There is a silence. It would be so easy to lie. To say that my father had my best interests at heart. But I am tired of putting on a front to the world. Or to myself.

'Yes,' I say. 'Very angry.'

Françoise had told me when our father was dying that she had wanted a father to protect her. But my father had not protected me. He had not guided me. He had tried to control me. And he had done the same with my mother.

The policewoman's voice is softer now. 'Angry enough to murder him?'

'No.'

But I can tell she doesn't believe me.

51

Françoise

I have no lawyer with me. I do not need one. I tell the truth. It is not difficult. My mother taught me. *'You have to remember the bits which are best to leave out, chérie.'*

The policeman interviewing me asks the same kinds of question as the coroner's.

'Yes,' I reply. 'I am sure I gave Harold the correct dosage during my shift before Emilee.'

'Harold?'

'Mr Gentle.'

'But you called him Harold.'

'He asked me to do so.'

'Can you describe your relationship with him?'

'He was a good employer,' I say.

'You also said he was your father. You did a DNA test which you showed him, and he later gave you fifty thousand pounds. Is that right?'

Ha! I should have expected this. 'So Emilee told you about the cheque, did she?' I say.

'Is that right?' he repeats.

'Yes' I say shortly.

'So, I will ask you one more time. Did you administer an overdose of morphine to Mr Gentle?'

'Non,' I say firmly. 'I did not.'

But I can tell he does not believe me.

This is not working out as I had planned.

52

Emily

The police thank me for my time and say they will be in touch.

I try to rush out but Nick catches up.

'You had an abortion,' he says.

It's not a question. Or an accusation. It's more like a kind of stunned statement.

We are walking side by side. My eyes are on the ground.

'Why didn't you tell me?'

I round on him. Forcing myself now to look at his kind, sorrowful face.

'For the same reason I told the police. You'd broken up with me. I didn't want you to stay because you thought it was the right thing to do. And that's what you would have done, isn't it, Nick? You'd have stuck by me.'

My old love pauses. He is looking at me now in the way he had looked at me all those years ago, when he'd suggested a walk across the cliffs, the day before our first A-level exam. It almost feels like yesterday. I had just turned eighteen . . .

'I can't,' I'd said. 'I have to revise for my A-levels.'

Nick made an 'Are you sure?' face. 'A break will do you good.'

I thought of my father, who was working in his study, and my mother, who was running an errand for our elderly neighbour. No one would know if I slipped out.

'But it's raining,' I pointed out.

'The best time to walk,' he grinned. 'There'll be fewer people around.'

He'd been right. On both counts. It was wonderful walking in the rain and playing silly games, like sticking out our tongues to catch the drops. And we didn't pass a soul.

'The rest of the world is tucked up at home with their cocoa,' Nick joked. 'I prefer enjoying all this with you.' Then he flung out his arms, embracing the sea and the cliffs and the air, which smelled so new and fresh. So romantic! Even if the weather was more like March than June.

We walked across the top of the cliff, past the old 'Dad's Army' lookout post from the Second World War 'Amaz ing, isn't it?' Nick said, pointing out the information sign next to it.

Yes. It was.

'If it hadn't been for our grandparents' generation, we'd be living in such a different world.'

'I agree,' said Nick solemnly. 'They made so many sacrifices. One of my great-uncles was killed in the war. His name is on the memorial outside the church, actually.'

'I'm sorry,' I said. 'I never knew that.'

'You know, when I was young, I thought, well, it's one of those things. But as I've grown older, I really appreciate everything that he and all the others did. My dad says it's why we should enjoy ourselves. He reckons that

Great-Uncle Freddie wouldn't have wanted us to go round all po-faced. He'd rather we had a good time and live life to the full.'

Nick's dad was very different from mine, then. 'My father expects me to live life to the full too,' I said. 'But that means working hard and not having too much time off.'

Nick slung his arm around me. 'Everyone needs a break, Emily.'

We'd reached an isolated dip in the cliff now.

I shivered from the breeze whipping up from the sea. 'You're cold,' said Nick. 'Let me warm you up.'

Then he led me to a sheltered spot below the cliff, where a clump of evergreen trees gave us shelter – not to mention privacy – and he took me in his arms.

I didn't mean to. But I couldn't stop myself. One thing led to another. Our bodies moulded together, as if they were made to fit. It felt so natural. So amazing. So right.

'You know,' he said, looking down on me afterwards, 'I will never find anyone else like you. Never.'

'And I'll never find anyone else like you again, either,' I whispered.

That had to be the day I'd got pregnant. It had been the only time.

When I got back, my mother had beaten me home. Dad, summoned from his study, was pacing the kitchen. 'Where have you been?' he demanded.

'Out for some fresh air,' I said, flushing deeply. Even though my fingers were white cold from the wind outside, my body was still hot from Nick's touch.

'You should have been revising,' he'd snapped.

'Come on, Harold,' my mother said. 'Everyone needs a rest at times.'

Just what Nick had said . . .

'Go and change out of those wet clothes, love,' she continued. 'I'll bring you a mug of Bovril to warm you up. They say on the radio that it's going to be wet all weekend.'

I stayed in my room for as long as I dared before my father knocked on the door and told me that if I didn't get cracking with my revision downstairs on the dining-room table where he could see me, I might as well not bother with the exams. But all I could think of was Nick. Would he think I was easy? What if he told everyone at school?

On Monday morning, he was waiting for me outside the gates. 'I've missed you,' he said.

The sun had come out by then. It shone down with a brightness that could only be matched by my heart. Then he took my hand and we walked into the first exam together.

Nick mouthed something at me from his desk. I could see what he was saying. 'I love you.'

'I love you too,' I mouthed back.

'Look at those two love birds,' someone whispered loudly. I blushed.

'Silence!' said the teacher who was adjudicating. 'You can turn over your papers now.'

And then, a month later, just after A-levels, my period didn't come. I kept expecting it to, running to the loo every hour or so. I waited another month to be sure. By then, my food tasted metallic. I knew that was a sign. There had been a girl in our class who'd got married all in a rush last year. She'd described everything in great detail.

What would my father say? My eighteen-year-old self knew all too well. He would be so angry. So disappointed. I wasn't sure which would be worse. And what about my nursing place, which was waiting for me in London? I'd always wanted a career that allowed me to look after people.

But that could wait, couldn't it? I loved Nick. And he loved me! We would get through this together. He'd already suggested a walk later in the week. I'd tell him then. But he got in before I did.

'I've been thinking,' he said, as we crunched our way over the stones by the sea. Our arms swung side by side. He hadn't made to take my hand or put his arm over my shoulder as he usually did. 'We're both going in separate directions soon. Maybe we should give ourselves a bit of a break. We don't want to get tied down, do we?'

My heart chilled. 'What do you mean?'

He wasn't looking at me. 'I just think we ought to see some other people, that's all. Then we can work out if we're really meant to be together. We're very young, Emily. Don't you think?'

'Not too young to do what we did,' I whispered.

This time, he did take my hand. 'It was perfect, Emily. And I'll never forget it. Let's just see how we feel about each other this time next year, shall we?'

How could I tell him I was pregnant? How could I 'tie him down'? And what about all that stuff he'd said about never finding anyone like me again? If he was that fickle, maybe he wasn't right for me after all.

'Fine,' I said, trying to hide the hurt that had welled up inside. 'If that's what you want.'

But my mind was whirling. My father would kill me. Mum would be so upset. And what about the life I had envisioned in London? Working hard at the hospital, drinks with friends in bars, building up a bright, shiny, exciting new life away from the dozy seaside village I grew up in.

I'm ashamed to say that I thought far more about that than of the baby itself. It's only as big as a seed, I told myself. Nothing more than that.

Then I remembered. In the phone box, which I sometimes used outside school to tell Mum if I was going to be late, there was a notice. It read *In 'trouble'? Need to talk?*

Below was a number for a clinic in Truro that could provide contraception and discuss options for unwanted pregnancies.

Could I do this? A picture of my parents' faces came into my head. The embarrassment they would have to endure if it became known that Emily Gentle was 'up the duff'.

So I pretended I was going shopping for the day.

'You deserve a treat,' said my mother. She'd pressed some notes into my hands. 'Buy yourself some clothes. There'll be some parties in London, I expect.'

She never knew the money was used at a private clinic to get rid of her grandchild.

Afterwards, I couldn't wait to get away from Willowmead. I threw myself into my training course but turned down invitations to parties. I convinced myself that nothing had happened. It hadn't really been a baby. It hadn't been formed.

Then, each one in our group was put on a different ward for two weeks' work experience. I was sent to the neonatal unit. One of the mums had just had a premature baby. It looked so tiny lying there in the incubator with all the wires.

'Will it survive?' I asked the doctor afterwards.

She'd nodded. 'Chances are pretty good, I'd say. Babies are resilient. Right from conception, in fact.'

Then she looked at me. 'Are you all right, Emily?'

'Fine, thanks,' I said stiffly.

But afterwards, as soon as I could, I rushed back to my room in the nurses' home and cried and cried.

Afterwards, I sat up. 'This won't do,' I said to myself. 'You might not be able to bring back your baby. But you *can* make sure that you help other babies into the world safely.'

'You're a natural,' said one of the senior midwives after I'd helped deliver my first baby.

'Really?' I said, glowing.

I stared at the little scrap, locked in his mother's arms, sucking at her nipple as if there was no tomorrow.

I still felt regret. But at least now I had a purpose in life to help distract me.

When I came home reluctantly for Christmas, I spent my time walking the cliffs on my own and keeping my head low. 'Your old friend Nick rang,' my father said when I returned from a long walk along the beach, shivering with cold.

My heart pounded. 'Thanks,' I said, trying to sound casual.

'Don't you want to call him back?' he said. 'It would be good for you to see your friends.'

'Actually, I'd rather spend my time with you and Mum.'

He nodded approvingly. 'That's nice. We both appreciate that. Don't we, Jean?'

A couple of days later, just before New Year, Nick and
I passed each other in the village. I just nodded.

He looked hurt. But how could I see him? I'd got rid of
our baby. I couldn't even blame him. It had been my decision. Too late, I realized, I should have allowed him to
have a say too.

The following summer, Nick brought home a girlfriend
from uni.

Her name was Sophie.

53

Emily

'Yes,' says Nick now, bringing me back to the present. 'I would have stayed if I'd known you were pregnant.'

His voice sounds as if he's trying to hold back tears. 'And I should have done. We are made for each other. I feel comfortable with you in a way I've never done with Sophie.'

Then his voice changes. 'Do you know why I ended it with you?'

'You said we had to have time on our own.'

'It was your father. He came to see me and said he didn't like the fact that we were serious. He said that I was jeopardizing your future and career. So I made up that stuff about us being too young. I know I shouldn't speak ill of the dead, but in my opinion, your dad could be rather manipulative.'

A cold feeling crawls into my heart. Much as I loved my father, it was true.

I listen with a sinking heart as Nick continues. 'I decided that I'd find you at Christmas and tell you everything. I rang you and left a message.'

'I know,' I say, remembering. 'Dad told me. But I was too hurt to call back. And . . . and after my abortion, I told myself I'd put you behind me to concentrate on bringing other babies into the world.'

Nick's eyes are wet. 'If I'd stood up to your father, it might have been so different.'

'I should have stood up to him too,' I say. 'But if we had got together, you wouldn't have had Billy.'

He presses his lips tightly, as if trying to hold himself together. 'I know.'

'Your little boy is gorgeous, Nick. You can never regret having him.'

'Of course I don't.' He takes my hands. 'But I do regret not having him with *you*. And I didn't know your dad could be so angry.'

'Shhh.' We are standing in a passage alongside the police station.

'Dad would have killed me if he'd known I was pregnant,' I whisper. 'Well, not killed. But he'd have been furious.'

'Yet he'd had an affair!'

'I know. Hypocritical, isn't it? The main thing for him was that he wasn't found out. It meant he could carry on being a family man.'

'If it was me,' he says,' I'd have wanted revenge.'

I make a noise in my throat.

He stops, takes my hands and looks right into my face. His questions tumble out, 'So be honest with me. Did you give your dad an overdose? Did Françoise suspect you? Did you give her the house to bribe her into keeping quiet?'

I'm about to speak. To tell him the truth. But then he lets me go and shakes his head. 'No. I shouldn't have asked you that because it puts me in a difficult positon as your lawyer.'

So much for his earlier declaration that I could tell him anything. I'm beginning to feel even more uneasy.

'I know you couldn't have anyway,' he continues. 'You're not that kind of girl. It had to be Françoise who did it. Don't worry. The police will find out sooner or later. They usually do.'

A shiver passes through me.

'And what about this hospital investigation?' he asks. 'Do you want to tell me about it?'

Tears are rolling down my face now. I find myself blurting it all out. Telling him exactly what happened. It's such a relief. He stands there, holding me. I don't care if anyone sees us. I've needed to tell someone about this for so long.

'And then, of course, there was the bike accident.'

Nick frowns.

He'd asked me about that after hearing the coroner mention it but I'd shrugged off his question. Now it seems right to come clean.

I close my eyes briefly. 'It was on my way back to the hospital. A fox shot across the road and I fell and hurt my head.'

Nick looks concerned. 'Did you get it checked out?'

'No. I didn't want to go anywhere near a hospital after what had happened.'

'I get that,' he says, letting me go. 'Please don't take this the wrong way. But I've noticed you've been quite forgetful at times. I think you ought to see a doctor.'

'There's no need,' I say quickly.

'Why? What are you afraid of?'

'Nothing,' I say quickly.

But inside, my heart is beating. What if there's something seriously wrong with me? I am adopted. I could have inherited some congenital disease from my unknown parents.

Or maybe I don't ever deserve to be happy or peaceful again.

Some crimes are unforgivable.

Like murder.

54

Emily

Françoise is waiting for me. She has already poured herself a whisky from our father's cut-glass decanter. I don't normally drink but I accept the glass she gives me.

'You told the police I was adopted.'

She stares at me. 'No I didn't.'

I almost believe her.

Zorro paws at us.

'He needs a walk,' I say.

'Then we'll both go.'

I'd rather be alone. But on the other hand, I might – with any luck – get her to say something about Dad's last night that incriminates her.

We down our drinks in one, put on our boots and set off down the cliff path, Zorro slightly ahead. Every now and then I call him back to keep him by my side. Françoise bends down to pat him as though she is his owner. This irritates me. At the same time, I don't like myself for being petty. Zorro likes this woman. He's usually a good judge of character.

But what if he's wrong?

'I think we need to tell each other what really happened,' she says, as we negotiate the muddy footpath. It's been raining heavily and the ground is slippery.

'I've already told the police everything I know,' I snap. 'What about you?'

'Well,' she says slowly, 'there *is* something I should have told the police but something stopped me. Maybe it's because, deep down, I don't want you to go to jail.'

Again, a shiver goes through me, just as it had when I'd been talking to Nick.

'What?'

She sucks in her breath. 'I know you gave our father an overdose.'

I go cold at the thought that she could be right.

'How can you be so certain?' I protest.

Françoise makes one of her exaggerated hand movements. 'Because after I took over from you on that last watch after midnight, I saw an empty bottle on the floor. You must have left it there.'

'That's impossible! Where would I have got it from?'

She gives one of her Gallic shrugs. 'Je ne sais pas. You tell me.' Then Françoise widens her eyes in that artful way of hers. 'Or is it possible you have forgotten, Emilee? Look at how you forgot to lock the car when we went away. The kettle you left on the Aga and almost burnt dry. The heater in the bathroom that you did not switch off. So many little things I have noticed.'

She almost sounds sympathetic, although I know this is just a trick to get me to open up. 'Have you always been like that?' she asks.

I think of Nick's words. Of the fall which I never got checked out. The bicycle accident. But surely too much time has passed for me to still have concussion? Then again, I know from what I've seen at the hospital that the effects of concussion can last for months.

What if I had got a bottle from somewhere without remembering and got Dad to take a slug? *'Have some,'* I can picture myself saying, holding the bottle to his mouth. *'It will take the pain away.'*

Or did I do this out of vengeance? I can almost see a different picture now, one where I'm forcing his mouth open. *'Have some more, you dirty old man. You deserve to die.'*

Then a third picture surfaces. One where Dad is begging me to get the bottle from the kitchen and give him more than he should have. Yet that wouldn't explain the second bottle in my bag.

I begin to tremble. 'I honestly don't know exactly what happened any more. I'm scared that I did it to help him,' I blurt out.

She stares at me.

'So he asked you too?'

'Too?' I question. My skin prickles. 'What did he say to you that night?'

She slips, but manages to right herself, grabbing a bush. I wonder if this is part of her drama – a stalling device.

'I will never forget his words. *"Françoise, if you love me, you will give me the rest of the bottle. This pain is too much. I cannot bear it any more."'*

She imitates my father's booming voice as if she is on stage. Is this what Françoise has been doing since she arrived. Acting?

'It is what they all say at the end,' she calls out, looking over her shoulder. She is slightly in front now, going down the steps before me.

'What who say?' I call out.

'The old people I look after. They have had enough of life. They want death to come fast and painlessly.'

Again, I go cold. 'And what did you tell Dad?'

She is standing still now. Her back to the cliff. Looking at me. I put Zorro on the lead. He's whimpering. One push and I could send her flying. The false daughter. Where did that thought come from? What kind of person is she turning me into?

'I told Harold I could not. That they would find out and then put me in prison. I said he was asking too much. And then . . .'

Her voice chokes. 'Then he got angry. He says . . .'

'Said,' I can't help correcting. Sometimes I wonder if she gets it wrong on purpose as part of this 'little girl lost' image. Her English can be so good at times.

'He said I did not deserve to be his daughter and that he would ask his real one. "*Emily may not be my flesh and blood. But I have brought her up to do what I expect of her.*"'

It was true. More fool me.

'So is that what he expected of you, Emilee?' she asks now. 'Did he want you to end it all?'

'Yes.' His words come back to me, as clearly as if I am speaking them out loud now.

'*Please, Emily. Do this one thing for me. I've been a good father to you all my life. You owe me this.*'

A seagull swoops overhead, screeching.

'And what did you say?'

Tears prick my eyes.

'I told him I couldn't and he said my mother would have wanted it. I told him that wasn't fair and then he said . . .'

305

I stop, choked with tears.

Françoise puts a hand on my arm. Is it in comfort or is she going to pull me towards the edge? I step back. 'You don't have to tell me,' she says.

But I need to. Despite everything that has gone on between us, I know that only someone who has spent time with Dad would understand.

'He begged me to go to the kitchen and give him more morphine. Again, I told him that I couldn't and then . . . then he said that if I loved him, I would.'

'So unfair,' murmurs Françoise.

'That's not the worst of it. He then told me something I will never forget. He said that . . . you were a better daughter.'

I expect to see a pleased look in Françoise's eyes. But instead she looks sad. Compassionate. 'C'est pas vrais. Then what happened, Emilee?'

My voice comes out in a howl. 'I said, "You win. I'll do it."'

'Do what?'

'Give him an overdose,' I weep.

Françoise gasps.

'But I didn't,' I add, tears running down my face.

She stares at me with what can only be described as a disbelieving look. 'Tu es certaine?'

'Very certain.' I am trying to be calm now. 'I said it because I was so hurt by him saying you were a better daughter. I wanted to be the better one by giving in to his demands. It was also to get him off my back. But I stood outside the sitting-room door instead of going to the kitchen, wrestling with my conscience. After a bit I realized that of course I couldn't give him an overdose. I'd just have to go back and tell him. But when I went in, I saw he had fallen asleep. I felt my own eyes closing too with the exhaustion and trauma of it all. I must have dozed off then until you came in.'

'And he must have woken up when you were dozing and helped himself to the second bottle,' she says. 'You would have seen it when you came back otherwise.'

'But where did the second bottle come from?'

Her eyes widen. 'I do not know . . . And why ask me to give him an overdose if he had the means to do it himself?'

'Because he might have seen suicide as giving in. He always told me that one shouldn't be frightened of anything in life – including death. Maybe it had something to do with his experiences in the war.'

Then Françoise motions me to a bench as if she realizes I am mentally exhausted. We sit down and stare at the sea while talking.

'But what happened to the second bottle?' I ask.

'I hid it,' she says coolly.

'Why?'

Françoise gives another shrug. 'I did not think it is right you should get into trouble for trying to help your father. He ask me to end his life and I guess he ask you as well. You did what he wants – or so I thought. I feel sorry for you.'

Sorry? Do I believe her? She looks genuine enough.

'Then how did it turn up in my bag?'

'Ah!' Françoise makes one of her dramatic arm gestures. 'That is because you phone the police about me and tell them you suspect I am a killer.'

'How did you know?'

'They tell me. I am angry with you.'

'So then you planted the bottle that you'd been hiding, putting it in my bag?'

'Yes.' She makes no attempt to lie. 'I have to throw them off the scent. I wear gloves, so there are no marks.'

If this conversation was taking place in court, we could both end up in prison – me for murder and Françoise for attempting to pervert the course of justice. But it's not. This is an argument between two sisters. A private one.

Françoise turns to me. She almost looks excited. 'It's like *King Lear*, n'est-ce pas? That play your father used to read to me. The one where the king asks his daughters how much they love him. Harold said it was one of his favourites.'

So he'd read it to her too? Just as he had done to me when I was about nine or ten. I feel a twinge of jealousy.

'I loved him very much,' I said.

She tilts her head to one side questioningly. Despite the seriousness of our conversation, I cannot help wondering how she manages to achieve such a smooth black line under her eyes. It always smudges when I try.

'Even though he was not nice to you sometimes, Emilee?'

Now it's my turn to shrug. 'It was just his way.'

Françoise pouts. 'I loved him too. Even when he shouted at me.'

'He did?'

'It starts soon after I arrive. I bought the wrong kind of milk for his breakfast. He ranted and raved about the inconvenience and the wastage. For one litre! Can you believe it?'

Yes. I could.

'I told him I had made a mistake,' says Françoise. '"Subtract the money out of my wages, Harold," I said. "But do not talk to me like that or I will leave immediately."'

I cannot help being intrigued. 'Then what?'

'He sulked for a bit but afterwards I persuade him to play a game of chess and he returns to his charming self. Of course, I had to let his bishop take my queen.'

We both make a wry smile.

'At other times he was frightened of the smallest things. He became upset when a cup of coffee spilled on the carpet and he thought your mother would tell him off. He said she was very fussy.'

'No,' I said. 'It was Dad who was like that.'

She shrugs. 'The old can get very muddled.'

'Dad told me that you broke a glass and that Zorro hurt his paw,' I say.

'Your father threw it across the room,' Françoise says flatly.

'That's not how he told it. He said you were trying to hurt Zorro.'

Her expression turns hot and angry. 'Do you honestly think I would do that?' she demands, reaching out to pat him. Zorro's eyes are fixed on her in adoration.

I have to be honest. 'No. But you must have been furious with Dad for seducing your mother. You had to grow up without a father.'

'Yes. I was. But I would not kill him for that.'

'Are you sure?'

She looks down. 'When he ask me to give him an overdose, part of me thinks that maybe he deserves to be in pain. I think about it for a moment or so. But my conscience, it does not allow it. So I swear I do not do it.'

I swallow hard. 'When the police interviewed me after Daddy died, I told them what he said about you trying to hurt him.'

She looks scared. 'And what did they say?'

'That they'd look into it.'

'They won't find any evidence,' she says confidently. 'Don't you see, Emilee? He was setting us against each other.'

Maybe she's right. How cruel. How hurtful. Yet he was in so much pain. By asking us both, he was banking on one of us giving in.

She stands up. 'We should return to the house now. There is going to be a thunderstorm. Look.'

The sky is darkening. 'But what's going to happen next?' I ask.

She shrugs. 'I do not know. Maybe sooner or later, the police will come for one of us.'

'Will you tell them what I have just told you?'

'No.'

'Why not?' I ask.

'I'm not sure.' She gives another of those big shrugs. 'It just doesn't feel right. What about you, Emilee? Will you tell them that I put the second bottle in your workbag?'

'No.' Yet something inside me still feels doubtful. 'Are you sure you don't know where it came from?' I can't help asking Françoise. 'You didn't get hold of it yourself somehow so you could overdose him?'

Her big eyes widen with hurt. 'I would not do that.'

But how can I be certain that she is telling the truth?

55

Françoise

We walk home in silence.

I can tell that Emilee believes I know where that second bottle came from.

But I do not. And, I think, neither does she.

Yet, at the same time, I might not believe me if I was in her position.

In fact, my heart goes out to my sister. She seems so pale and fragile; today, even the little make-up she usually wears is absent.

I cannot hurt her any more. It is not right

'Shall I make us a cheese omelette for lunch?' I say, when we get back to Willowmead House. Once more, I am struck, as we go in, by the spacious hall, the steadily ticking grandfather clock, the deep luxurious rug on the polished floorboards, the gracious staircase that spreads its way up to the first and then the second floor like a fan. It is so beautiful!

And it could all be mine. If I want it.

Yet houses are like people. They need to be owned by good people if they are to be truly lovely. And after what I did, I am a bad person.

'I'm not hungry,' says Emilee quietly.

'Nonsense!' I declare briskly. 'You must eat or you will not manage. Just a light one.'

I whisk the eggs and add grated Cheddar with a pinch of ginger, some spinach leaves and chopped garlic before heating it on the Aga. I place it before her and – yes – see her picking up her knife and fork. She prods it gently and then takes a mouthful. Then another.

There! I knew she would not be able to resist. I learned from the best. My mother, who had learned from her mother, and hers before her. An omelette might seem like a simple thing. But there are hidden secrets to it. Just as there are with people.

Then I make another for myself and join her. As we eat in silence, I look around the kitchen with its big Aga and the knots in the old wooden table where Emilee is sitting, staring into space as if she is somewhere else.

Harold's chair is at the head. Empty. But I sense his presence.

To my left is the huge pine dresser which is studded with dinner plates, pink wine glasses, a row of matching pottery mugs with blue and green fish on them as well as little trinkets hanging from cup hooks. Photographs, too. Some in frames, others propped up against plates.

I gaze enviously at these pictures of Emilee as a child with her parents, Emilee as a teenager, Emilee as a midwife. I have seen these before because I took all these things off the dresser when I arrived and gave it a good dusting. How it needed it!

But now I see some other photographs that were not there before. My eye is drawn to one of Harold in uniform from the war. Even though he is only a boy in this one, I can still recognize that strong nose and his height. He's standing with a group of other soldiers, their arms around one another. Their actions look as though they are on holiday. But there is a scared look in their eyes.

Emilee sees me looking. 'I found it in his things,' she says. 'He'd always refused to talk about the war so I was surprised he'd kept it.'

I get up and look at the other new photographs too. Emilee on a pony. Emilee and her father swimming.

'You have had an easy life,' I say.

'You don't know everything,' she replies. 'Photographs don't always tell the truth.'

This is true. Maman and I never took pictures. '*We cannot afford a camera,*' she used to say when I was young. '*Besides, the best pictures are the ones which stay in your head.*' Yet there are others too – darker pictures which will not go away.

The wind has picked up. It is rattling the windows. I can hear the sea outside, roaring. Zorro is settled in his basket by the Aga.

'That time I nearly drowned,' I say. 'You could have left me. Why didn't you?'

She makes a face as if this is obvious. 'Because I could not allow someone to die. My job is to help people into this world.'

I shrug. 'And mine is to help them into the next.'

Emilee cuts in. 'It's ironic, isn't it? We are both at opposite ends of life.'

'Oui. But there are times when . . .'

What am I saying?

'There are times when what?' asks Emilee. Again, there is a sharp tone. Or is it fear?

313

'Nothing,' I say quickly.

Zorro is leaping up, barking furiously. There is a hammering on the front door. We both get up and reach it at the same time.

It's the solicitor, Nick. His hair is wet. It is raining.

'Something has happened,' he says.

56

Emily

He couldn't take the guilt any more apparently.

'Joe has approached the police with some evidence,' Nick tells us. He is standing in the hall, his raincoat collar turned up.

I take Nick's wet coat from him. It feels strange to touch something he's just been wearing. I can hardly look at him but I must. 'What kind of new evidence?'

Nick addresses me, but I notice he keeps glancing at Françoise too. 'When your father began to go downhill, he told Joe that he'd managed to get hold of a bottle of morphine on the black market.'

'What?' I gasp. 'But how?'

'Joe didn't know.'

'Where did Dad keep it?'

'Joe didn't know that either.'

Françoise's eyes glitter. 'It is unfair. If he has this bottle, he should not ask us to overdose him.'

'He asked *you* to do that?' says Nick in a 'you must be kidding me' kind of voice.

'Separately,' I say.

I can feel Françoise stiffening beside me. I can feel her anger.

'But neither of us could do it,' I continue. 'I didn't

know he had his own supply, but my guess is that Dad was too proud to commit suicide unless it was a last resort.'

I don't tell him that Françoise and I have already talked about this. 'He was banking on one of us agreeing to do what he wanted,' I continue. 'Like we usually did.'

Nick looks appalled. 'You mean he'd prefer that one of you got prosecuted instead?'

I shrug. 'Possibly, I'm afraid. When we didn't agree, he had to resort to Plan B and do it himself.'

'And you definitely didn't give him that overdose?' persists Nick. 'Out of love?'

'I was tempted,' I say. 'But it goes against my ethics as a nurse and midwife.'

'I am tempted too,' says Françoise. Until now she'd been silent. 'But I do not because . . .'

She seems to falter. Is she going to tell him about planting the bottle in my bag? I hope not. Otherwise Nick might be obliged, as my solicitor, to tell the police. Then she would get into trouble. And despite everything, I'm not sure I want that after all.

Then she seems to recover herself. 'I do not because it did not feel right.'

'Harold Gentle was a clever, manipulative man,' says Nick slowly. 'It must have been hard to stand up to him.'

This isn't the first time he's used the word 'manipulative'. It almost sounds as if he has a personal grudge against Dad for separating us. Maybe Nick really had loved me as much as he'd said.

'Will they charge Joe?' I ask.

'Apparently not. He didn't do anything wrong intentionally. He just didn't tell anyone. So the police have dropped the case.

'By the way,' he adds. 'Have you read your father's memoir yet?'

He is diplomatically looking at each one of us in turn as he speaks.

'No,' I say.

We've both been too busy trying to establish our innocence.

'But we must!' says Françoise excitedly. 'Don't you see? We might find out who our father *really* was. Harold Gentle – he is a mystery, but we can unravel him together. It could explain a great deal.'

But part of me is afraid. What else has my father done?

France, 1944

We lie together, breathing each other in. 'Your body is so soft,' I murmur.

She arches her back. Her nipples are stiff. I feel myself stirring again.

'I love you, Antoinette,' I say. 'I think I fell in love with you from the minute I heard you play the waltz on the piano.'

She ruffles my hair. 'You are such a sweet boy, Harold.'

'But do you love me?' I demand.

'Yes. Of course I do. What good is life without love? It is the only thing which war cannot take away from us.'

And then it happens.

The barn door opens.

The rifle cracks.

'Antoinette!' I scream.

I throw myself over her in protection but it is too late.

My love lies bleeding in my arms.

'No,' I cry. 'No!'

I leap up. Wrench the pistol from the German soldier.

And turn it on him. Shoot him.

Dead.

Then I sweep up Antoinette in my arms and start to run.

Her eyes are glazed.

'You're going to be all right,' I tell her desperately. 'You will be. I promise.'

But I am lying. Not just to her. But to myself. The truth is too much to bear.

I dash into the farmhouse. There are bodies everywhere. Her father. Her mother. Gently, I place Antoinette next to them. Dear God! Everyone is dead.

Then there is a whimper from inside a cupboard. I open it. Sitting there, shaking, is a small child. Antoinette's little sister. Someone must have put her there before the soldiers came in.

I pick her up — she doesn't protest — and run into the lane outside. By the grace of God, a truck is approaching. It is British.

'Leap in,' yells the driver. 'Bring the kid with you.'

She is rigid with fear. I try to reassure her as best I can but she says nothing. When we get to the next village, I give the child to the authorities. 'Will she be all right?' I ask in my halting French.

'We know the family,' I am reassured. 'There is an aunt who can look after her.'

Eventually, I am returned home to England.

Not as the young boy who had left.

But as a man who had seen too much.

57

Emily

The coroner closed the case after giving an open verdict on Daddy's death. It now seems a fitting time to read his memoirs. To be truthful, I'd partly delayed this because I was scared of finding out something about my father that I couldn't accept. But Françoise was right. We have to know the truth behind this man who had changed both our lives. Not just for his sake but also for ours.

So the two of us sit down together by the fireside, with Zorro stretched out alongside us.

'I do not understand why he is angry with me when I suggest he write down his life stories,' says Françoise, 'when he is doing it anyway.'

'I'm not surprised, though,' I answer. 'He wanted to keep it private. On his own terms.'

I have to admit I am curious as well as apprehensive. It takes us a while, but eventually we piece together the torn-out pages from his notebook, bearing his shaky, spidery writing, each one under the heading FRANCE, 1944.

It's like doing a jigsaw puzzle of my father's heart. And it explains so much.

We take turns to read it out aloud.

I can almost hear my father's voice.

I gulp as this young boy describes how he tried not to

show his fear; how he buried one of his comrades; how they were taken in by a kindly farmer.

How he had fallen in love with the farmer's daughter, Antoinette.

'He confided in me about Antoinette when he is dying,' says Françoise slowly.

I am hurt. 'He never talked to me about her. What else did he say about her?'

'Nothing.'

But I am sure there is something she is not telling me.

'Voyons! Let us read on.'

We shudder when he describes how she had been shot in his arms.

Françoise's eyes are wet. 'It is so sad.'

I nod, unable to speak.

There are more memories too.

When I came home after the war ended, I found out that the girl with blonde plaits in our street, the one I had sent the Valentine card to, had been killed. Another innocent victim of a deadly war.

I could not bear it. I wanted to cry, but soldiers don't do that. So I threw myself into my work. And then I met Jean. Later, we had our beloved Emily.

But I could never forget Antoinette. No one will ever be like her. She died because of me.

Françoise gives a little gasp. 'He says this too on his deathbed.'

This is too much. 'Why didn't you tell me?'

'I didn't want to upset you.'

My father's voice is so clear as I continue to read his words.

I should not have slept with Céleste. But her dark hair and youthful beauty reminded me of Antoinette, you see. It was such a shock when she arrived to look after Emily. I thought my true love had come back and for one moment, I gave into temptation.

I stop. I'm not sure I can go on.

'Let me,' says Françoise gently. 'He has told me this already.' Her voice is thick with tears.

I cannot explain myself. I had never been unfaithful to Jean before. And never again after that. Céleste, too, felt guilty. She left soon afterwards. No one knew. I do not think Jean suspected. I certainly didn't realize Céleste was pregnant. But now, here is a woman who claims to be her daughter! I do not want my precious Emily to be upset. Yet I owe something to this young woman, Françoise. And on top of it all, I am dying. What should I do?

58

Emily

It's his last entry.

'So that's why he gave you that cheque,' I say sharply. 'It was guilt.'

Françoise shrugs. But her eyes are still wet with tears.

'It looks like that, n'est-ce pas? But remember, I rip up the cheque.'

'Why?'

'I already told you. Because I did not come here for money. I come for love and recognition.' She snorts. 'I do not get that from your father but the cheque proved that he saw me as his own flesh and blood.'

I resist the temptation to say that Dad might just have been buying her off. On the other hand, that had never been his style. Then again, the father I knew at the end was not the father I had thought I'd known.

'You have the house now,' I point out. 'I have signed the paperwork.'

'That does not mean I have accepted,' she replies quickly.

I don't understand this woman. Yet I no longer hate her. In fact, part of me admires her. If she's telling the truth – and I'm beginning to think she is – Françoise tried to protect me by hiding that second bottle that turned up out of nowhere. But then she planted it in my bag! She protected me at times and tried to get me into trouble at others.

Françoise Alarie is a walking contradiction.

Yet maybe so am I.

As these thoughts whirl round my mind, I cannot help noticing the Christmas lights winking across the road from the village. Their jollity is at odds with the sombre mood in our house.

'What was Christmas like for you and your mother?' I ask impulsively.

A soft look comes over Françoise's face. 'We would save up for months beforehand to get each other a present. I usually bought Maman her favourite perfume made of lavender and roses by the local chemist.' Her eyes soften with tears. 'She wore it every day. Right to the end. I had to dab it on her wrists because she was too weak to do it herself.'

Then Françoise's voice grows stronger, as if forcing herself to be brighter. 'We would also save up for some treats: sweet pastries, strong cheeses. Maman was very popular. The bank manager would always send us a big box of chocolates and the local dignitary who had commissioned a portrait would present us with a bottle of good wine. But the best present was having time off with Maman. What about you?'

'My mother cooked for days beforehand to make a huge Christmas lunch for just the three of us,' I said. 'We had turkey and pigs in blankets . . .'

'Qu'est-ce que c'est?'

Françoise's English is impressive but I forget there are certain phrases which must sound very odd. 'Pigs in blankets are sausages wrapped in bacon.'

She throws back her head and laughs. 'How funny!'

I giggle. 'I suppose it is.'

Then I fall silent for a minute, thinking of the other things that had happened at Christmas.

When I was younger, my father used to come carol singing with me and my friends. 'You need an adult with you,' he always said. 'Just to make sure you're safe.'

'Safe' was a word he used a lot. '*Look carefully when you cross the road to be safe. Don't run. It's not safe. You might fall.*' And, later, when I started dating Nick, '*Make sure you don't do anything you shouldn't.*'

'*Harold!*' my mother would say. '*You can't protect Emily against everything. She has to learn from her mistakes. It's part of growing up.*'

'*I'm just telling her to be safe when they go out,*' he'd retort sharply. '*No fast cars or anything that might be dangerous.*'

'I have to tell you something,' Françoise says, breaking into my thoughts. 'Your father, he tells me some of these stories about the war when he is alive. So I knew some of them before he wrote them down. Not the ones about Antoinette but the stories about landing in France.'

'Why didn't he tell *me*?' I ask, hurt.

'I think he always tries to protect you,' says Françoise.

Her explanation takes the sting out, but somehow I still feel second best.

Then I think of something. Did that overprotective nature explain why Dad hadn't told me I was adopted? Instinct tells me he'd tried at the end. Perhaps he couldn't find the courage to do so.

'Dad was terrified that something bad would happen to anyone he loved,' I say to Françoise. 'Maybe that's because of what happened to Antoinette. He would get furious if Mum or I did something that might be risky. Once, my mother drove into a tree when she'd taken a bend too fast. I was about thirteen at the time. I couldn't understand why he was so cross. She wasn't hurt. No one was. But he kept talking about what *might* have been.'

I take a gulp of the claret that we've helped ourselves to from the cellar, where the bottles were carefully arranged and ordered according to date. 'That wonderful childhood that I told you about. It wasn't idyllic. Not underneath.'

'He was a proud man,' says Françoise.

Before, I might have been annoyed by the way she speaks as if she knew my father as well as I had – or even better. But everything has changed now.

'I think,' she continues, 'it is why he wanted us to give him an overdose even though he could do it himself. He did not want to be the one to give in. "I fought to the last." That's what he kept saying when he told me about the war.'

'He *did* fight to the last,' I say. 'He almost got us both arrested by leaving that empty bottle without any explanation.'

'This is true.' Françoise drains her glass. 'But he was too feeble to leave a note.'

Mentally or physically, I wonder. Maybe both.

'Tell me,' she says, 'what kind of man was Harold? Really, I mean. Deep down.'

'He could be selfish,' I say. She nods. Somehow, I knew that Françoise was thinking that too. 'But I still love him. I can't switch off over thirty years of that. He and Mum will always be my real parents. I have no intention of trying to find my biological father. No one can match the man who brought me up.'

She winces. I've struck a nerve. It can't be easy meeting a man who should have raised her too.

'You know,' she says, topping up my glass, 'when I first saw Harold, I thought he was the most charming man I'd ever met.'

I can't help but give a sardonic smile. 'He was good at putting on that front.'

'Gentle too.'

'Only by name,' I say. 'Not always by nature.'

'I found that out myself,' says Françoise.

My skin prickles. 'How? He didn't hurt you too did he?'

'Too?' she replies.

'Nothing much,' I say quickly. 'The odd warning hand on my arm.'

'Vraiment?'

I find the words spilling out. 'A bruise,' I gulp. 'That's what I told myself. Just a smack across the arm after he had caught me smoking a joint with my friends one night. He yelled at me that cannabis can damage your brain. "Don't you ever do that again!"'

And I hadn't. Even after the bruise had faded from my skin, the memory lingered.

'How can someone profess to keep you safe and hurt you at the same time? Why did I love him so much? It was only after I left to work in London that I realized. Keeping someone safe and keeping them under control can be two very similar things.'

'That's terrible,' she breathes.

'What did he do to you?' I ask. I don't want to know, but I must.

'It was when I'd been here about a fortnight.' Her hands are clasped around the stem of her glass. Her voice sounds dreamy. 'He had been talking about some of his legal cases. He was such a good storyteller.'

I nod. 'He was. What he didn't know, he made up.'

I think back to when my mother and I would hear him tell someone about a situation we had been in with him. Frequently, he would elaborate. Make it more interesting. Sometimes, there was only a kernel of truth. But his tales enthralled people. And that's what he liked. To be an entertainer. To be as far away as possible from the man who was scared inside.

'Then he asked if I would play him something on the piano,' said Françoise. 'Instead of our usual rock and roll, I chose a waltz by Chopin.'

Her face clouds. 'It was as if I had pressed an electric switch. He leaped up and began shouting and screaming. He came up to me, his face furious. I was so scared that I ducked down behind the piano. "You must never, ever play that! Do you understand?"'

'Antoinette's music,' I whisper, thinking of the notes we'd just read.

'Exactement,' nods Françoise. 'But I did not know that then. I said I was sorry. But I was scared. I tell you, Emi-lee. I feared he was going to strike me. And then his face changed. It was as if he was someone else. "That's all right. Now play me something else, can you?" he said.'

I could see the scene so clearly. Hadn't I gone through so many others like that myself? Dad's 'little moods', my mother would call them. We would go along with them. Tiptoe around him. Then he would be back to his kind, usual self. That was the pattern I'd grown up with. That was the pattern I'd stuck to. We all had to do what he wanted or he would have a tantrum.

'He lied when he told you I'd given up the piano because it was boring,' I say now to Françoise. 'It was because he told me I should spend more time on my school work. He was always manipulative.'

She nods.

'It's why I couldn't keep my baby,' I whisper.

Her face goes still. 'You were pregnant?'

Tears run down my cheeks as I tell her about the abortion.

I am sobbing now. Françoise actually reaches over and holds me in her arms. 'It was a mistake,' I weep. 'I threw my grief into supporting other women to have babies. Taking my pleasure in theirs, but all the time wondering what might have been. Wondering if I should have told Nick. Waiting . . . waiting for the right man to come along so I could have a baby I could keep.'

'I am so sorry,' murmurs Françoise. 'You know, when I first met you, I hated you.'

'Really?'

'Yes. You had everything I didn't. A father. A lovely home.'

That's what I'd thought at the time.

'But then Harold began to play those games. Giving me those earrings that had belonged to your mother.'

'I was so hurt,' I say. 'I thought you had persuaded him to give them to you.'

'I know,' Françoise shrugs. 'I apologize. I went along with it because I felt he owed me. I was the daughter who got nothing. But then, I started to realize what a monster he was.'

'No,' I say, wondering, at the same time, why I feel the need to defend him. 'Not a monster. A man who had suffered.'

'Perhaps. The point is, Emilee, I didn't want to like you. But now I find that I do. In fact, I want you to have your mother's earrings back. Look, I have them in my pocket to give you.'

She brings them out. I open the box and finger them lovingly. I can see Mummy wearing them. She might not have been my blood mother but to me she will always be my real one.

'Thank you,' I say.

Maybe I've been wrong about Françoise all this time.

'You should have his pen back too,' she adds.

'No,' I say, although I would have liked it. 'You must keep that.'

Then she reaches out her arms to me and I find myself hugging her back.

'I always wanted a big sister,' she says when we draw away, each slightly embarrassed.

'But we're *not* sisters,' I point out. 'I am adopted.'

'It's not blood that counts. It's spirit that brings you together.' Françoise now takes my hand. It is warm. I feel an unexpected hope in my heart.

'I thought you were trying to hurt Dad,' I say. 'I even found some herbs in your bedroom and took them with me to London to get them checked out. I was so ashamed when the health shop told me they were used to treat sinusitis.'

'So that is where they went!' She laughs, throwing her head back almost gaily. 'Remember how you asked me what that "yellow powder" was when I added it to Harold's coffee? I said it was turmeric but I could see the doubt in your eyes.'

It's true. I didn't trust her then. Do I trust her now? I want to. But I'm still not sure.

'In the old days,' I say, 'you might have been seen as a witch.'

She throws back her head and laughs again.

It introduces a note of levity into the solemnity.

'What shall we do now?'

'What do you mean?' she asks.

'Will you carry on living here?'

Françoise tilts her head in that coquettish way of hers. It doesn't irritate me as much as it used to. It's part of her, just as I twist my hair between my first finger and thumb when I'm talking. 'I told you already,' she says firmly. 'I will not accept. But I appreciate the gesture.'

'I may not be able to afford to give it to you anyway,' I say grimly.

She frowns. 'Why?'

'I have to go up to London again.' I cannot hide the fear in my voice. 'My case is being heard by the Nursing and Midwifery Council. And I don't know what's going to happen.'

59

Françoise

Of course, I knew quite a bit about Harold Gentle before I decided to meet him. And Antoinette too.

It was all in my mother's letter.

Ma chère fille,

I am not the kind of woman who has an affair with a married man. You must believe that. I promised myself that I would never reveal this to anyone. But I've thought long and hard about it all and decided that sometimes a promise has to be broken. So I am going to tell you how it happened . . .

When I was a young woman, I took a job as an au pair for a family in Cornwall. The mother, Jean, had an active social life and the father, Harold, worked so hard as a lawyer. They needed help in bringing up their little girl, Emily.

Harold could be such a gentleman one minute and then a beast the next. Always with his poor wife. But rarely with me. I understood because he had fought in the war. My mother had told me stories of the occupation. So many lives were destroyed. So many minds. I had an uncle who was never the same again. I suspected this was the case with Harold.

I grew to care deeply for this family. The daughter, Emily, was so sweet. She appeared clearly in awe of her father. I started to paint her portrait in my spare time. The mother, Jean, said she wanted to buy it when it was ready. But she did not know that I was beginning to fall in love with her husband. I knew it was wrong. And of course I was aware there was a fifty-year age gap or more. But he was so kind. So attentive. An extraordinary man. You never knew where you were with him. This was part of the attraction.

Harold had gone through so much as a soldier in France. I did not suspect until one day, I played a waltz by Chopin. He burst into tears like a child. Luckily, his wife was not in the room at the time.

'Antoinette,' he sobbed. 'Antoinette.'

Then he started to yell at me. 'She's dead!'

The poor man was hysterical. But somehow, I managed to soothe him.

'I loved her so much,' he had sobbed. 'You look like her, with your dark hair. It was my fault that she died.'

That's when he told me about a girl called Antoinette, whom he had loved and lost during the war. She would play waltzes on the piano sometimes, to distract the Germans while her father, a farmer, hid English soldiers.

My heart went out to him. I kissed him gently on the cheek and, well, one thing led to another.

Then I discovered I was pregnant with you, ma chérie. I did not want to tell Harold or his wife. I knew he loved her. And he adored Emily. It was the war that had made him angry. I could not break up a family. Jean was a sweet woman who was so kind to me. I should never have done what I did. My only defence was that I was young and easily swayed.

So I returned to France. I took Emily's portrait with me. It was almost finished and I thought that maybe I might complete it. But I never had the heart. Nor could I bear to throw it away. This little girl was your half-sister. One day, I thought, if you ever

found out, you might like to see what she looked like. I put the
Gentles' address on the back so you would know where to go.

Maman had made it so easy for me.

Do you remember me telling you once that everything is possible
except one thing?

Yes! I had often wondered what she meant but did not want to press her. My mother did things in her own time. And now, it seems, she was doing so from beyond the grave.

I was referring to love. It is not possible to forget it, even when it is
wrong. And I loved Harold. I really did.

I can almost hear my mother sigh and yet smile at the same time.

Back home, I was courted by a man whom a mutual friend
introduced me to. I told him I was pregnant but he said he would
bring you up as his own.
   This was the man you thought was your father. But he was
jealous of my love for you and jealous of Harold in England,
even though we had no contact. We were not suited. So he left. I
may have behaved badly, but I don't regret any of this, ma chérie,
because Harold gave you to me. I am too scared to tell you
face-to-face in case you judge me. So I am leaving this letter for you
to read after I am gone.
   I beg you, now and for ever, please forgive me.
   Your always-loving Maman x

I knew that I was risking Harold's wrath when I played those waltzes on Emilee's beautiful piano.

Yet I had to. I hoped it might encourage Harold to confide in me and tell me more about Antoinette and how she had reminded him of my mother. Then I could tell him about me. His other daughter.

Yet I cannot talk to Emilee about this yet. I feel she has had too much to take in. One day, perhaps.

Right now, I have to help her with two things. First, I made her promise to go to the doctor.

'You need to get your head examined in case you have an injury,' I said.

'Nick says so too.'

'Then what are you waiting for? I will come with you to your appointment.'

And it turned out I was right. Emilee has delayed concussion. It must have been affecting her memory ever since.

So that is one problem solved. But there is another one ahead. Next week, we will go together to my sister's big hearing in London.

60

Françoise

Nick wants to come too but Emilee asks him not to. I think she is too ashamed. I feel flattered that she accepts my company.

I am given permission to attend because of Emilee's medical condition. The doctor has given me a letter to say I am her 'carer'. It is ironic, n'est-ce pas?

Now, she stands in front of all these people in a big room. It is not a court of law but it feels like one. My heart goes out to her. She looks so pale and scared when she is called to the front to give evidence.

Emilee's voice is almost a whisper.

'The birth wasn't totally straightforward. The baby took a while to turn due to the contractions slowing down. But everything was fine.'

I see tears swimming in her eyes.

'He was a beautiful little baby boy. Usually there would have been another midwife on duty with me. But we were short-staffed. I delivered the placenta and membranes, which seemed quite ragged – but that can be normal.'

She glances at the panel of people who are in charge of deciding her future. One of them seems to nod.

'In fact, part of it was missing.'

She pauses for a minute and then continues. 'I'm usually

so careful. But I wasn't concentrating as much as I should have been in the sluice room. I had a date that night. I was excited.'

Her face flushes, as if she didn't mean to say that last part.

'Then I heard George's voice and went back . . .'

'For the record,' says a sharp-faced woman, 'would you clarify who you mean?'

Emilee goes a dark red. 'George Chester. The new consultant obstetrician. He said he'd "come back shortly" to check up on mother and baby. But he didn't. Then, when I went up to give my statement at the maternity unit where I work, he denied this. I'm not passing all the blame onto him. But if he had come back, he might have realized something was wrong.'

My sister bursts into tears. 'He was the man I was meant to have a date with that evening. I thought he might be the one for me – but he wasn't the man I thought he was.'

I gasp. No wonder Emilee has been acting so strangely ever since I met her. She has been carrying such a weight.

'There's something else, too,' says Emilee. 'My dad. He died recently. He was old – in his nineties – and I'd been worried about him. I've had a lot of pressure. It's why I've made a few mistakes. I didn't tell anyone the reason because I didn't want people to think I couldn't cope.'

Her head hangs down.

Emilee has finished now. Next, others give evidence. I watch as solemn-looking men and women talk with their furrowed brows. Emilee's previous mistakes are referred to. Two drug errors where she'd given patients the wrong amount of sedative: both had been too small rather than large but this can be damaging as well. Then there was the case of a woman whose sutures had come apart and led to severe bleeding and infection. Emilee was responsible for that too. All took place in the last four years. Is that a coincidence that this was when her mother died? I do not think so. She would have been grief-stricken and worried about her father. Our father.

But there are also some glowing character references. 'This nurse was responsible for saving the life of a baby and mother during a breech birth,' according to one doctor. 'She is an asset to any midwifery team.'

My heart rises with hope. Maybe then they will excuse her.

Then someone else speaks: a sharp-eyed woman with a no-nonsense manner.

'But the truth, as Emily Gentle has already proclaimed, is that she failed to check the placenta and membranes thoroughly in the sluice room because she was distracted by the sound of George Chester's voice next door. If she had, she would have realized that part of the placenta was still in Mrs Smith's body. Nor had she counted the number of swabs. There should have been five. Instead there were four. One had been left inside, along with the rest of the placenta. The result was that Mrs Smith developed an infection and suffered a haemorrhage. She had to have an emergency operation and could have died. And all because Emily Gentle had not been concentrating, as she freely admitted.'

Emilee is weeping silently. 'I am so sorry,' she is whispering.

My hand creeps out and holds hers. She squeezes mine back.

'Fortunately both mother and baby are well but it could have been a very different story,' adds the speaker.

A midwife is now claiming that since George Chester was in a senior position, the 'onus' should fall on his shoulders. 'He had promised to return but he didn't.'

Now he is being called to give evidence.

'I did not return because I was delayed in another ward,' he says flatly.

'In that case, you should have arranged for someone else to take your place.'

'There wasn't anyone.'

I do not like the look of this George. He has a hard face. My mother always said that full lips were a sign of generosity. Harold had a thin top lip, which is said to be a sign of meanness.

He thumps his hand on the table. 'You know how under-resourced we are. We work every hour that we can – and more. We're knackered. Besides, an infection takes time to develop. It would not have been obvious so soon.'

I can see his point. But I can see some people here are shocked by his anger. Maybe this will help my sister's case. I secretly hope he loses his temper even more.

There is a break. I am glad. It is exhausting to listen to all these people who are criticizing Emilee. Yes, she made a mistake. But just listen to all the lovely things that other people have said about her. They cannot deny she cares. A second mother told us how Emilee had saved her life – and her baby's – by acting quickly during a complicated delivery.

We go out of the room to get water from the machine.

Emilee is very quiet. I hold her by the arm. Then a woman comes towards us with a pram. Emilee stops. Her face goes white.

'Oh,' says Emilee. 'What a lovely little boy.' Then she holds out her hands to the woman. 'Mrs Smith, I am so very sorry. To think that he might have grown up without a mother. I cannot believe I made such a terrible mistake.'

Stop, I want to say. *This is making it worse.*

Tears are rolling down Emilee's face.

But the woman is glaring at her. 'I should think you *are* sorry,' she says. 'I could have died. It was only due to the skill of the surgeon that I survived.'

'Believe me,' says Emilee. 'I would do anything, *anything* in the world, to repeat that day and do it right.'

'So would I,' says the woman. Then she walks on.

Emilee is sobbing now, so loudly that I have to take her into les toilettes. I put both my hands on her shoulders and shake her. 'You have to stop. This is not going to achieve anything. You have to pull yourself together and get back in there. If you're struck off, you are struck off. At least then you can get on with the rest of your life.'

I blot her face for her with a paper towel. 'You're more like an older sister,' she says. 'Not a younger one.'

This is the first time she has called me her sister. I feel a lump in my throat.

'Well, one of us has to be in charge,' I say briskly, to hide my emotion. 'Now, let us go. They're about to make a decision.'

61

Françoise

'This is a very serious error,' says the woman who seems to be in charge of the panel. 'Emily Gentle's mistake could have risked the life of a woman. George Chester should not be blamed.'

Despite my earlier words of encouragement, I shiver in my shoes for Emilee.

'If it were not for her glowing previous record and her obvious remorse, my ruling might be more stringent. There is no doubt that her fitness to practise is impaired.'

My heart pounds with ferocity. Goodness knows what Emilee's is doing.

'I therefore rule that Emily Gentle should be disbarred from practising for a year and then be allowed to return to midwifery, providing supervision conditions are met in full.'

'She should be struck off!' calls out the boy's father. 'My wife and I can still pursue our own private legal action, you know!'

But right now, it seems she is free to go.

Yet Emilee is silent.

'Are you not relieved?' I ask as we make our way out.

'How can I be?'

'A year will go fast,' I protest.

'It's not that,' says Emilee. 'It's knowing that Mrs Smith could have died and that her baby might have grown up motherless. Besides, what if the Smiths do take private action against me?'

'Then we face that when it comes,' I say firmly.

'We?'

'Absolument.'

George Chester sweeps past us without even glancing at Emilee. 'You must allow yourself to be free of blame,' I say firmly.

'I'm afraid that is not quite true,' she says quietly. 'But I have learned a lesson.'

'Maman used to say that every stage of life is a lesson, whether it is a triumph or a mistake,' I say. 'Now we will go home.'

I link my arm with Emilee's. 'It will be all right. You will see. You will work again.'

'No one will want me.'

'Possibly not at first. But there will be opportunities. I know it.' I hesitate for a moment. 'May I give you a piece of advice?'

'You've never asked permission before,' she says, half-smiling.

'Do you mean I'm bossy?'

'Sometimes.'

'Touché! It's something Maman used to say. Never hold a grudge against anyone. Always forgive. If you hold anger and resentment inside, it is like taking poison and expecting the other person to die.'

She nods slowly. 'I get that. But do you forgive everyone who has hurt you, including Dad?'

'I am working on it,' I say.

*

342

On the train back to Cornwall, I try to lighten Emilee's spirits by offering to give her a makeover.

'Here? On the train?' she asks.

'Why not?' I retort, getting out my make-up bag.

A little girl across the aisle watches us intently. She reminds me of myself at that age, observing my mother getting herself ready for the day when she was well.

'Now let me plait your hair,' I instruct.

'No,' she whispers. 'Honestly. I don't feel I deserve it after the inquiry . . .'

'Stop,' I say. 'That is behind us now. Besides, I want you to look your best.'

'For what?' she asks.

'For yourself, of course. Trust me. It will make you feel better.'

I work with my tongue between my teeth, the way Maman did when doing my hair.

'There,' I say. 'Look in my mirror.'

I hand her the powder compact.

The little girl is still watching. Emilee flushes. 'I don't look like me.'

'You don't like it?'

'Of course I do. But I keep thinking about the Smiths.'

'That's understandable,' I say. 'Yet if you let mistakes go round and round in your head, you will never learn from them.'

She smiles sadly at me. 'Was that one of your mother's sayings too?'

'No,' I say firmly. 'It is my own.'

When we arrive at Truro station, we head for the taxi rank.

'May I offer you a lift, ladies?' asks a voice.

'Nick,' says Emilee, flushing. 'How did you know we were on the train – or is this a coincidence?'

He glances at me. I shrug. 'I rang him,' I say simply.

I admit I was wrong about Nick. And even though I did not care much for Emilee in the early days, I felt protective of her because of the way Jean-Luc had treated me and how Harold had taken advantage of my mother. I couldn't just let it go. But I admit that maybe I was wrong to interfere by leaving that message on Emilee's phone about Nick kissing his wife.

The last few weeks have shown me that Nick is a good man. He also likes the look of the new Emilee, judging from his eyes. I did the right thing to 'do her up' on the train!

When we reach the village, I tell them to go back to Willowmead House without me. 'I have some shopping to do. I will see you later.'

Then I leave them to it.

I head for the post office. As usual, there is a long queue because the post office woman is chatting to the person in front of me. I stand, impatiently, wishing she would hurry up.

'Have you heard about Mavis?' she says in a loud whisper.

I can't help overhearing their conversation . . .

'Hello,' says the post-office woman when finally I reach the counter. 'What can I do for you?'

'Actually,' I say, 'I've just realized I need to be somewhere.'

She seems a little annoyed. But I do not care.

344

There has been a question that has been niggling away at the back of my mind for some time.

And now, thanks to the postmistress's gossip, I know exactly what happened on the night Harold died.

At least, I think I do.

62

Françoise

Joe does not seem pleased to see me. So I get straight to the point.

'I know you've never liked me much, Joe.'

He doesn't attempt to deny this. Just sits there, pipe in hand, in his vegetable plot at the back of his terraced cottage. I wonder how old he must be. In his eighties perhaps? But he is still nimble, always trimming hedges and digging.

'And I didn't like *you*,' I continue. 'But you misread me. I wasn't here to "get presents out of Harold", as I heard someone say at the funeral.'

Joe empties his pipe and grinds the ashes into the earth with his boot, as if he would like to stamp on me like that. 'Look, missy. Don't you get smart with me. I know why you came to Willowmead House. Harold told me.

'He used to tell me everything. We would talk in the greenhouse. Sometimes I'd come into the house and top up his whisky glass for him. Later, when he couldn't move, we talked through his bedroom window when I was up the ladder, cleaning, attending to the creepers and what have you. He told me about the DNA test you took. You're his bastard daughter by that fast-and-loose French woman who came to look after young Emily.'

Blood boils in my heart. I want to slap him. 'How dare you talk about my mother like that!'

'Well, it's true, isn't it? She seduced him.'

'Hah! So he didn't tell you everything, then.'

His eyes are hard. 'I know everything I need to. You came here when your mother died to see if you could get your hands on Mr Gentle's money.'

'I do not want his money, you old fool,' I spit. 'I want justice. Not just for me but for Emilee too. She deserves to know the truth. I know your secret.'

He's glaring even harder now. 'What do you mean?'

'You knew Harold through the war, didn't you?'

He goes very still. A red flush creeps up his neck. 'Don't talk such rot.'

'Emilee has been going through old photographs that Harold had tucked away. There was one of Harold and his troop. She didn't notice. But *I* did. And I recognized you.'

I expect him to deny it. But his face collapses.

'That wasn't me,' he mutters. 'I was too young to enlist. That was my father. Albert.'

'Your *father*?'

To my surprise, tears are welling up in the old man's eyes. His voice has a catch to it. 'Harold served with my father in the war. He was just a lad and my father took him under his wing. Gave him some whisky when he was scared – that kind of thing. Then their truck was bombed by the bloody Jerries and my dad . . . my dad died. Harold buried him in the grounds of a French farmhouse, even though the other men just wanted to leave his body without a decent grave.'

'I know that story,' I gasp. 'Harold told me about

burying a man who was kind to him. But I didn't realize it was your father. When I spotted the likeness in the photograph, I thought it was you.'

'He told you stories about the war?' asks Joe. 'But I thought he'd only talk about that to me.'

'Maybe he felt comfortable with me too,' I reply smartly.

Joe makes a harrumph noise before carrying on. 'My dad had been carrying a photograph of my mum and me. Harold went to the trouble of tracking us down when he got back from the war to tell us about Dad's final moments.'

His voice thickens. 'He was a real gent, was Harold Gentle. He gave my mother some money to help us out. I was a kid then. Later, when he moved here, he wrote and asked me to help out with the garden. He made out like I'd be doing him a favour. But he knew I needed a job.'

I swallow hard. 'But you helped Harold too, didn't you?'

He nods. It's all coming out now. It's as though I have opened the floodgates.

'Harold got a medal for shooting that German and saving the farmer's little girl after the rest of her family had been slaughtered and his own troop shot. He went to law school in London and became a lawyer down here. Oh yes. Harold Gentle would be very jolly with everyone else, but he confided in me. Only I knew how much he had suffered – and continued to do so.'

There is a silence. There are men and women like this still in France, I remind myself. They are the elderly who remember the fighting. And there are their children and grandchildren who inherited the anxieties and stresses of their parents.

'It must have been difficult,' I say.

'It was.' He sucks in his old wizened cheeks. 'I used to give Harold the odd cigarette for his nerves.' His face is wistful for a moment. 'Said it reminded him of the fag my dad had given him after they arrived in France.'

My ears prick up. 'Really? And did you give him that secret bottle of morphine too?'

I watch his face carefully.

It goes rigid. He is silent.

This is no more than a guess. Again, I expect him to deny it.

But he says nothing.

I have to crack him. Not just for me but for Emilee too.

'I found an empty bottle after he'd died,' I say. 'Was that a present from you?'

I was taking a chance and I knew it. If Joe told the police about this, I'd be in deep trouble for not telling them.

'There wasn't a pharmacy label on it,' I add.

Still Joe says nothing.

'You'd taken it off before you gave him that bottle, so no one knew who it belonged to, hadn't you, Joe?'

He stiffens.

Oui! I've struck a nerve.

'You hoped that by keeping quiet you'd save your skin and that maybe, just maybe, I would be blamed.'

His eyes bore into mine. I would not have wanted to face this man on a battlefield.

'But your conscience got the better of you. You were probably worried that Emilee might get arrested. So you went to the police and told them part of the truth. You said Harold told you that he'd got hold of his own supply of morphine on the black market. You didn't confess that it actually came from you.'

'You can't prove that,' he snaps.

'I just have. I can tell from your face it's true.'

Again, I am only guessing, but it's amazing how far you can reach the truth this way. Perhaps it is me who should be the policeman.

'*Stay calm*,' says my mother's voice in my head.

'Do you realize how much trouble you could get into for supplying a prescription drug?' I ask. 'Did it come from your sister-in-law?'

This was another lucky discovery. It had been the conversation in the post office which I'd heard earlier today. The reason for my visit to Joe.

'*Have you heard about Mavis? You know Mavis – her brother-in-law does the garden at Willowmead House. Well, she's back in charge of the sewing committee. It will do her good after looking after her sister. They say it was bad at the end, even though she was on these really strong painkillers. Liquid morphine, I heard. Terrible, isn't it?*'

'You can't go to the police without evidence,' he says when I recount this. But there's a hesitant edge to his voice.

'I have no intention of handing you in. I just want to know the truth. Admit it, Joe! It's eating away at you inside, isn't it? You feel guilty about murdering Harold.'

'I didn't murder him! I only gave him the bottle to help the pain. I didn't know he was going to take the lot.'

I've cracked him!

'So you admit it,' I say triumphantly.

'I just wanted to put Harold out of his pain,' he repeats

furiously. 'I didn't expect Miss Emily to be blamed when he died.'

So I was right.

'You hoped *I* would be, didn't you?' I demand.

He scowls. 'Yes, to be honest. I thought they'd see you as the likely culprit. There's folk here what reckoned you were out for what you could get.'

'All I ever wanted,' I say softly, 'was a father. You know what that's like, don't you, Joe? You were only a baby when your own father died. No wonder you would have done anything for Harold. Why don't you tell me exactly what happened?'

He is shaking. I feel sorry for him. Joe Evans is an old man. But that doesn't excuse his crime.

Something gives in his face. 'I told Harold about Mavis's sister dying and how she'd been on liquid morphine too. I had the bottle on me, as it happens. It was still half full. I was going to hand it in to the chemist after cutting back some shrubs at Willowmead House. You can't just put medicine in the bin, you know. It's not safe in case someone gets their hands on it. But first, I went up the ladder to have our usual chat through his bedroom window.

'When I told him about going to the chemist, he begged me to give the bottle to him instead. "Just in case I need it", he said.'

Joe's voice grows thick. 'I told him I couldn't. I didn't want to be responsible for something going wrong. But then he got angry. You know how Harold could do that.'

Oui. I did.

Joe continues.

'He told me that I owed him, especially after he'd buried

my father and looked after Mum and me. He also made me promise not to tell anyone – especially Miss Emily. She and her mother hadn't even known that Harold knew my dad, or that he'd helped us financially. '"It's our secret," he'd always said. "I need to put the war behind me."'

'But he did tell me some stories towards the end,' I say.

'I feel sorry for Emily,' mumbles Joe. 'They should have told the lass she was adopted. I told Harold that, but he thought that too much time had gone by to tell her the truth.'

He looks down. 'I felt bad letting that slip to the police when they talked to me.'

'What do you mean?' I ask sharply.

He wipes the tears from his face with a grubby hand. 'The police interviewed me after Harold's death. They wanted to know if I'd seen anything suspicious. Then they asked me questions about Miss Emily. That's when I told them she wasn't his real daughter. I wanted to distract them, like.'

I shake my head. 'She thought *I* had told the police she was adopted.'

He hangs his head.

I pause. 'Something tells me that you have suffered like Harold did. It was not easy growing up during the war.'

'And how would *you* know that?' he scoffs. 'You're just a kid. You lot have had it easy.'

I think of the stories I was told in my old nursing home by ordinary men and women who had survived to tell tales of horror during the German occupation.

'Maybe you're right,' I say. 'But the effects pass down through the generations.'

Something crosses over his face.

'Do you have children?' I ask.

'No.' His voice falters. 'I didn't fancy bringing them into a world that can be so cruel.'

'I am sorry.'

To my surprise, I see more tears welling up in his eyes.

I have misunderstood this man. Just as he has misunderstood me.

'I'll take my leave now, Joe. I may not see you again.'

He stops me in my tracks. 'I heard Miss Emily has given you the house. Suppose you're going to sell it now?'

I'd thought about it. But in truth, the simple fact that Emilee has chosen to give it to me is enough. It proves she has accepted me as her father's child. And that is sufficient for me.

'I don't want it. It doesn't belong to me. It's Emilee's. So don't worry. Your job will be safe. I'm leaving because I've done what I wanted.'

In fact, this isn't quite true. Yes. I had finally met my father. But I hadn't had the universal recognition I had dreamed of. '*This is Françoise!*' I had imagined my father saying to the village. '*She is my daughter.*'

Instead, I'd had to announce it myself at the inquest. But it didn't feel as good as I thought it would.

In fact, I felt rather ashamed. It wasn't just the furtive looks later from the people who passed me in the street.

No. It was because I had hurt Emilee at a time when she needed me most.

My sister.

Until I'd come to England, Emilee had just been the

little girl my mother had looked after. But now, she means so much more to me.

I also hope I have set her free. Not simply by showing her how to make the most of those cheekbones with my highlighter and blusher, as well as wearing brighter colours and plaiting her beautiful, flame-coloured hair.

Or by writing privately to Mrs Smith (through the hospital, which agrees to pass my letter on) and telling her exactly how sorry my sister is and what she has had to go through with our father. 'Please do not take this any further,' I pleaded. 'She does not know I am writing but I beg you to forgive her.'

No. I have also released Emilee by helping her see that it is never too late to make a fresh start.

She has released me too. With her at my side, I have learned to forgive my father.

And now I get ready to go home to France. I have cleared my head and my heart.

I, like Emilee, have the chance to start a new life.

63

One Year Later

Emily

'But you have to be with me,' I tell her.

Françoise's voice is faint on the phone. It's not a great connection. Either that or she is doing her nails at the same time as talking to me while holding the mobile between her ear and shoulder. It wouldn't surprise me.

'Nick is your birthing partner, Emilee!'

'But I want you too. You're my sister. And you're qualified.'

'What does your husband say about this?'

'He agrees.'

Nick had changed his mind about Françoise in the last few months. 'She's all right,' he'd said to me. 'Rather stubborn. Then again, so are you. No – don't take that the wrong way! I admire that.'

When Françoise said she was going back to France, I realized that I didn't want her to leave. The baby-faced policeman called round to confirm that the police had closed their investigation. Thanks to Joe's testimony, they believed Dad had killed himself with a supply of liquid morphine that he had somehow got hold of on the black market. Of course, it was suspicious that it had ended up in my workbag, but there was no evidence to build a case against me. Or Françoise.

To my surprise and relief, I had heard nothing from the Smiths about taking their own legal action. But I will carry the guilt of 'what might have been' for ever.

And now I must live life without the sister I've only just found.

'I have to go home,' she'd said, hugging me tightly. 'You will be fine. I have my path to follow.'

'You should consider the medical profession,' I said.

'We will see – my whole life is ahead of me.'

That was one year ago. So much has happened since then. I thought that maybe I would never hear from Françoise again. But she rang to say she'd been accepted on a nursing course.

'That's wonderful,' I said. 'You are a natural.'

'Thank you. I think so too.'

I've learned that Françoise's confidence isn't as brash as it might seem. It's a cover for all the things she lacked when she was growing up. In particular, a father.

After that, it became a habit that we would call each other twice a week.

'So much nicer than a text or email, don't you think? It is more personal.'

'You're right,' I said.

'Besides,' she added, with a lilt to her voice that, if we were face to face, would doubtless be accompanied by a twinkle in her eye, 'I can probe you more easily this way about Nick. Now tell me, how is it going?'

'Good,' I said hesitantly. 'Surprisingly good.'

'Then why the catch in your voice?'

'Because we're talking about him moving in with me.'

'To Willowmead House?'

'Yes.'

Before leaving, Françoise had declared she wanted no part of the house. So I decided to sell it. Too many bad memories.

'Are you sure you want to leave the home where you grew up?' she'd asked. 'Maman always used to advise that after something big has happened, one should not make un grand changement too fast.'

So I promised to give it a bit of time.

But then I had a birthday, which steered me closer to forty. I'm embracing my age now but it does make me aware that there are some things I need to get on with. Nick took me out to dinner. 'I'm not sure I want to celebrate,' I protested when he ordered champagne.

'Well, I do.' He held his glass against mine. 'I know you've been through a really tough time, Emily. But I can hardly believe my luck. I'm finally with the woman I've always loved.'

'You mean that?' I asked. 'Even though, without telling you, I went through with an —'

I stopped, unable to finish the sentence.

'Yes,' he said. He knew what I was going to say.

That's when he suggested something else which took me by surprise.

'You're sure?' I gasped.

'Surer than I've been of anything else,' he says.

'And Billy?'

'I had to run it past him first of course. He loves the idea!'

'*Ah*,' Françoise had breathed down the phone when I recounted this. '*A happy ending! How romantic.*'

And so Nick moved into Willowmead House with me, with Billy coming every other weekend and also during the school holidays. Almost immediately, my family home was filled with a peace I had never felt before. We turned my old bedroom into a den for Billy, with a train set on the dining-room table from downstairs. It got a bit scratched – my father would have had a fit – but I didn't care. The table was the perfect size.

'Cool!' breathed Billy when he saw it, his little face lighting up.

We've also put a big map of the world on his bedroom wall with lots of fact posters about the sea and the creatures living in it. 'Wow!' he said, reading one of them. 'This says they think that ocean animals first appeared around six hundred million years ago. Did you know that?'

'No.' I laughed. 'But I do now!'

It all seemed so natural. As if it was meant to be. My long-term concussion had finally subsided, thanks to treatment. This was partly medical and partly what my father might have called 'new-age' intervention with a counsellor. I won't say I felt like my old self because I didn't want that. Instead, I was a new Emily. A happier one.

The hardest part was starting work again when I was allowed to. I didn't want to go back to the old hospital in London with all those staring faces. Besides, it wasn't practical. How could I be so far away from Nick and Billy?

Instead, I took a part-time job at the local maternity hospital – under supervision, according to the regulations that had been imposed on me. It took me a while to gain my confidence and I always triple-checked everything I did. But so far, touch wood, nothing has gone wrong. On the contrary, they seem pleased with me.

Knowing too that I was adopted makes the miracle of birth even more special. I often think of my poor biological mother, who had died before she could give birth to me. How extraordinary that they had literally cut me out of her body! When I helped at my first caesarean after returning to work, I was almost paralysed with fear. But then I remembered the brave doctor who had saved me and that gave me strength.

All this made me yearn even more for a child of my own. It wasn't a subject I had discussed with Nick. I didn't want to frighten him off. Yet neither of us was getting any younger. Besides, he had Billy.

'There's something I have to tell you,' said Nick, when we celebrated our first month of living together. My heart sank. We were lying in bed, his arm around me.

Almost the same words he had used when we were eighteen. My heart chilled.

'Please tell me you don't want a break,' I said quietly.

'No – on the contrary.'

He was stroking my tummy button. Round and round. 'The thing is . . . Billy is always asking for a brother or a sister. What do you think?'

'A baby?' I said, stunned. 'You want us to have a child?'

'Why not?'

I could think of any number of reasons. Because I didn't have the one we could have had all those years ago. Because I am scared I don't deserve such happiness. Because I really, really want one too but am terrified it might go wrong.

'Let's see how it goes, shall we?' I said. 'Right now, I'd like to get to know Billy better.'

He held me to him. 'I'd like that too.'

Not long afterwards, Sophie married a man she'd been seeing for some time. She didn't seem to mind that her little boy spent every other weekend with Nick and me.

We had everything I'd dreamed of. Well, almost. We had picnics on the beach. I helped Billy with his home-work. Took him to surf school. Made his packed lunches. Played hide and seek.

Billy and Zorro became soul mates. 'I'd always wanted a dog,' he said, cuddling up to him by the Aga. Zorro gave him a big lick on the face. It might not be very hygienic but I hadn't the heart to stop them. Those two were joined at the hip.

'Mum and I used to do this on the beach,' Billy said one day, when it was just him and me. We were painting shells and stones. 'She used to look out for you.'

My skin prickled. 'Really?'

'She said she wanted to know what you looked like.'

I had a fleeting memory of that flash of pink watching me one day from the woods by the sea. I'd thought it was Françoise. But maybe it had been Sophie. I don't blame her. If another woman had turned up in my ex's life, I'd have wanted to see what she looked like too – especially if she was spending time with my child.

And then I started to feel sick.

My breasts were tender when Nick touched them. They were bigger, too. I had that metallic taste once more.

I didn't need to take a test.

I knew. I knew!

'That's wonderful!' said Nick, when I told him. His eyes were shining with tears. Then he held me tenderly. 'We'll get married.'

'We don't have to,' I said.

In fact, I wanted to – but I was also scared of repeating history. I didn't want Nick to marry me out of duty. I could bring up a baby alone. I was a different woman. Stronger than before.

'But Emily,' he said, cradling my face in his hands. 'I want to.'

The whole village came to the wedding.

'I am so glad you are better now,' said Sally from the post office. 'You were in quite a state that time I saw you near the station when you came home.'

I vaguely remember someone saying 'hello' yet I can't be certain. But it wouldn't be the first time I'd forgotten something after that head bump.

'I thought you seemed a bit dazed. You told me you had fallen off your bike in London. None of us thought you were quite right afterwards. After your father died, I told the police about the accident. I thought it might help. I hope I wasn't speaking out of turn.'

I'd never been able to work out who it was. But now I knew. She'd only been doing her best. It's what I love about Willowmead. Everyone looking after each other.

Françoise was busy taking her final nursing exams and couldn't be with us at our wedding. 'I'm sorry, chérie. I will be with you in spirit,' she had trilled down the phone. 'Mind you, I would have given anything to be there, just to see you walking down the aisle at four months pregnant!'

Françoise had a good sense of humour, I was

discovering. When we chatted, I found myself being less serious. 'It is good that we are so different. We complement each other. N'est-ce pas?'

I decided, after a great deal of thought, not to try and trace my real parents' families. What good would it do? My parents, for me, were the ones who brought me up. My father had had his faults. But he was still my dad.

I hope that he'd be proud of me now. Especially after what Joe revealed during a quiet moment at the wedding reception. 'Your father told me something before he died,' he said. 'He knew you were in trouble over some hospital business. He'd found a letter in your bedroom.'

The letter that said I had to go to London to give a statement! I remember the slight smell of cigarette smoke too. So it was Dad who had unsealed the letter after having a secret fag from Joe. Not Françoise, as I'd thought at the time.

'Why didn't he say anything to me?' I asked.

'He said you had to learn to stand on your own two feet,' Joe said.

He was right.

And that's exactly what I am doing. Except now, there are three pairs of feet.

Soon to be four.

64

Françoise

It is soon after the wedding when I receive the letter. At first, I think it is a joke. But then it is all over the internet. Apparently, one DNA company has had a glitch in the software. Certain customers in the last few years have been given a positive match, when it should have been a negative.

It is apparently impossible to know who is affected. But everyone is being offered a free second test.

But I can't have one. Because Harold is dead. How can I take a strand of his hair or a scraping of his skin?

And then I remember. I had given Emilee my hair, had I not? She was going to take a sample of Harold's too, so she could send both off to a different company for a second opinion. So I ring her.

There is silence at the other end when I tell her.

'Are you still there?' I ask.

'Yes.' Her voice sounds different. 'I'm sorry, Françoise. But I threw away the results before reading them. I was going through a bit of an avoidance stage then, to be honest. It was like not opening an exam-result letter so I didn't have to worry either way.'

'So you lied! You said they showed a positive match between me and Harold,' I say.

'Actually, Françoise, you jumped to conclusions because I'd given you Willowmead House. Remember our conversation? It was outside Nick's office after the will reading. You said, "I presume you give me the house because you have the results of the DNA test which you did."'

'And you confirmed that.'

'No. I said "When things go wrong, it's important to put them right." I didn't contradict you, because I felt guilty. I couldn't be certain I hadn't overdosed Daddy because of my memory loss. Part of me also felt sorry for you because of my father's terrible actions. So I felt the least I could do was give you my home. After all, your own DNA result had shown Daddy was your father.'

'But now it might be wrong,' I howl. I cannot help it. 'Can you get in touch with them?' I beg.

'I can try.'

A few hours later, Emilee calls me back. 'I am sorry. They are no longer in business.'

It is as though the forces of nature are in league against me!

There is only one person I can think of who might know more.

So I take the train down to Lyon and go into the bank.

'I would like to see the manager,' I tell the clerk.

'I regret that he is busy.'

'Please tell him it is Françoise Alarie,' I say.

Immediately I am ushered into his office.

I hand him the newspaper cutting. 'Please do not try to fob me off,' I say. 'My mother told me she was pregnant with Harold Gentle's child. You say the same. But now I wonder if I may not be his child after all. Do you know of any other men who might have fathered me?'

The shock – and guilt – on his face is answer in itself. He does not even need to say anything.

I stare at this short little squat man with kind eyes.

'*You*?' I ask.

He goes bright pink. 'Sadly, not. Your mother and I had known each other as teenagers and she confided in me. Please. Sit down.'

I do not usually obey. But my legs are shaking.

He blushes. 'I was always sweet on your mother. But she never felt the same about me. Nor did she care for the man she married. She only did so to give you a respectable home. But he had a temper I did not know about. It was a blessing when he left.'

'I remember feeling a great weight lifting when he went,' I say. 'My mother used to say that as long as we had each other, we would be all right.'

He nodded. 'You were *everything* to Céleste. My wife and I were not blessed with children and it was a grave disappointment to us both. I would often visit. I tried to give your mother money to help you both but she was proud. She would not take it.'

I remember them coming round. The bank manager and his wife. The poor woman. 'Did she ever suspect you had an attraction to my mother?'

'No. I played my part well.' He blushes again. 'And nothing ever happened.'

I stand up. 'Thank you for helping us when my mother was alive.'

'It was an honour. You have spirit, Françoise. Like your mother.'

And then my mobile rings.

It is Emilee. 'It turns out that the old records are still available. So I've got the results.'

65

Emily

'Try not to push, Emily,' says the midwife. She looks very young. Yet she seems to know her stuff.

How many times had I told other women the same thing? But it isn't until now that I know how difficult this is.

'Remember our classes,' says Nick. 'Distract yourself. Think of something that helps you relax.'

I close my eyes. I imagine running through the woods and down to the sea. Playing with Zorro. Throwing a ball to Billy, who is shooting up in height, like his dad had done at that age.

'I can't wait to have a brother or a sister,' he's been saying for months. 'I'm going to love it SO much.'

'You can push now,' says the midwife.

Push. Push.

'I can see the head,' says Nick. His voice is like a child's; it sings of magic at Christmas. Just like the sparkly festive lights outside.

'You are doing great, Emilee!' trills Françoise, who is holding my hand. 'Now, close your eyes and in between those contractions, imagine that sunshine is pouring down on your head and washing through your body.'

'How can I meditate when I'm giving birth?' I gasp.

'Emilee, haven't you learned? You can do anything,

anywhere. You are the strongest woman I know – apart from me, of course!'

I am so grateful that she came over for the birth. But I can't help worrying about her. It would be nice if she could find the right person to share her life with.

'There was a man once . . . when I was younger,' she'd told me during one of our many long phone calls from France. 'His name was Jean-Luc.'

Françoise had sounded dreamy. I had never heard her like this before.

'He wanted me to go to Paris with him, but I could not leave my mother. So he went without me. Later, I found he took a friend of mine instead.'

I got the feeling that Françoise was once bitten, twice shy. That she's not as resilient as she appears.

'It's a girl!' cries the midwife. Her voice sings out like mine used to when I helped deliver another living soul into the world.

But this is different. This is *my* baby.

'Give her to me!' I call out. I'm aware, as I do so, that I ought to say 'please'. But I just want her. I am screaming out for her. I want this baby more than I have ever wanted anyone. Even Nick.

I hold my daughter in my arms. She is wide awake. Bawling lustily. Her eyes are the same colour as my husband's. She has my short stubby fingers. And weirdly, she has the same determined look that Françoise and my father shared.

'She is beautiful,' says Françoise. Tears are running down her face.

'What are you going to call her?' asks the nurse.

'Hope,' Nick and I say at the same time.

We'd agreed on this beforehand if we had a girl. Because that's what she represents. *Hope*. Hope shines through all obstacles. All wars. All impediments. All misunderstandings. All lies. All secrets.

Hope is the start – the beacon – of our new beginning.

'She has a middle name too,' I say. I glance at Nick nervously. We hadn't discussed this beforehand but now it feels right. I am pretty sure he will understand.

'What's that?' asks the midwife.

'Françoise,' I say. I reach out my hand to this woman who had waltzed into my life so unexpectedly, but now feels like flesh and blood.

'Merci,' she whispers. Then she glances down at little Hope. 'Bless you, ma petite,' she says.

'Billy,' I remember. 'We need him here.'

Jenny, whom I'd helped when she got burned at the bonfire party – and who is now a friend – is waiting outside with him. I hear his footsteps running along the hospital corridor and her words as she races behind him 'Billy! Wait!'

He comes rushing in. The magic on his face is like all the Christmases I have ever known, rolled into one. His eyes are locked on little Hope's face and she seems to stare back at him with equal adoration.

'You've got a little sister, Billy,' says Nick.

'You can hold her hand if you want,' I add.

Carefully, very carefully, he strokes each little wrinkled finger in turn.

'When you're older,' he says, 'I'm going to teach you to swim. I'll tell you all about the life cycle of a turtle. Did you know that they break out of their eggs with a special

369

tooth that they have grown? And we'll take Zorro for long walks on the beach. Won't we, Mummy?'

It's the first time he's ever called me that. Until now, it's just been Emily.

I feel a pang for Sophie, his real mother, who would surely be hurt if she heard this. I would have been. But I've also learned something. Family comes in all sorts of shapes and sizes. And it's not blood that matters. It's love.

66

A Year Later

Françoise

I have had more time to reflect.

And this is what I think.

Birth and death are beginnings.

Both are endings too.

Hope's birth is emblazoned on my heart.

Just like Maman's final moments on earth. It is as clear as today.

'Please, Françoise,' my mother had beseeched. 'Put me out of my agony.'

I stared at the bottle of tablets in my hand.

'I cannot, Maman. I am sorry. I cannot do it.'

'If you loved me, you would.'

A shiver went through my very bones. How could I kill my own mother? This wasn't fair. Just as it wasn't fair she should die of cancer at such a young age.

'But I *do* love you,' I said.

'Then do as I ask.' Her thin arm reached out for mine. Her cold fingers gripped my hand. 'The pain is too great.'

So I did it. Not from her own bottle. That would be too obvious. But from a supply I 'borrowed' from the home.

Just in case. This wasn't the first time Maman had asked me, you see. And I could not bear the idea of her suffering the same agony that my poor friend Maurice had gone through.

'Thank you,' she murmured.

The effect was extraordinary. I watched her breathing more steadily. The pain drained from her face. I knew it was only temporary, but at least she had some relief.

'Now, Françoise,' she whispered, 'I have to tell you something.'

She coughed. I realized with a start that her lips looked dry. I gave her some water quickly.

'Happiness is not always possible, you see, ma chérie. But the good news is that lovely things often come from what feels like sadness at the time. I am talking about your father.'

'You have heard from him?' I asked, scared. 'Is he back? What if he tries to hurt us again?'

'Not that one,' she said.

I put my arm around her. 'Gentle,' she murmured.

Her speech was becoming unclear.

I thought she was speaking English for some reason. When Brian Montague lived here, he sometimes gave us conversation classes.

'I am trying to be gentle, Maman.'

'No. *Harold* Gentle.'

Then Maman had closed her eyes.

She was finally at peace.

There was gossip, of course. Suspicion. The doctor said her end had come faster than he'd thought. (Just like Harold.) He'd questioned the dosage I had given her. I swore I had followed the instructions. I almost believed this myself. No one reported any missing medicine from the home. I was lucky about that.

It is why I covered for Emilee at first. Why I hid the second bottle, which I thought she had got hold of somehow to put our father out of his pain, just as I had done with my mother. (I did not know then that Joe had given it to Harold.) Then, when Emilee told the police she was suspicious of me, I put this second bottle in her workbag to make her look guilty. That's when the police found it. Trust me. I am not proud of this.

Did I feel guilty about ending Maman's life? Yes and no. There are times in life when you have to lie. Not just to save your soul, but to save the souls of others. Like Harold, my mother would not have wanted it known that she did not have the strength to endure her end.

There was no post-mortem. Perhaps her local dignitary friend saw to that. Did he suspect? Possibly. Who knows?

But my wrongdoing had haunted me. It still does. It always will.

It was why I could never have given Harold his wish. I could not have killed my father as well as my mother.

Me – I will not have children. It is too much pain. Too much responsibility.

Mind you, I have lovers! No one like Jean-Luc, of course. He meant too much. I prefer men for whom I do not care, because then I cannot get hurt. I need to be able to stand on my own two feet. Young is good too! They are, in my experience, more capable in bed. And they do not want commitment.

Yet the only person I want right now is my mother. If only I could talk to her.

Instead, as I often do, I curl up on my bed in the pretty apartment I rent in Montmartre, and reread the letter from Maman that the bank manager had given me after her death.

My eyes swim with tears. If only I could tell her that of course I understand. Of course I forgive her. It is why I wrote to her before, when I was in England, but changed my mind when I'd got to the post office.

So much time has passed since then. But finally I feel ready.

I pick up my tortoiseshell fountain pen; the one which Emilee had insisted that I kept.

Dear Maman,

You will not believe what happened when I went to Angleterre . . .

I cover several pages, telling her exactly what had happened, including Joe's confession, and the headstone in the graveyard of Willowmead Church:

HAROLD GENTLE, BELOVED
HUSBAND OF JEAN
AND FATHER TO EMILY AND FRANÇOISE

'You included me,' I said to Emilee. She had linked her arm in mine. 'You are his daughter too,' she said simply. 'It felt right.'

My story is almost finished, Maman. Yet there is one more thing to tell you. Something so exciting! You see, I have Hope.

Hope is my pretty little goddaughter. I adore her as if she is my own. Indeed, her middle name is Françoise! I was so moved when Emilee and Nick called her that. 'It's because you are part of the family,' my sister had said to me.

I have visited Hope at Willowmead House. She is enchanting! Charmante!! This summer, she and her parents bring her to me in Paris. I read her Winnie the Pooh even though she is so young. I buy her pretty dresses. When she is older, she will be able to come and stay with me on her own. I will show her the Louvre. I will take her out to dinner. I will give her advice on love!

Maybe, one day, when Hope is ready, I will (if Emilee agrees) tell her why I had to find a man called Harold Gentle. The young soldier. Lover. Father. Grandfather. Old man. But the best part of it all, I will tell Hope, is that I found her mother – my sister – too.

I am sure you can see little Hope from wherever you are, Maman. And Harold too. You would both adore her. And Billy – Nick's son – he is so sweet. He wants to be a marine biologist when he grows up.

Then, with tears in my eyes, I make my signature.

With love, as always, from your adoring daughter, Françoise.

I place the letter inside a sealed envelope, marked 'Maman'. I do not address it. I tuck it under my pile of cashmere jumpers, in the bottom drawer of my armoire. Its purpose is completed. My heart feels lighter.

Then I put on those beautiful sapphire earrings, which Emilee had insisted on giving back to me after Hope's birth as a gift for being there.

Of course, when Hope is old enough, I will pass them on to her. But right now they are, as she said, 'an emblem of our love'. I glance in the mirror.

Perfect, Françoise Alarie, if I say so myself.

If there is one thing my father has taught me, it is that life is for living.

And then I take myself off to meet a handsome young man who's waiting for me, right now, in my favourite restaurant near Notre-Dame . . .

Epilogue

Emily

How could I tell Françoise the truth? It would have broken her. I could tell that from her anguished howl, when I said the DNA company was no longer in business.

I'd desperately hoped the old records would not be available. Then we genuinely wouldn't know one way or the other.

But they had been.

When I saw the results, I didn't know whether to be relieved or disappointed.

Either Céleste had genuinely got it wrong (which meant she had been playing around). Or she had deliberately misled her daughter by telling him that Harold was her father in the hope he might help her both financially and emotionally.

I cannot bring myself to believe that Françoise has been lying all along. I have grown to know this woman far better than the day when she opened the front door of Willowmead House and asked who I was.

'What did it say?' Françoise had asked when I'd rung to tell her.

I thought of what I had told Nick during our trip to Fowey.

I had one done too, using hair from each of them. The results arrived the same day you read the will. Apparently, Dad never knew her mother was pregnant. Or so he claimed to Françoise. At least, that's what she told me.

I hadn't said I was too scared to open the results and that I genuinely didn't know. Instead, I'd used my words carefully, to make him presume she was Dad's child. Just as I had done with Françoise.

But now the truth was in my hands.

I could see her there in Paris, glass of wine in her hand, pretending to be cool on the outside even though she would be trembling on the inside. Not that long ago, I might have delighted in telling her the truth. But not now.

'You are definitely Harold's daughter,' I told her.

The relief and laughter in her voice was proof, as if I needed it, that I had done the right thing in lying. 'Vraiment? I am so glad.'

I understood that. Not just because Harold Gentle was a good man at heart.

Or because Françoise and I have each found a 'sister'.

No. It is because everyone needs somewhere to belong.

Even Céleste, who had led us all up the garden path, either deliberately or not. We may never know.

Life is a jigsaw. I have learned that. And sometimes the most unlikely pieces slot together.

I waited for her to ask me for proof. To see a piece of paper confirming it.

But she didn't ask.

Perhaps, deep down, she senses the truth. That I lied.

That Harold Gentle's two daughters are related neither to him nor to each other.

It doesn't matter, as long as both of us go along with it.

Besides, we all have our secrets. And the longer you pretend something, the more real it becomes.

Acknowledgements

I would like to thank the following for playing their roles in *We All Have Our Secrets*:

The wonderful Katy Loftus and the rest of the incredible team at Penguin, including Victoria Moynes, Harriet Bourton, Lydia Fried, Jane Gentle, Ellie Hudson, Georgia Taylor, Ella Horne, Julia Connolly, Dead Good, Page Turners, the sales teams and everyone else!

My amazing agent, Kate Hordern.

My brilliant TV and film agent Italia Gandolfo, Founder/ CEO Gandolfo Helin & Fountain Literary Management.

Trevor Horwood, who is everything a writer wants in a copyeditor.

Proofreaders Sarah Barlow and Sally Sargeant for their on-the-spot eyes.

Hayley Smith, Small Business Consultant at Myriad Virtual Assistance.

Mark Camp from Visit Cornwall

Introtweet Ltd.

The Nursing and Midwifery Council.

Nicky Wallace, midwife, who spoke to me so movingly about the magic of delivering a baby.

Dr Jacqui Williams, Midwife and Midwifery Educator (any mistakes are mine). Thank you for being so patient with all my questions.

Philip C. Spinney, HM Senior Coroner for Exeter and Greater Devon and his team (any mistakes and tweaks are mine). I really appreciate the time you gave to me and our Zoom calls.

The incredible Zorro! Thanks to my cousin Robin for 'lending' me his dog.

Lucie Langevin, conference interpreter and translator (any mistakes are mine).

Cristelle Macdonald – my first cousin once removed – who also helped me by checking French words.

Frances Ionov, who kindly talked to me about good practice for end-of-life care, including compassion for the elderly.

Sarah E. C. Byrne, who kindly donated to the charity Young Lives vs Cancer in a character-naming auction.

David Wingett, who also kindly donated to BBC Children in Need for his name to be used in my book.

My family.

Writer friends including The Freelance Media Group and Prime Writers.

Bloggers, reviewers, booksellers and readers. Thank you.

Words on p.166 from *Winnie the Pooh* by A. A. Milne.

This novel is a work of fiction. Names and characters are the product of the author's imagination and any resemblance to actual institutions, companies, incidents, settings or persons, living or dead, is entirely coincidental.

blood sisters

THREE LITTLE GIRLS. ONE GOOD. ONE BAD. ONE DEAD.

Kitty lives in a care home. She can't speak properly and she
has no memory of the accident that put her here.

At least that's the story she's sticking to.

Art teacher Alison looks fine on the surface. But the surface is
a lie. When a job in a prison comes up she decides to take it –
this is her chance to finally make things right.

But someone is watching Kitty and Alison.

Someone who wants revenge for what happened that
sunny morning in May.

And only another life will do . . .

Praise for Jane Corry

'A fearsomely good thriller'
Nicci French

'I raced through this'
Teresa Driscoll

'So many brilliant twists'
Claire Douglas

the
dead
ex

HE CHEATED . . . HE LIED . . . HE DIED.

Vicki's husband David once promised to love her in sickness
and in health. But after a brutal attack left her suffering with
epilepsy, he ran away with his mistress.

So when Vicki gets a call one day to say that he's missing,
her first thought is 'good riddance'. But then the police find
evidence suggesting that David is dead. And they think Vicki
had something to do with it.

What really happened on the night of
David's disappearance?

**And how can Vicki prove her innocence,
when she's not even sure of it herself?**

Praise for Jane Corry

'Compulsive, edgy and fabulous twists!'
B. A. Paris

'Few writers can match Jane Corry'
Cara Hunter

'Totally hooked me'
Peter James

I Looked Away

**YOU MADE A MISTAKE.
BUT THEY'RE SAYING IT'S MURDER.**

Every Monday, 49-year-old Ellie looks after her grandson Josh. She loves him more than anyone else in the world. The only thing that can mar her happiness is her husband's affair. But he swears it's over now and Ellie has decided to be thankful for what she's got.

Then one day, while she's looking after Josh, her husband gets a call from *that woman*. And – just for a moment – Ellie takes her eyes off her grandson. What happens next will change her life forever.

Because Ellie is hiding something in her past.

And what looks like an accident could start to look like murder . . .

Praise for Jane Corry

'Sensitive and thought-provoking'
Adele Parks

'Thrilling, emotional and pacy'
Claire Douglas

'Dark, sinister, compelling'
Nicci French

I Made a Mistake

IT STARTED WITH A KISS . . . AND ENDED WITH MURDER.

In Poppy Page's mind, there are two types of women in this world: those who are faithful to their husbands and those who are not. Until now, Poppy has never questioned which she was.

But when handsome, charming Matthew Gordon walks back into her life after almost two decades, that changes. Poppy makes a single mistake – and that mistake will be far more dangerous than she could imagine.

Someone is going to pay for it with their life . . .

Praise for Jane Corry

'Gritty, real, interesting and clever'
Gillian McAllister

'Clever, compulsive and twisty'
Claire Douglas

'Absolutely brilliant'
Angela Marsons

The Lies We Tell

**YOU DID WHAT ANY MOTHER WOULD DO . . .
AND NOW SOMEONE ELSE'S SON IS DEAD.**

Sarah always thought of herself and her husband, Tom,
as good people. But that was before their son Freddy
came home saying he'd done something terrible.
Begging them not to tell the police.

Soon Sarah and Tom must find out just how far they are
willing to push themselves, and their marriage, to protect
their only child . . .

As the lies build up and Sarah is presented with the
perfect opportunity to get Freddy off the hook, she is
faced with a terrifying decision . . .

Save her son . . . or save herself?

Praise for Jane Corry

'Everything I love in a book'
Lisa Jewell

'Jane Corry's best yet'
B. A. Paris

'Brims with suspense'
Louise Candlish

my husband's wife

FIRST COMES LOVE . . . THEN COMES MARRIAGE . . . THEN COMES MURDER.

When lawyer Lily marries Ed, she's determined to make a fresh start. To leave the secrets of the past behind.

But when she takes on her first criminal case, she starts to find herself strangely drawn to her client. A man who's accused of murder. A man she will soon be willing to risk everything for.

But is he really innocent?

And who is she to judge?

Praise for Jane Corry

'Jane Corry is the new queen of the psychological thriller'
Kate Furnivall

'Chilling and suspenseful'
Elizabeth Haynes

'Twisty, feverish and utterly gripping'
Eva Dolan